Robert Reid

The Emperor, the Son and the Thief

BOOK 2

THE SON

THE EMPEROR, THE SON and THE THIEF

Copyright ©2021

Robert Ferguson Reid has asserted his right under the Copyright Designs and Patents Act 1988 to be identified as the author of this work.

This book is a work of fiction and except in the case of historical fact any resemblance to actual persons living or dead is purely coincidental.

❖ ❖ ❖ ❖

To Charis – my thanks for all your help
and encouragement.

❖ ❖ ❖ ❖

ACKNOWLEDGEMENTS

❖ ❖ ❖ ❖

Firstly, thank you to all those of you who have read "The Emperor" and given me such positive feedback on the story. It is this as much as anything that has encouraged me to continue writing the story of Audun and the red fire.

Many thanks to my daughter Charis, who has once again read a first draft of the manuscript and given me lots of constructive ideas for improving the story.

Grateful thanks to the editorial team, who have done a great job correcting the many mistakes in the early manuscripts.

To the design team, thanks for your creativity in the cover layout and detail in the map.

Finally and most importantly, thanks to my wife Phyllis for her forever love and for putting up with a missing husband hiding in his grubby office tapping away at the computer keyboard. Loved you yesterday, love you still, always have and always will.

RFR
June 2021

ABOUT THE AUTHOR

❖ ❖ ❖ ❖

Robert (Bob) Reid grew up in Scotland's beautiful border country. Hawick was home until it was time to go to university in Edinburgh. A degree and a PhD in Chemistry followed. It was in Edinburgh that Bob met and married Phyllis. Work opportunities took them south, and their son Simon was born in Cheshire and their daughter Charis some years later in Swindon. Highworth, near Swindon, became home in 1982. It still is home and has become a special place to Bob and Phyllis.

Bob's career of forty years was initially in technical management, then general management and business consulting. Work generally took priority over creativity. Semi-retirement in early 2018 created the time, family and friends the encouragement, for Bob to develop his writing.

His first novel *White Light Red Fire* was published in April 2019 and is a historical fantasy loosely based on the Scottish wars of independence of the early 14th Century. *The Emperor* was the first of a trilogy based in the same lands as *White Light Red Fire* but placed two hundred years later, in the early 16th century. *The Son* continues Audun's story and the story of the red fire.

The third book, *The Thief*, is currently being written.

AMAZON REVIEWS OF
WHITE LIGHT RED FIRE

❖ ❖ ❖ ❖

A Terrific Read

This is one of the most engaging novels that I have read in a very long time. The author has created a world that draws you in from the very early stages and keeps you hooked, and caring about the outcome, until the thrilling climax. The battle scenes are realistic, very well constructed, and don't fall into the same trap as many with a magical twist that use the magic as a short cut. The multitude of characters and dominions, each with their own ambitions, lends the book an often overlooked degree of plausibility, and is helpfully supported by maps and a character summary. You are left with a great feeling of a journey travelled, as well as an eagerness to delve further. I was given this book as a gift, but will certainly buy the sequel.

❖ ❖ ❖ ❖

Cracking Good Yarn With A Satisfying Ending

I read this book over a period of two weeks as a treat - it really was! Well paced, not overly complicated and characters you can believe in. For Fantasy and battle scene lovers like me, you will enjoy being transported to a place where people have extreme survival fears, an advanced technological age has been and gone and there are hints of the influence of a higher being. There's a touch of romance that does not distract from the whole, but links to the human experience of the characters. The story is begging for a sequel, which I will snap up as soon as it's published. I suggest you read this book and watch out for the next!

❖ ❖ ❖ ❖

A Wonderful Story

Robert Reid, in my opinion, is an excellent author with a vivid imagination. His well constructed story has so many facets in that his tale includes conflict, justice, drama, fairness and love with a mystical element thrown in. There are just enough characters to make life in this imaginary land interesting but not too many to cause confusion. The maps are also helpful, ensuring the reader does not "lose the plot" along the way and adds to a really good read. I look forward to Robert's next book with anticipation.

AMAZON REVIEWS OF
THE EMPEROR

❖ ❖ ❖ ❖

Great Start to a New Series

I had already read and enjoyed White Light, Red Fire. It serves perfectly as a primer for The Emperor (book 1 in The Emperor, The Son and The Thief series) but isn't really necessary to enjoy this book. Although I would describe the book(s) as fantasy, there is little actual magic, no dragons etc. The story is told almost as history rather than fantastical happenings. Something I found quite refreshing. I really enjoyed the story telling in The Emperor, and author Robert Reid's writing just seems to get better. I eagerly await the next book in the series.

❖ ❖ ❖ ❖

Fabulous follow-up to ***White Light Red Fire!***

There's been peace across the kingdoms for 200 years since the end of White Light, Red Fire – but that is about to change. The Emperor picks up the story and moves it along at a satisfying pace. It's easy to get hooked and the pages turn quickly. A slightly smaller (or so it seems) cast of characters and a straightforward start to the trilogy that brings The Emperor, The Son and The Thief into focus and links them together.

This first book shows us the aspirations of The Emperor and his eagerness for a fight. The evil of the Red Light is ever-present and the threat it represents sits menacingly in the background. The book gallops along and we learn the history of the Son and the Thief along the way.

A really engaging and enjoyable read that

follows-on well from White Light, Red Fire and finishes leaving the reader keen to uncover the next steps in the second book of the trilogy.

CONTENTS

❖ ❖ ❖ ❖

Prologue

Map

Two Hundred Years Earlier

Introduction from Book 1 – The Emperor

Chapter 1	Mora	1
Chapter 2	Audun	24
Chapter 3	The Staff of Power	36
Chapter 4	Questions and Answers	63
Chapter 5	Sparsholt	76
Chapter 6	The Dragon's Message	90
Chapter 7	The Empress	113
Chapter 8	The Sorcerer	128
Chapter 9	Explanations and Revelations	144
Chapter 10	Fields of Fire	158
Chapter 11	Unforeseen Consequences	173
Chapter 12	A Wizard's Name	189
Chapter 13	Hillfoot	209
Chapter 14	An Unexpected Arrival	225
Chapter 15	The Cult of the Staff	235
Chapter 16	Juice of the Yew	243
Chapter 17	Trouble at the Mill	258
Chapter 18	The Guardian	277
Chapter 19	Iskala	287
	List of Characters	294
	Geography of the Land	298

PROLOGUE

❖ ❖ ❖ ❖

Like all Bala weddings, this was to be a simple ceremony. Alastair Munro was to conduct the proceedings and the couple's rings would be swapped from the right to the left hand.

Elbeth and Angus embraced, stepped back and each took the other's hand. The rings on the third fingers of their right hands shone with white intensity, dimmed and then reappeared on their left hands. Between their right hands a silver quaich appeared with the Cameron motto shining brightly: *Aonaibh Ri Chéile*, 'let us unite'. And united they were.

But then, as the couple lifted the ancient wedding cup to their lips, Munro once again heard his old mentor's voice from beyond the grave, and this time it carried a warning: "To your right Alastair, evil stalks here in the shadows!"

Alastair spun to his right to see an old beggar pointing his raised staff at the wedding party. Oien! It could be none other. As a flash of red fire left the staff, Alastair pushed his hands forward, palms outward, and then drew them apart. A white wall appeared in front of him, consuming the red flame.

Oien raised his hand and another red bolt shot out, again quenched by the white light. Alastair advanced on the old alchemist and Oien hurled more and more deadly bolts of red fire. As Alastair closed on him, Oien knew that his power was as nothing to this white force. He started to beg for mercy, but Ala Moire's voice echoed in Alastair's head: "It is too late; take him in your embrace. Forgiveness, if it is to be granted, is for a greater power."

Alastair Munro took the alchemist in his arms and felt all the anger and the lust for power which had corrupted the old man's soul. He placed his arms around the other man's shoulders, clasped his hands and stepped back. The white wall now completely enclosed Oien, and as it brightened in intensity it hid him from view. Flashes of red seemed to bounce around inside the wall and then began to fade away. The wall became a shimmering wave, like a mirage in the desert. Gradually that too vanished, and all that remained where Oien had been was a piece of dull red rock.

From "White Light Red Fire"

The Island of Andore and the Neighbouring Countries

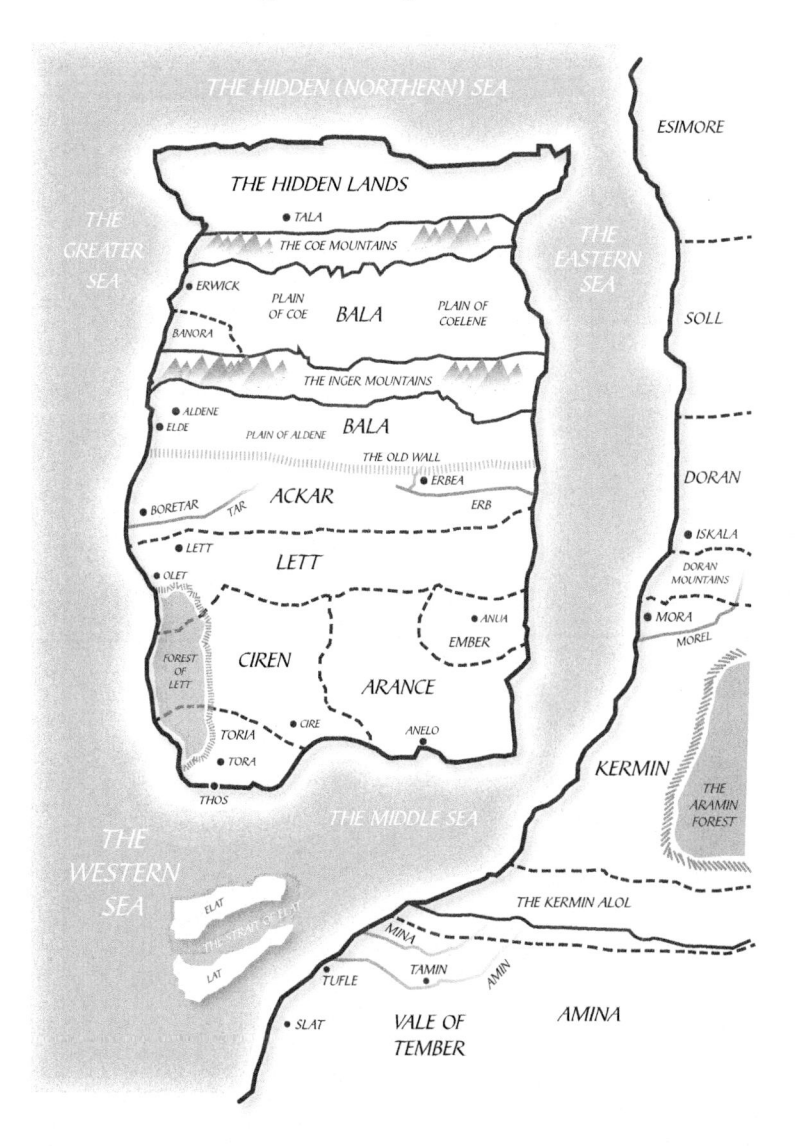

TWO HUNDRED YEARS EARLIER

❖ ❖ ❖ ❖

On the island of Andore, the late 13th Century of the Third Age was a time of brutal conflict. Powerful warlords fought for supremacy, kings raised armies to defend their lands and the people lived in fear. By 1298 King Dewar the Second of Ackar and Lett had quashed all resistance, and every kingdom on Andore swore fealty to the Ackar King.

The rich country of Amina lay across the Middle Sea, south of Andore. In 1299, King Dewar led a great army over the sea, intent on conquering Amina and thereby extending his dominions and further increasing his power and wealth. The two armies met on the Vale of Tember, close to the Amina capital of Tamin. The battle raged for two months and ended in stalemate. The Dewar and his army were forced to return to Andore, but the King promised he would return and conquer.

In 1300 an old alchemist called Oien arrived at the mighty stronghold of Boretar, capital of

Ackar and the seat of power of the Dewar Kings. In the Second Age the alchemist had learnt how to harness the power of a rare mineral, a red stone called othium, which in that earlier time had been used to fuel the industrialisation of the world. The Second Age had been brought to a sudden end when meteorite storms rained down on the planet and drove man back to his earliest beginnings in caves and remote valleys.

Now the alchemist had returned, and he offered the King an alliance. The power of othium and the red fire, together with the King's armies, would destroy all who stood against them. The Dewar would be able to fulfil his promise to conquer Amina, and the alchemist would again begin his journey towards world domination. First, however, he needed an army to march north, because he knew that the last unexploited seams of othium lay trapped in ancient mines in the Inger Mountains.

In the peaceful province of Banora, in the country of Bala, lived a farmer called Alastair Munro, who was unaware that he had an inheritance. He had been gifted the power of the white light, and he would need to learn how to harness this power to withstand the evil of the red fire.

For two years battles raged across the lands, one side fighting for conquest, the other for freedom. Othium-powered weapons wreaked havoc on defending armies. The red fire was hard to resist, but the white light was stronger. Gradually the tide turned and the freedom fighters regained control of their lands and their cities. The stage was set for the final battle.

The opposing forces met outside the Ackar city of Erbea in 1302 and the forces of good won the day. The alchemist escaped and was about to take his revenge at a wedding ceremony when he was bound by the white light. All that remained was his heart, or maybe his soul, encapsulated in a piece of red rock.

Dewar the Third succeeded his father and the new king promised a time of peace and prosperity. History would call him the Peacemaker.

Now, two hundred years on, a new Emperor seeks to rule the world, while an illegitimate son sets out on a path towards revenge and a thief begins to learn his trade. It is time for the alchemist to return.

FROM BOOK 1 - THE EMPEROR

❖ ❖ ❖ ❖

The southern lands of Kermin and Amina were separated from the large island of Andore by the Middle Sea and the Eastern Sea. In 1496, Alberon, King of Kermin, also inherited the throne of Doran and declared himself Emperor of the North.

Kermin was a rich country, due its fertile farmlands and to the gold found in the Doran Mountains. The capital, Mora, boasted its wealth all too clearly when the sun reflected from the gold-plated turrets on the Emperor's castle. The country of Doran to the north, with its capital, Iskala, was by contrast poorer, with the small farmsteads scattered across the Doran Plain only productive during the short summer months and locked in by snow during the winter.

Despite the riches of the lands over which he ruled, Alberon lusted for more power, and like Dewar the Second, two hundred years earlier, he turned his ambition to the south, to the wealthy country of Amina, where his brother-in-law was king. Bertalan, King of Amina and brother to Alberon's wife Sylva, refused to swear fealty to the Emperor and prepared for war. In 1507, the armies met in battle in the Kermin Alol.

The Kermin Alol, the hill country on the border between Kermin and Amina was ideal land for defensive actions. Silson, Duke of Amina and Commander in Chief of the Amina forces, deployed cannons for the first time in battle. Outthought and outfought, the Kermin army was forced to retreat. Humbled, Alberon had to sue for peace and the treaties were signed in Amina's capital, Tamin, in 1508.

In 1486 a maid was banished from Mora after falling pregnant and being accused of being a witch. Ragna was Alberon's first love, but it was a forbidden one, and so the mother and her unborn child were sent home to the mother's parents' home in Tamin, the capital of Amina.

Thirteen years later the Empress, Sylva, discovered the existence of the illegitimate child and tasked her brother, Bertalan, to seek out the mother and child and remove the potential threat to the dynasty that her own son, Aaron, would one day inherit.

Ragna and her son escaped Tamin and journeyed to Boretar, the capital of Ackar on the island of Andore. A sea captain and merchant whose name was Ramon befriended the pair. Sadly in 1503 Ragna died and the son, whose name was Audun, became Ramon's stepson. On finding out that the Emperor in Mora was his natural father, and blaming him for his mother's death, Audun vowed to have his revenge.

After breaking his leg in an accident in 1507, Ramon had decided to take a sabbatical, to read more of the books in his library. Audun took command of his stepfather's caravel, the *Swan*, and by 1509 he had become an accomplished sailor and captain.

The majority of vessels that traded across the seas in the early 16th century were carracks and caravels. Carracks were large ships, with their distinctive three or four masts and prominent aftcastle; they were the workhorses of the seas, able to voyage even through winter storms. Caravels were the little brothers of the carracks, lighter and more manoeuvrable, with two or three masts and lateen sails. They carried smaller loads, but their speed gave them some advantages across the trade routes.

As well as being a sailor, Audun was an amateur historian, having read many of the ancient volumes in Ramon's library. He was particularly drawn to the histories of the wars that had raged across Andore, Kermin and Amina in the early 14th century

Aldene, the capital of Andore's most northern country, Bala, had been one of the focal points in the wars of the 14th century. North of Aldene, Bala was bisected by the Inger Mountains and in 1300 these mountains held one of the few remaining sources of a mineral, a red stone called othium. In 1301 the armies of King Dewar the Second of Ackar invaded Bala to acquire the land and to tear the red stone from the mountains.

An ancient alchemist called Oien knew how to harness othium's power and wield the red fire. The details of the conflicts of the 1300s had been recorded in Angus Ferguson's history book, *"White Light Red Fire"*. The history described the end of the alchemist: "*the white wall now completely enclosed*

Oien, and as it brightened in intensity it hid him from view. Flashes of red seemed to bounce around inside the wall and then began to fade away. The wall became a shimmering wave, like a mirage in the desert. Gradually that too vanished, and all that remained where Oien had been was a piece of dull red rock".

Audun had first visited Aldene in 1504, when, close to the castle dungeons, a flash of red light attracted his attention before a disembodied voice had seemed to call to him, saying *"I am here Audun"*. During this visit Audun received a gift of the book *White Light Red Fire*, and having read the history he had pondered on the resting place of the red rock and wondered if it somehow still held the essence of the alchemist and his power.

Audun knew he needed power if he was to get his revenge on his father, the Emperor. He returned to Aldene in 1507 and his search for the red stone was successful. The stone's red light had guided Audun to an ancient cave deep below Aldene Castle. The light shone from an old casket with red discs decorating the side panels. Audun removed the stone in its casket from Aldene and for two years it travelled with him in his locker on the *Swan*. The stone had remained stubbornly inert, but Audun still hoped that it was the source of power that would help him challenge the Emperor. His hopes increased when the stone began a metamorphosis after he had first revealed his existence to his father.

Fourteen-year-old Raimund and his best friend Aleana were thieves and pickpockets. Both had been orphaned in the pestilence of 1501 and taken in by Rafe, master of the Den of Thieves. Rafe and his two adopted teenagers were the only residents in the Den since new laws had been introduced in 1507 to reduce crime in Mora. However the Den of Thieves, in the old dilapidated warehouse close to the old port of Mora, had secrets, and the trio were comfortably wealthy.

Before his parents died in 1501, Raimund's family had lived in a small cottage in the tradesmen's quarter of Mora. Due to several outbreaks of disease in the area the old cottage had remained uninhabited for several years.

1509 was a time for recovery and rebuilding in Kermin and Mora. The fields of the Kermin Plain were once again planted with wheat, oats and maize as the treaties between Kermin and Amina held. Whilst the country was rebuilding, the Emperor was focused on rearming. The conflict in the Kermin Alol in 1507 had changed the face of warfare. Cavalry charges and pike battalions still played an important part, but it was clear that the power of the black powder, gunpowder, was the weapon of the future. Alberon needed to replace the cannons that had been lost in the mud of the Kermin Plain in 1507. Knowing that he could not continue to be dependent on importing weapons from Ackar, he had sent a team of smiths to the Ackar ironworks to learn the techniques needed to forge cannons. The team were led by the master smith Wayland Henry, and it was now time for the smiths to return to Mora with their equipment.

Late in 1508, with winter snows blocking the roads, the Emperor instructed his Chancellor, Aracir, to hire a messenger to carry his instructions to the smiths in Ackar. Aracir knew of two men who would be able to successfully complete a winter mission. One of the huntsmen, the brothers Valdin and Vidur, would accept the contract.

In February 1509 Ramon was preparing his new

vessel, a carrack called *Lex Talionis*, for a journey from the port of Olet, in Ackar, to Mora. The carrack was carrying a heavy load of iron components from the ironworks in Ackar. A stranger, whose name was Valdin, had negotiated the large contract on behalf of Aracir, the Chancellor of Kermin and a certain Duke of Alol. Ramon suspected that the goods he would be carrying would be in breach of the 1508 treaties, but the contract was significant and sufficient to pay off the debt he owed for the refurbishment of the carrack. As *Lex Talionis* sailed south, so the *Swan*, with Audun at the helm, travelled in the opposite direction returning to Boretar. On his arrival back home in Cross Street, he would learn about his stepfather's departure and face a puzzle that would help him to decide his next move. It was time for the red stone to play its part. It was time for revenge.

CHAPTER 1

Mora

❖ ❖ ❖ ❖

Ramon knew it was a tight schedule to get *Lex Talionis* loaded and ready to sail in the three weeks before the February full snow moon. If the carrack could leave the port of Olet by the third week in February, with the moon, then Mora could be reached by mid-March, dependent on the weather of course.

If his suspicions about the cargo he would be carrying were correct then the sea route would have to avoid Tufle, Amina's port. This would mean a longer and possibly more hazardous journey via Thos in Toria and Anelo in Arance.

The crossing of the Eastern Sea from the Andore coast to the Morel estuary which lay south-west of

Mora would be the most challenging part. However, the promise of a sea journey and testing the mettle of his new carrack made Ramon tingle with anticipation.

First though, before he left his home in Cross Street, he needed to compose messages for his stepson, Audun, describing his departure and the cargo he was carrying. He also needed to try to leave some explanation of the various messages that had been delivered by Valdin.

A book of poems written by the so-called Bard of Bala, who Ramon knew was in fact the 14th century warrior poet Angus Ferguson, was rebound to show Audun's name on the cover sheet. Maybe Audun would understand what subtlety was behind this cryptic message from the Duke of Alol.

The letter that Valdin had carried requesting that the *Swan* transport the iron goods to Mora was placed alongside two other letters. The first outlined the contract that had just been signed and stated that *Lex Talionis* would be at sea for about three months before returning to Boretar. Ramon also described his plans to negotiate contracts for additional cargoes on the outward journey, to be collected on the return trip. This letter also hinted at the type of cargo he would be loading at Olet and the risks involved.

The second letter summarised the visits of Valdin, describing the huntsman in some detail. Ramon, in particular, described the strange tattoo on Valdin's palm, an open viper's mouth which appeared open and ready to strike and then to do so as the palm closed. Ramon described this in the letter and asked Audun to look at a couple of old manuscripts, as this viper tattoo vaguely reminded him of something he had once read.

Finally he instructed Audun to continue working the *Swan* round the Andore coast, saying that they would probably meet at either Anelo or Thos in May. Ramon locked the door of the house in Cross Street and headed for the port. The carrack, *Victoria*, was bound for Tufle, Amina's main port, but as a favour to his friend, the ship's captain had agreed to detour via Olet.

As Ramon was boarding the ship in Boretar, Valdin was already racing south on his black stallion, Onyx. His destination was the foundries at the Ackar ironworks. He was not looking forward to breathing the smoke-filled air again, but he had to inform Wayland Henry of the new destination port for the equipment. Fortunately, whilst the smith may not have been good with his letters, he was an excellent organiser, and when Valdin reached the forges the first wagons were drawing up to haul the goods overland.

The worked iron was neatly stacked ready for loading and Valdin suddenly understood why this cargo could never have been transported on a caravel like the *Swan*. Each of the long iron tubes must weigh between two and three tons, and there were ten of them. Alongside these were multiple large wooden cores, dozens of iron balls and multiple other forged items. Valdin suddenly worried that even a large carrack might not be capable of transporting such weights.

Valdin instructed Henry to transport all the equipment to Olet, then pulled Onyx round and headed south west. He had better check again with Ramon to confirm that the carrack could indeed carry such a load.

In the second week of February 1509, a large convoy of wagons began clattering onto the dockside in Olet. Ramon had already hired the dock workers, and the slings, cranes and scaffolds were all ready and prepared to load the cargo.

The first wagons carried the ten-foot-long iron tubes, along with a lot of the other forged items. The wooden cores, iron balls and iron straps followed. Ramon had assured Valdin that the weight would not be a risk, as *Lex Talionis* could carry two hundred tons without sitting too low in the water. Indeed Ramon had purchased additional goods that he would sell on in Anelo.

Depending on the weather, the carrack would stop briefly at Thos, in Toria, to take on some fresh supplies. It wasn't the weight of the load that was critical but the order in which the goods were stored on board. It was essential that *Lex Talionis* was not left top heavy so the iron tubes would be the first to be loaded into the base of the hull as the additional ballast would improve the ship's stability in rough seas. As the slings and pulleys creaked under the strain, Ramon's suspicions were confirmed. *Lex Talionis* would be carrying components for cannons to Mora.

Ramon reflected on this again, as he had done before accepting the contract. This was a high-risk cargo and there had to be some reason why the shipment needed to reach Mora by mid-March. Knowing that the peace treaties between Kermin and Amina had been signed the previous year, Ramon persuaded himself that the components he would be transporting must, in some way, be related to the peace treaties. After all, he was a sailor and a merchant and he had no interest in the politics of the southern lands. Most importantly, on completing this contract the fees would more than cover the debt he had incurred in the purchase and refurbishment of the carrack.

Putting aside his concerns, Ramon returned to oversee the loading. Everything went according to plan and with the full snow moon lighting the way, *Lex Talionis* set sail from Olet and made its way into a calm Greater Sea.

Miles further south Audun was preparing to leave Thos, guided by the same full moon. The unusually calm late February weather offered him a chance to get the *Swan* safely back home to Boretar. With Thos disappearing in the distance Audun had no way of knowing that he would pass his stepfather sailing in the opposite direction.

The *Swan* docked at Boretar in the first days of March. Thanks to a brief stop in Olet, to shelter from a sudden winter gale, Audun knew that *Lex Talionis* had taken to the seas some days earlier, but he had no idea why.

Stepping into the house in Cross Street, Audun found it strange that his home was empty. During the past year he had been accustomed to returning home to find Ramon settled in his library with a pile of books in front of him. Audun did of course know that his stepfather had grown tired of being a landlubber and pined to be free again on the open seas. He presumed that this explained the unexpected departure of the carrack from Olet; perhaps Ramon had decided that now that it was fully fitted it was time to give *Lex Talionis* a sea trial.

Audun settled back into his rooms and the maidservant brought him his evening meal. It was late in the evening when he lit the candles in the library and saw the packages laid out on the table. Quickly scanning the letters, Audun took in the news. His stepfather was bound for Mora, carrying a cargo of iron components. Audun noted his stepfather's opinion that the iron work was most likely for the construction of weapons. That in itself was of concern. Did Ramon know about the Amina gunships that had patrolled the Morel estuary in the previous year? Maybe that was the reason for the urgent contract to travel the winter seas and so avoid any renewal of the stop and search patrols at the mouth of the Morel.

Audun was further shocked that the contract had been delivered by Valdin, with whom he had enjoyed a meal only a few weeks earlier, in Thos. Audun noted Ramon's warning about the man's tattoo. He had seen it when Valdin had boarded the *Swan* in Slat, but had paid little attention to it.

Next Audun opened the small package addressed to him. The book of poems, copied from the original version written by Angus Ferguson, had a bookmark in the page containing the poem that had almost certainly broken his mother's heart. Audun sat back and took a deep breath; this could only have come from his father, the Emperor. Now Alberon knew who he was and where he was. He had been too rash in the moment in Tufle nine months earlier when he had first given his father a hint of his existence.

Audun then studied all the documents in more detail. The explicit instruction that the *Swan* transport the weapons was clearly ridiculously impractical, but it suggested that the Emperor was now playing some sort of game with his illegitimate son.

The last book lying on the table was open at the final page. It was a translation of an ancient Aramin myth. Ramon had scribbled a note and left it lying next to the open page: 'Why did you insist on naming the new carrack *Lex Talionis* and what has this to do with your past?'

Audun spoke quietly to himself. "Yes my dear stepfather, once we agreed the sea route for the carrack was to be between Andore and Mora it could only have one name, and it bears a message that maybe in the future I can explain to you. *'Lex Talionis'*: for justice and for what was done. I hope one day you will understand, Ramon."

Finally he rose from the table and started flicking through some of the old manuscripts as Ramon had suggested. An old book titled *History of the Doran Mountains* provided an answer. It carried a full-page copy of a tattoo, a serpent with an open mouth ready to strike with the tail wound round some form of curved dagger.

Suddenly Audun's attention was drawn. He turned a few more pages and found the answer. The curved blade was a skilatu, the favoured weapon of the assassins who had lived in the Doran Mountains a century earlier. Audun again took a deep breath. Had Valdin's mission been to kill him, but back in Thos he had not yet received his instructions? Audun wondered; had he been saved by the weather and the wild winter seas? Was his father playing some sort of word game with him or was he ordering a permanent solution? Either way it was time to prepare to move to Mora. *Lex Talionis, An eye for an eye, a tooth for a tooth, a life for a life.* It was time for justice, time for revenge.

As the winds filled the sails and blew through his black hair, Ramon realised he had forgotten how much he enjoyed the feel of the rolling of a ship under his feet. As it turned, out *Lex Talionis* was a fine ship. Despite the weight of the cargo, the carrack sailed steady and true.

Thos had been a short stopover to top up on fresh supplies. Whilst in the port, Ramon learnt that the *Swan* had left Thos a week earlier. It was a strange thought that his stepson had probably passed somewhere nearby travelling in the opposite direction on the Greater Sea. Ramon hoped that the weather had held and that the *Swan* had sailed safely home.

The conundrum about the name of the carrack still bothered him. He wondered if Audun was now reading the letters in the library. He murmured to himself, "I thought I knew the boy, but I wonder if I know all of his history. Something, or someone, in Mora holds his secrets from me."

Following a two-day stop in Anelo to negotiate contracts for the return journey, *Lex Talionis* headed out onto the Eastern Sea bound for the Morel estuary and on to Kermin's capital, Mora.

A dull mid-March morning welcomed the carrack into the Morel estuary. The port was now only an hour or so upstream. In Anelo Ramon had learnt about the previous year's blockade and he was relieved that there had been no sign of the Amina war boats as *Lex Talionis* approached Kermin waters.

It had been several years since he had last visited Mora and Ramon was looking forward to revisiting some of his old haunts in the city, but for now his task was to get the carrack safely berthed and unloaded. He was crossing the main deck to find Wayland Henry to tell him to go on shore and gather the necessary dock hands and equipment when Valdin caught up with him. "Captain, I have one additional instruction that I have not shared with you. The cargo will not be unloaded until I return to give the order."

Ramon shrugged. "As you wish. If you're reporting back to your Chancellor you might return with the rest of my payment. I presume you have the letter with the details we agreed?"

Valdin nodded. "Yes I have. Please keep all the men and the cargo on board until I return."

Aracir was annoyed that Valdin had agreed to the additional gold payment, but the huntsman had signed the document in Aracir's name and the Chancellor was a man of his word. Valdin was told to return to the carrack, deliver the payment, inform the Captain of his follow-on orders and then leave.

Aracir in turn left his office to report to the Emperor.

"My lord, your goods from Ackar have arrived at the port. I have sent Holger with a troop of guardsmen to quarantine the vessel, and we have spread a rumour in the port that it may be carrying disease. That should keep any inquisitive passers-by some distance away. From my man's report there are ten large iron tubes on board and multiple other metal components. It will take some time to complete the unloading and we will need to get heavy lifting equipment and men. The latter may be difficult if the dock hands are fearful of infection."

Alberon waved his hand dismissively. "I wouldn't have suggested spreading the rumour if I didn't have a solution. Holger knows his instructions. The vessel is to be moved through the swing bridges to the old port this evening. He should already have sent a message to get the wagons to the port by dusk. Lifting gear has been in place near the old warehouses for the past week in anticipation of the ship's arrival, and the guardsmen are to be paid extra wages to complete the unloading. They have been told that the sickness rumour is not true. I am certain that King Bertalan will have spies in the city, and in the port, and I cannot risk him learning about this shipment. The equipment must be loaded onto the wagons and across the bridges by dawn tomorrow. Wayland Henry and the smiths will travel with their iron. Morserat confirms that the new forges are ready near Iskala and that the routes across the mountain are just about passable. Once all this is complete, Holger is to arrest the Captain of the *Swan* and instruct the ship to leave our port."

Aracir coughed. "The equipment has not been carried on the *Swan*, sire. The caravel was not capable of carrying such a load on winter seas."

Alberon banged the table. "I gave specific instructions that the *Swan* was to carry this equipment."

Aracir was calm. "My lord, it was not possible. A caravel would have sunk under the load within a short distance of leaving port. The carrack, *Lex Talionis,* has made the journey successfully and I believe is captained by the master of the *Swan*."

Alberon smiled. "Excellent, you will bring him to me once the ship has left for the sea. *Lex Talionis* is a strange name for a ship. What does it mean?"

Aracir shrugged. "I have no idea."

Valdin was back on *Lex Talionis* and deep in discussion with Ramon. "Captain, we both know what the equipment is that we have shipped from Ackar. It is essential that no word of this cargo gets to King Bertalan in Tamin. I know all the instructions we received were from some unknown Duke of Alol, but my guess is that the orders came from the Emperor. I have spoken briefly to my brother Vidur, who is a confidant of Ingrid, the Queen Mother, and he says he has never heard of a Duke of Alol."

Vidur of course had his own secrets to keep. Moments later a cohort of guardsmen led by Holger, Captain of the City Guard, arrived at the dockside. Valdin continued. "I am sorry Captain Ramon; your ship is quarantined for now and will move through to the old port this evening. I am to tell you that once the goods are unloaded you are to turn round and sail back to Anelo. Neither you nor any of your crew will be allowed to set foot in the city."

"But the men have been at sea for weeks now and they need shore leave!" protested Ramon.

Valdin held his hand up and continued more formally. "Captain, the ship is suspected of carrying disease and hence the guard is here to ensure that no one leaves the vessel. You will return to sea in the morning." He softened slightly. "Ramon, you have been very well paid for this trip and I am sure that for a little extra gold the crew will not miss their shore leave. My job is done." With that the huntsman shook Ramon's hand and left the ship.

Holger stepped forward and saluted. "Captain, from now until you leave Mora, you and your ship are under my command. You will do exactly as I tell you."

It was a long night and dangerous work. Unloading the heavy metal items from the hold in the dark was slow and cumbersome. By the next morning only five of the ten tubes had been loaded onto the wagons and were heading north.

Aracir reported back to Alberon, who was concerned about the delay. "This is not good enough! The longer the equipment is visible on the dockside the more chance there is that news gets to my brother-in-law."

Aracir again calmed his Emperor. "Nothing is left visible on the dockside. The first wagons left before dawn and the task will be completed tonight. All the remaining goods are still hidden in the hold of the carrack."

Alberon had another question. "Have you met the captain? What is he like?"

Aracir shook his head. "I have only seen him from a distance when I was getting Holger's report. He would appear to be in his late forties, maybe early fifties. An old sea dog and an excellent captain would be my guess. He certainly negotiated a handsome deal to deliver your cargo."

Alberon nearly said, *"That can't be my son"*, but he caught the words just in time and instead said, "Are you sure he is the captain of the *Swan*?"

Aracir nodded. "From what Holger has learned from the crew, his name is Ramon. He is the owner of the *Swan* and *Lex Talionis* is a new addition to his fleet. His stepson, Audun, is captain of the *Swan*, which they believe is at its home port in Boretar."

Alberon suddenly realised the connections and the

mistakes. "I look forward to meeting Captain Ramon, but for now, is Morserat's nephew still in Mora?"

Aracir nodded. "Yes I believe Soren is."

"Good, then I have a task for him. I need him to leave today for Iskala and inform his uncle that the goods are on their way. Morserat will know what that means." Alberon gave a wry smile. "You can enjoy a year of peace, my Lord Chancellor, there's plenty of time for you to replenish the treasury. This time next year my cannons will be travelling back across the Doran Mountains."

The next night the rest of the metalwork was unloaded from the carrack. The heavily loaded wagons had again crossed the bridges over the Morel before sunrise and were on their way to Iskala, the capital of Doran. Wayland Henry and his fellow smiths had departed with the last of the wagons.

Ramon was resting in his cabin whilst some of his crew were preparing *Lex Talionis* for the return to sea when there was a polite knock on the cabin door. Holger stepped into the room. "Captain, the swing bridges will open within the hour and your vessel needs to depart the port whilst the tide is high. I presume all is ready?"

"Yes we are almost ready to sail but it is a pity that we cannot enjoy some of Mora's pleasures before we leave," Ramon told the Captain of the Guard.

It was a moment Holger was not looking forward

to. "Captain, your crew may not be allowed entry to the city but unfortunately you will be. On orders from the Emperor I am to arrest you for smuggling weapons into Kermin. Under the 1508 treaties signed between Kermin and Amina, no imports of weapons from Ackar are permitted."

Ramon was stunned. "What are you talking about? My contract was paid by Kermin's Chancellor and my suspicion is that the goods we carried were at the order of the Emperor himself. I have not broken any treaties."

Holger knew that Ramon was indeed telling the truth, but he was a good soldier who followed orders. "Captain, it has come to light that you were smuggling the weapons into Mora for shipment on to the rebels led by the Duke of Alol, who is currently gathering his forces near the Aramin forest."

Ramon rose angrily to his feet. "Holger, this is made-up nonsense, just like the rumours of my ship carrying disease. Am I supposed to believe that a rebel duke could organise the delivery of tons of metalwork to the Emperor's capital and the Emperor would simply let it vanish out into the Kermin Plain? It is ridiculous, preposterous!"

The two guardsmen stepped out from behind Holger, who looked apologetic. "I am sorry sir, but I have my orders to follow."

Ramon was given a short time to brief Vasilli, his second in command, on the situation and he quietly asked the first mate to find Audun and report the situation to him.

Ramon knew that somehow this "mistake" was bound up in Audun's secret past. He stood on the dockside as *Lex Talionis* turned round and headed west on the Morel. He had hoped to spend some time revisiting his old haunts in Mora, but a prison was not among them.

At the house in Cross Street, Audun was also worrying over plans. That morning he had checked the casket on the *Swan* and found that the red stone remained stuck in the same state of transformation, the upper half a perfect red orb and the lower half a rough red stone. Audun had hoped that the stone would give him some guidance. He again reflected that he had acted rashly nine months earlier in Tamin, and with his father's knowledge of where he lived and of the name of the ship he captained, it was likely that his life was in danger. Yet he wondered; if the Emperor wanted him dead, surely Valdin could have delivered that contract, either on the *Swan*, or by waiting in Boretar until Audun returned? It didn't make any sense.

Audun then considered the voyage his stepfather had undertaken, and remembered the letter from the Regents of Kermin, his father's parents, banishing him and his mother from Kermin. The final words echoed in his mind: *"However, if the maid Ragna or her child is apprehended anywhere within our territories the maid will be condemned as a witch and her child a sorcerer. The penalty for witchcraft is death."* It then made some sense. Alberon did not want him quietly eliminated; he wanted him in Mora on trial for sorcery. That way his father would remove the illegitimate son without getting blood on his own hands.

It was clear to Audun that he could not simply sail the *Swan* to Mora and step off into the city. There were three possible options: sail to Tufle and cross overland to Mora, volunteer on another ship bound for Mora, or use the cove north of the Morel where he had run the black market goods during the blockade in 1507 and early 1508. The latter would be the most dangerous if the Amina patrols were reinstated, but it would also be the most covert way of reaching the city.

Audun again reflected on the book of poems. Remembering his mother's heartbreak, he spoke quietly to himself. "I won't make it that easy for you father. Maybe you will understand if Ramon explains the name of the carrack."

Ramon was bored. He might not be in a dungeon, but the suite of rooms in Mora Castle, where he was being held, was beginning to feel claustrophobic. Fortunately the rooms held a large number of books, so Ramon passed the time reading. He was still mystified as to why he had been put under house arrest, but with guards at the doors there was little he could do but wait.

A week passed and Ramon's only visitors were the servants who brought him his food. The guards were also friendly and happy to join in with a card game when none of their senior officers were watching.

It was a wet afternoon and Ramon was sitting with a book in hand when he heard a sudden clanking of metal and shuffling of feet. Ramon knew this must be an important visitor, as the guards were clearly coming smartly to attention.

The man who entered the room was half a head shorter than Ramon and the fair hair was flecked with touches of grey. His cloak was embroidered in gold and Ramon recognised the golden eagle, one of Kermin's royal emblems. So this was the Emperor, Alberon.

As the Emperor reached out a hand Ramon was instantly struck by the ice-blue eyes, so like those of his stepson. Alberon smiled. "Captain Ramon, I am sorry that it has been necessary to have had you incarcerated here for these past few days but you do understand the sensitivity of our situation. Berin, the self-proclaimed Duke of Alol is claiming he has a right to my throne. Fortunately my spies informed me of the Duke's plot and we have been able to confiscate the weapons you transported. They are now safely under my control."

Ramon knew these were lies on top of fiction, but he had little room to manoeuvre so he kept his reply simple. "If you say so my lord, but I did not know, I understood I was fulfilling a contract on behalf of your Chancellor."

Alberon waved away the comment. "Yes Captain, it is all rather complicated, but enough of that, I have other questions I need you to answer."

Ramon sat back in the chair and waited, not knowing what questions an Emperor could possibly pose that he could in any way answer.

"You have a son I believe who is captain of the caravel called the *Swan*?"

It was a strange question, but Ramon answered. "Yes, but he is my stepson."

Alberon leant closer, as if he was going to dissect every word in answer to the next question. "Please tell me his story, captain. How did you meet your stepson?"

Ramon was somewhat perplexed, but he told Alberon the story; how Audun and his mother had left Tamin at night, the evil husband, the flight to Boretar and the mother's death. Alberon listened intently. So this was what had happened to Ragna and her child. His love affair with the maid seemed as if it had happened in a different lifetime.

Once Ramon had finished his story, Alberon leant back. "I have one final question Captain. *Lex Talionis*, what a strange name for a ship. What does it mean?"

Ramon smiled. For a minute he had the upper hand and different pieces of a jigsaw were beginning to form in his mind. "My lord, it is the title of a poem, a ballad, an ancient myth, said to originate from the Aramin tribes and their lost city of gold, Aram."

Alberon grew more interested. "I know of some of the myths and one day I will send an army to the Aramin forest to rid myself of the vermin living there. Maybe I will even find the golden city, but I don't know of the ballad you refer to. Please enlighten me."

Ramon was on safe territory now and he spoke with the authority of one well versed in ancient texts.

"Lex Talionis is a poem, or probably more correctly a ballad, that tells of the demise of Althred, the last king of the Aramin. Althred and his capital Aram were consumed by a red fire brought down on them by an evil enemy. The ballad tells that Althred's second wife, Karun, was hungry for power and jealous of the baby recently born to the regent Queen. Karun led the enemy through the forest to reach Aram and laughed as the city burned. The king's baby son, Adun, escaped the destruction and the ballad says that one day the child will return and seek revenge. The ballad does not describe the return of the son, but ends with the lines that define the child's intent. I can recite them for you:

Lex Talionis
An eye for an eye
A tooth for a tooth
A life for a life
Not my revenge

Justice
Not for revenge
For justice

Lex Talionis
Not for what is now
But for what was done
Betrayal of love
Escape of a son
Not for revenge
For justice
For what was done.

"My stepson insisted that the carrack should be named *Lex Talionis*, although I have no idea why this was important to him. It would have been much simpler to name the ship 'The Revenge'."

At these final words, Ramon thought the Emperor shuddered slightly and went a little pale. It passed in a second as Alberon regained his composure.

"Captain, I have information that says that the *Swan* was guilty of running contraband to Kermin during the past winter and as a result your stepson is a criminal. You will be detained here at my pleasure until Adun presents himself before me to answer these charges."

Ramon instantly noted the slight change in emphasis. The Emperor had said Adun, from the ballad, not Audun. Was he concerned about a mythical child or a real man?

"It is not correct that the father pays the price for the sins of the son, so you will remain here as my guest," said Alberon. "You are welcome to access most areas of the castle but you will not be allowed to leave the castle grounds. I have a large library which you are welcome to make use of." With that Alberon walked out of the room, leaving Ramon pondering the pieces of the jigsaw that he was still juggling with in his head.

CHAPTER 2

Audun

❖ ❖ ❖ ❖

It was mid-April and Audun was once again guiding the *Swan* into the dockside at Thos. The port was particularly busy because the favourable spring weather meant that the sea routes were navigable by most sizes of ship. The caravels were mostly tied up at the dockside, whilst a number of the larger carracks were moored in the harbour. Dozens of small boats were ferrying goods back and forth to the carracks.

Audun spotted *Lex Talionis* moored mid-harbour. He let out a sigh of relief; hopefully Ramon had made a successful trip to Mora. When Audun had learnt about the voyage and the cargo being carried, he was concerned about his stepfather's safety. These concerns were amplified by the fact that the instruction had been to ship the goods on the *Swan*. If the Emperor in Mora understood the meaning of 'Lex Talionis', then Audun might have inadvertently added to the risks Ramon was taking.

Quickly organising the unloading of the *Swan* and leaving everything in the hands of Danill, his helmsman, Audun jumped onto one of the small ferry boats and headed for *Lex Talionis*. Time for a glass or two of wine with Ramon and sharing of the stories they both had to tell.

As Audun climbed aboard the carrack he was met by a solemn-faced Vasilli, Ramon's second in command. Vasilli said nothing but gripped Audun firmly by the arm and led him to Ramon's cabin. Once inside, Audun pulled his arm away. "Vasilli, what is going on? Where is Ramon? Why are you doing this and no word of welcome?"

Vasilli took the seat behind Ramon's desk. Audun had known Vasilli for half a dozen years. The first mate had always been Ramon's right-hand man and whilst Ramon had been enjoying his year's sabbatical, Vasilli had been second in command to Audun on the *Swan*. He had never seen the other man as flustered as he was now.

Audun was impatient. "Well go on, tell me where Ramon is and why he is not on board?"

Vasilli seemed to try to collect his thoughts but failed.

He simply blurted out, "Ramon was arrested in Mora."

Audun recognised the tension in the other man. "Relax, Vasilli. Tell me about the journey and what happened at Mora, but take your time."

Vasilli slowly described the cargo that had been loaded at Olet, the sea journey and the reception at Mora. "I don't know why the authorities at Mora quarantined the vessel. We had no sickness on board but the city guard effectively took control of the ship. As soon as we had unloaded the cargo we were instructed to leave port immediately. That was when Ramon was arrested."

That evening Audun was sitting alone in the Sailor's Rest toying with his meal. Too many thoughts were fighting to get to the top of his consciousness. He told himself to calm down and think about it all logically. He started running through all the parts of the puzzle in his head, trying to fit them together in chronological order.

Valdin, the man with the tattoo, could have been sent to kill him but had not done so. Had that been luck, or was it just fortunate timing? No, Valdin was not sent as an executioner. If he had been there would have been no need to demand that the *Swan* transport the metalwork to Mora.

Audun knew that the book of poems was delivering a message from his father, and it was good fortune that the Emperor was not knowledgeable about travel on winter seas or about the carrying capacity of a caravel. So it was clear that his father did not want him eliminated, but it was also clear that Alberon wanted to deal with his bastard son in Mora. That was why Ramon had been arrested.

Audun had unwittingly drawn his stepfather into the web of intrigue. His thoughts halted at the word 'stepfather'. Ramon was really the only father he had ever known and the one he loved. His real father existed only as an enemy, a target, a goal. It was time to fulfil his destiny, time to avenge his mother. "I will play your game Alberon, and it will be played out in Mora," he whispered to himself.

In mid-May 1509 the *Swan* was crossing the Eastern Sea towards the coast of Kermin. The caravel's destination was the cove north of the Morel where Audun had landed the black market goods in the winter of 1507.

Lex Talionis and the *Swan* had both moored at Anelo earlier in the month and learnt that the Amina gunboats had returned to their stop-and-search duties and were once again patrolling close to the Morel estuary. The *Swan* was carrying an innocent cargo, but Audun knew he could not simply sail the caravel up the Morel to Mora.

Vasilli was once more Audun's second in command, although he was mystified by the younger man's orders. The *Swan* was to moor in the cove and transport Audun to the shore, and then Vasilli was to return to Anelo. He was to remain with the *Swan* and only trade between Anelo, Thos and Tufle. The gold that Ramon had been paid in Mora had been moved to Audun's cabin on the *Swan*, and Vasilli had access to these funds if they were required. Danill, Vasilli's brother and senior helmsman on the *Swan*, was to sail *Lex Talionis* back to Boretar and continue to trade as normal, but he was not to return to Mora.

The early summer sunlight was glinting off the gold clad turrets of Mora Castle as Audun walked into the city through the northern gate. It was an impressive sight, but Audun was looking beyond the gold. So that is my father's home, and my birthright, he thought. High on the castle's central turret, two flags flew lazily in the light summer breeze. One was the flag of Kermin. The white background with four golden stars had been the emblem of the Kingdom for centuries. Flying high above the national emblem was a much larger flag. On the light blue background it showed a bright yellow sun held in the hands of a tall man. Audun had seen the Emperor in Tamin and smiled to himself. "Father, you seem to have grown in the past couple of years!"

It was Audun's first visit to the Kermin capital, and he paused at the city gate to take in his surroundings. The Doran Mountains sat proudly to the north with their snow-capped peaks creating a stunning backdrop to the castle towers. The wide avenue directly in front of him was tree lined, with large houses on either side. This was clearly where Kermin's nobles and rich merchants had their homes. At the end of the avenue he could see the main gateway leading into the castle. Whilst it was highly unlikely that he would be recognised, he felt reluctant to walk openly past his father's front door, so he turned south, following a smaller street which he presumed led to the centre of the city.

A short distance from the gate he found himself in busier streets, full of the citizens of Mora going about their daily business. The city had clearly fully recovered from the deprivations of the winter of 1507-1508. Audun wondered if the people had already forgotten about the suffering that they had gone through as a result of his father's lust for power and Empire. Had the people forgiven the Emperor, or were they too afraid to take action? One thought led to another, and Audun wondered where his stepfather was being held. Ramon was probably somewhere in the castle and he would need to find some way to get a message to him.

First, though, as he planned to stay in the city, he needed a home base. It would be risky to be seen at the docks as it was very likely that he would meet fellow sailors that he knew. Similarly, renting rooms in a tavern might result in encounters with old acquaintances. Whilst Audun was travelling light, and was modestly dressed, his pack contained more than enough gold to purchase a small dwelling. Sitting next to the bags of gold was the casket containing the red stone.

The Golden Fleece tavern sat at the boundary of the Merchant's Quarter and the tradesmen's quarter. Audun had paid for five nights' board, hoping that would give him sufficient time to find more permanent accommodation.

It was early evening and the tap room was getting noisy as the customers enjoyed their ale at the end of the working day. A big brute of a man was holding court with his cronies at the centre of the serving area. From his corner seat Audun heard him complain to his fellows. "The cottage is cursed, I'm sure. It's been quarantined twice in the last few years and when we've managed to let the place the occupants all complain that it's haunted and leave within a few months. It belonged to my wife's sister and husband and I've been trying to rid myself of it for years, but no one wants to buy a cottage that has supposedly twice harboured the pestilence."

Audun walked towards the group, looking to refill his tankard. He deliberately bumped into the big man, causing him to spill some of his ale. For a big man the brute was surprisingly quick. He planted his jug on the counter at the same time as his large fist grabbed for Audun. "Fool, you have spilt my ale! I will make you lick it up from the floor before I get you to replenish my jug."

Audun had lived most of his life amongst sailors, and on the docksides you had to know how to protect yourself. He ducked the swinging fist, and as he stood back up the point of his dagger was already at the man's groin.

He spoke quietly. "I apologise for spilling your beer, and I will refill your jug, but as for licking the floor? Move wrongly now and it will be your balls that need to be swept up from the floor." The man froze as he felt the sharpened point prick his groin. "I may have a proposition for you and I suggest we walk slowly back to my table and I will order a refill for our jugs," continued Audun.

Casually the big man nodded to his cronies as though nothing was wrong. "This man seems to want to do some business with me. I will rejoin you shortly."

Audun's blade had done a trick of its own and was now surreptitiously located under the other man's armpit. Any slip there would be fatal, so the man carefully walked side by side with Audun and took a seat at the table. Audun shouted over to the serving girl. "We need two more jugs over here please."

Pacified, the other man seemed to relax. Audun held out his hand. "My name is Adun and I believe you may have a cottage for sale?" Audun was not sure why he had simply shortened his name other than to try to keep some sort of anonymity in Mora. Why he had chosen the name of the mythical Aramin child he would never recall.

The man opposite gripped the offered hand and tried to make light of his embarrassment. "That dagger of yours weaves a magical dance, I am impressed. Yes I have a cottage for sale, or to rent, depending on your preference. My name is Arvid. When we finish our ale I will show you the cottage. It is only a couple of streets away on the edge of the tradesman's quarter."

The early evening light was fading as Arvid unlocked the front door and he and Audun stepped into the dusty front room. "You can see it is not much of a place and it's in need of some repairs. It belonged to my sister-in-law and her husband, but they died of the pestilence eight years ago. There was another outbreak in this area a couple of years later and the cottage was again quarantined. Since then it has been difficult to rent and impossible to sell. People seem to view the place as being cursed because of its history."

Audun smiled. "I'm not much of a believer in ghosts or curses and I think this will suit my purpose fine. I'm not certain how long I will be staying in Mora, but as long as you offer a fair price I will take it on six months' rent provided you have it cleaned and tidied before I move in."

Arvid haggled as best he could, but he knew that whatever deal he got from Audun was likely to be the best he would get. Eventually a price was agreed.

The pair shook on the deal and Audun concluded the arrangement. "I'm staying at the Golden Fleece for the next few days. Come and find me there when the place is ready and I will pay you what we have agreed."

Audun spent the next few days familiarising himself with Mora's streets. His discreet enquiries as to where Ramon might be were met with blank looks, which largely confirmed his expectation that his stepfather was being held in the castle. Audun moved into his new home in the first week in June.

Having largely explored the city, Audun was at a loose end and was relaxing in the garden at the rear of the cottage. The June sun was warm and he was half asleep when a wasp decided to interrupt proceedings. Standing to rid himself of the irritating insect, Audun was stunned when a bolt of red fire suddenly flashed through the cottage. It lasted only a moment before it was quenched.

Puzzled, he walked through the cottage and opened the front door. Had he heard a knock on the door just as the fire erupted? There was no one there, but an ancient staff lay propped up against the cottage wall. The staff emanated a strange amber glow.

He picked it up and turned back into the cottage's main room. The casket was on the table at the far side of the room and Audun immediately saw that the discs on the sides of the wooden box were glowing bright red.

He rushed over to the casket. It was almost exactly two years since he had taken the piece of dull red rock from the dungeon far below the castle in Aldene, the capital of Bala. He paused, suddenly reluctant to look inside the casket. He remembered his terror in the dungeon and his fear when faced with the power of the red stone. Now he heard a voice, seemingly from inside the casket. It repeated the words he had last heard in Aldene's dungeon two years earlier. *"Audun, I know that you have read about me in the histories. I have been locked in this prison for two hundred years. I cannot return to the world in my old form but I still have power. That power is yours now. One day we will return to Mora and you will have your revenge."*

Audun had concluded some time ago that the disembodied voice must be that of Oien, the alchemist who had ruled the world in the second age, lusting for world domination. He had used the power of the rare mineral othium to fuel vicious conflict and destruction in the early fourteenth century. It must be Oien whose essence was somehow entrapped in the piece of red stone.

Audun had waited for two years in the hope that the power of the old alchemist would help him exact his revenge on his father. Was the waiting over? Had the old alchemist returned? Yet he hesitated. He recalled the stone beginning to transform in Tufle a year earlier, when he had first seen his father. The bottom half had remained unchanged, a rough piece of red rock, but the upper hemisphere had become smooth and unblemished; the dome's deep red mirror had reflected the sunlight that had come in through his cabin window that day. Had his patience been rewarded? Was Audun now being gifted the power to reach for his destiny and avenge his family?

With a mix of fear and anticipation, Audun opened the lid of the casket. What had once been a rough piece of red rock was now a mirror smooth, deep red, round orb, with amber sparks flashing from the shining surface. The metamorphosis was complete.

He closed the casket and looked over at the ancient wooden staff, which he now saw was covered with ancient motifs that meant nothing to him. The staff too seemed to be alive; amber sparks were running down over the carvings. Audun felt his fear rise again. What was the purpose of the staff, and where had it come from? The answer seemed to come from the ether: *"The staff and I are one. Now you have the power."*

CHAPTER 3
The Staff of Power

❖ ❖ ❖ ❖

Mora Castle sat on a rise looking down over the city. The gold-clad turrets, glittering in the June sunlight, were a statement to the wealth of the Emperor. The citizens of Mora had largely recovered from the tribulations of the winter of 1507-1508.

The war that the Emperor had instigated in 1507 with Kermin's southern neighbour, Amina, had been a disaster. Bertalan, the King of Amina, had outwitted and out-manoeuvred his brother-in-law. The caravels, with falconets mounted on their prows, had closed off all access to the river Morel and Mora's port.

The battle in the hill country of the Kermin Alol had been won by the Amina defenders, who had deployed culverins in action for the first time. The cannons, the falconets and the culverins had become the weapons of the future. The winter of 1507-1508 had been one of deep snow and starvation in Mora. In the spring of 1508 peace treaties had been signed between the countries, and with trade routes reopened, by 1509 life had largely returned to normal in Kermin and Amina.

In June 1509 the Emperor was not resident in Mora Castle. He had crossed the high Doran Mountains which formed the northern border between Kermin and its northern neighbour Doran and was travelling towards his second capital, Iskala.

Alberon was by birthright King of Kermin and King of Doran, and by threat of conquest he was also overlord of Soll, the country to the north of Doran. In 1496 he had crowned himself Emperor of the North, but his ambition for Empire also stretched to the south. Whilst Kermin was rich from its trade and the gold found in the Doran Mountains, both Doran and Soll were relatively poor.

By contrast, Amina, Kermin's southern neighbour was fabulously wealthy, as its capital, Tamin, and the nearby port of Tufle controlled much of the trade with the countries on the island of Andore that lay across the Middle Sea. In addition Tufle's shipyards built almost all of the vessels that plied their trade across the southern seas. Bertalan, the King of Amina, and his wife Aisha were childless, so Alberon's desire to extend his empire to the south could be settled through succession. Alberon was married to Sylva, Bertalan's sister, and as long as Bertalan and his Queen remained childless Alberon's sons, Aaron or Elrik, would succeed to the Amina throne when he died. Once crowned, the new king would swear allegiance to his father, thereby cementing the Empire.

Alberon however was not a patient man and was not prepared to wait on future possibilities. In 1507, at the Emperor's command, Kermin declared war on Amina. The war had been a catastrophe for Alberon, a humiliation, and as he rode towards Iskala he remembered the disrespect he had been shown in Tufle and Tamin a year earlier. He had signed the treaties in 1508; it had been his only option, as he had needed time to regroup and rearm. Now Alberon needed cannons, and it was for that reason that he was riding towards the Doran capital, Iskala.

Audun sat at the table in the old cottage staring into the casket as if mesmerised. A myriad thoughts were cascading through his head. The rough piece of red stone was now a perfect shining orb, but it sat in the round base of the casket seemingly at peace. The completion of the metamorphosis must mean something, but what? Was it now time to march up to the castle and settle things with his father? Could he release his stepfather, Ramon, from Mora's prison? Oien had promised him power, and whilst the deep red orb had a fascination, it showed no sign of being a weapon of power.

Audun had been playing a game of words with his father, and that game had brought him to Mora, but Alberon was one of the most powerful men in the world and Audun could see no way to confront his father without an army at his back. How could he raise an army?

Audun thought about the game so far, and the letters he had left for Alberon on the Emperor's flagship, *The Eagle*. That was almost a year ago and it had brought him to his father's attention. Audun remembered the coincidence of meeting with Valdin, who may have been an assassin sent to eliminate him. The carrack had been named *Lex Talionis* to send a deliberate message to the Emperor, and Audun had not realised that this would cause Ramon to be arrested and detained in Mora. Audun also remembered the equipment carried by the carrack. *Lex Talionis's* cargo had been the essential components to manufacture modern weapons, falconets, culverin and bombards. Audun thought that maybe these were the weapons he needed to have at his command, not the deep red orb.

As he rode through the small town of Iskala towards the castle on its rocky promontory, Alberon's thoughts mirrored those of his illegitimate son. If he was to wage a second war against his brother-in-law he needed to have weapons of destruction. Bertalan had used cannons in the battle in the Kermin Alol and on board the ships that had blockaded the Morel estuary. The weapons had been imported from the ironworks in Ackar on the island of Aldene, and 1507 was the first time the cannons had gone to war. In the Kermin Alol the culverins had torn huge holes in the lines of the attacking Kermin foot soldiers, whilst the falconets on the prows of the caravels had stopped any ships moving into or out from Mora's port. The treaties signed in 1508 prohibited Kermin from importing weapons from Ackar, but Alberon, for once, had been ahead of the game and in 1507 he had sent a team of master smiths to Ackar to learn how to build cannons. The treaties said nothing about Kermin developing its own weapons.

Alberon was in Doran to inspect the progress his smiths had made. He was met at Iskala's castle gate by his uncle, Morserat, who was the Duke of Doran and Commander in Chief of Kermin's armies. He was also Alberon's proxy ruler in Doran, but the two men were not friends. The fifty-year-old Duke disliked his nephew's arrogance, recklessness and impetuousness. Morserat took Alberon to the Emperor's richly appointed apartments in the castle and informed him that the next day they would travel down to the plain and assess the progress being made at the forges.

The village of Sparsholt was an hour's ride north from Iskala, and the smoke from the forges could be seen some distance away. Sparsholt was a new construction on the Doran Plain. The forges and neighbouring cottages had been constructed during the summer of 1508; Alberon hoped that the remoteness of the location would keep the work there well hidden from any of his brother-in-law's spies.

Master smith Wayland Henry was in charge at Sparsholt, and he was the first to greet his Emperor. Alberon dismounted. "Well Master Henry, I hope you are making progress here."

Wayland bowed. "Yes sire, the furnaces are all fully operational and we are beginning the construction of the weapons. We have only been here now for two months, but when the Duke informed me of your imminent arrival in Iskala we worked day and night to get one of the culverins prepared for demonstration."

Alberon nodded. "Good, lead on and show me."

The beast was mounted on a gun-carriage further north on the Doran plain, half a mile from Sparsholt. The ten-foot tube that had been transported from Ackar was now fully formed, with muzzle, trunnion, chase and breech. The whole culverin was decorated with forged images of wild animals.

In addition to Wayland and his assistant smiths, Sparsholt was also the new home for five gunners. Osian and his gun team had been present at the debacle in 1507 when Kermin's cannons had sunk in the mud of the waterlogged Kermin Plain, miles behind the battle lines on the Kermin Alol. The gunners had been recruited by Morserat in late March and had travelled from Mora to Doran with the iron components and the smiths. Now it was time for them to demonstrate their prowess.

Osian and his team stood to attention and saluted as the Emperor and Duke reined in close to the culverin. Osian stepped forward. "Welcome, my lords. I hope Wildfire's power will impress you."

Alberon looked quizzically at Morserat. The Duke explained. "Gunners like to give their weapons names and these are usually dictated by the symbols forged on the barrel by the smiths. Since Osian and his team were here as the culverin was being forged they had an opportunity to request the characters and the names. Osian named the culverin Wildfire and asked the smiths to forge the appropriate motifs and hence the images on the barrel of the wild animals being consumed in a dragon's fire."

Alberon smiled and nodded to Osian. "A good choice of name Osian, and wild fire will be what my artillery will deliver to our enemies."

Osian gave the orders and the culverin was primed, loaded with the ball and the powder ignited. The iron ball sailed out across the plain and on landing bounced forward on the hard ground. Alberon smiled, imagining

Amina foot soldiers being obliterated by the bouncing ball. He turned to Wayland Henry. "A good start, Master Henry, but there is a lot of work to do if we are to be ready to bring the artillery across the Doran Mountains next spring. I will return in a couple of months and hope to witness much more of your wild fire." With that the Duke and the Emperor turned their horses and rode back to Iskala.

In his rooms in Iskala, Alberon was daydreaming about how his army would defeat the forces of Amina. In his mind's eye he could see Wildfire being rolled across the Tamin Plain ready to obliterate the walls of Bertalan's capital. One thought led to another, and Alberon remembered the humiliation of the previous year and the old nag that he had been forced to ride from the port of Tufle to his brother-in-law's castle in Tamin. That triggered the memory of the crowds jeering at him as he rode through Tamin's streets and the one face still so clearly etched in his mind, that of the young man with the fair hair and ice-blue eyes, smiling as he mouthed the words, *"One day I will come for you Alberon and I will have my revenge."*

Alberon now knew that the young man was Audun, his own illegitimate son, the product of a love affair of his youth. For the umpteenth time he wondered if he should have had the bastard son eliminated. It would have been easy to give the order to the messenger his

Chancellor, Aracir, had sent to Boretar to organise the shipment of the iron components now being worked on in Sparsholt's forges. Alberon recalled the name of the carrack that had transported the iron from Olet to Mora: *Lex Talionis*. Audun's stepfather, Ramon, had captained the carrack and whilst Alberon had hoped to arrest the stepson, Ramon was able to explain the message delivered in the carrack's name.

> *Lex Talionis*
> *An eye for an eye*
> *A tooth for a tooth*
> *A life for a life*
> *Not my revenge*
> *Justice*
> *Not for revenge*
> *For justice*
>
> *Lex Talionis*
> *Not for what is now*
> *But for what was done*
> *Betrayal of love*
> *Escape of a son*
> *Not for revenge*
> *For justice*
> *For what was done*

These, he now knew, were the final lines of an ancient

ballad, a myth that had been passed down through generations by the savage tribes living in the Aramin forest. Alberon was amused and intrigued. He rather admired the bravado shown by the son he hadn't even known existed until twelve months ago. What was the boy going to do, arrive at Mora with an army and lay siege to the city to claim his birthright? Alberon's wife Sylva had suggested the possibility nine years ago when she discovered Alberon's letter to his teenage lover. It was as preposterous now as it was back then – a bastard son, a ship's captain, raising an army to storm Mora? Alberon laughed quietly at the ridiculous thought.

In Mora, Audun was wrestling with the same problem. If he was going to get his revenge, how could it be achieved? He thought of his mother Ragna, dying in Boretar of a broken heart five years earlier. She had been the Emperor's first lover, but she and her unborn child had been banished from Kermin by Alberon's mother Ingrid, now the Dowager Queen. Audun remembered the letter, still tucked in his sack, the letter that accused his mother of using witchcraft to seduce the young prince, the letter that by connection would allow his father, the Emperor, to sentence him to death for being a sorcerer, born of a witch.

Audun spent two days aimlessly walking Mora's streets hoping for some inspiration. In the cottage the red orb shone but remained silent. If his days consisted of aimless wanderings, his nights were restless, filled with strange dreams and nightmares. He would dream he was back in Tamin where Arin and Amelia, his grandparents, had lived, but he was not in the little house in Rose Street, he was in the dungeon of Tamin Castle, a silent onlooker as his grandfather was being tortured. Over and over again Audun would hear the torturer demand, "Tell me where your daughter and grandson are and we can end all this pain." The dream would flip to the richly adorned family rooms in the castle and Audun could see King Bertalan reading a letter from his sister. Sylva, Alberon's wife, needed her brother to seek out her husband's ex-lover and her bastard child. The dream would switch back to the dungeon, and he would see his grandfather lying dead on the dungeon floor and wake with a start.

Now awake and reluctant to return to a disturbed sleep, he would pace the cottage floor. The old staff and the orb seemed to be enjoying a slumber that he could not himself find.

At other times Audun would dream that he was back in the ancient cave below Aldene Castle, carefully replacing the piece of red rock in the casket that now sat in the room next door. He would relive the fear he had felt when he had first seen the red light emanating from the dungeon's depths and first heard the disembodied voice instructing him to go deeper into the cave, to his doom or his destiny.

Then suddenly his dream would become a nightmare. He was holding the old staff, the hilt now crowned with the red orb, and as he lifted the staff, red fire erupted from the tip. He could see the fire coalescing and fireballs illuminating the vista in front of him. One moment it was soldiers that were consumed and in the next moment cities were burning and he could see men, women and children running, living torches, as their cities were burnt to the ground.

He would wake drenched in sweat. He recalled no details other than the flames, the death and destruction, and he did not recognise any of the burning cities.

In addition to being a seasoned sailor and ship's captain, Audun was an amateur historian. He had been fortunate that his grandfather and mother had taught him to read and more fortunate still that his stepfather, Ramon, had a large collection of old books in his library in the house on Cross Street in Boretar. Audun was particularly fascinated by the period of history around 1300 when wars of conquest were waged across the island of Andore and in Amina.

After two restless nights Audun was sitting in the tap room of the Golden Fleece lost in thought. The red orb and the old staff had some sort of connection in his nightmares, but what? He was searching his memory of the history books, trying to piece together what he knew chronologically, and he started with the oldest book he had ever read. The book's title was *The Evils of the Second Age* and the author had a strange name, 'Ala Moire'. The book was written hundreds of years ago but told of an even earlier time. Audun had learnt of the council of five and what was effectively the age of a rare mineral called othium. In the Second Age the red stone had powered conquest and aggression followed by industrialisation and the expansion of man's power beyond the planet. The author wrote of the enslavement of the people of the world, conscripted into the othium mines and industrial factories. The closing lines of the book were short: "Then God intervened and the meteorite rains fell across all the lands."

Audun knew that according to the history an alchemist called Oien had led the tyranny of the second age, but also that the alchemist had somehow survived the meteorite rain. Audun's thoughts moved to the histories of two hundred years earlier. *The History of the Kermin Alol, 1270 to 1303* gave much more detail of the battles fought near his home city of Tamin. The terrifying power of othium's red fire wielded by the old alchemist, Oien, was described in detail in the chapters describing the battles of 1301.

Audun searched his memory for references to a staff with a red orb wielded by the alchemist. Nothing came to mind; Oien knew how to harness the power of othium but there was no mention of his staff. The thirteenth century wars in the Kermin Alol and on

Aldene were ended before the gates of the Ackar city of Erbea. Audun had read the history book many times, Angus Ferguson's *White Light Red Fire*. Recalling the author's name distracted Audun as he recalled the book of poems written by the same author and the poem that had driven his mother Ragna into terminal depression and heartbreak.

> *We met in the north on a spring day*
> *I am sure now it was our destiny*
> *Tender moments in the Nath*
> *With the sand at our backs*
> *Somehow fate set our path*
> *A love that would last*
> *Now in our winter years*
> *Smile Elbeth my love*
> *Shed no tears*
> *White gold our rings*
> *United we were*
> *United we will always be*
> *My love for you*
> *Is for all of eternity*

This was the poem that his father had read to his young lover, Ragna, twenty-three years earlier. It was the poem that had first caused Audun to seek retribution and revenge.

Shaking off the memories of his mother and

recognising that his thoughts had been distracted, Audun rose to refill his jug with ale. Returning to his table, he focused back on the history as it was recorded in *White Light Red Fire*. If his memory was correct, Oien had used his staff as a weapon in the battle at the pass through the Inger Mountains and again in the final battle for Erbea in 1302.

Gradually Audun reworked his way through the history. In 1300 Oien had used the red rock othium to power machines and weapons but had also, at times, used a staff to demonstrate his own personal power. Audun could not recall any reference to the staff holding a red orb at its hilt, but then in 1300 the alchemist himself could have been the orb. Audun again remembered the last reference to the alchemist in *White Light Red Fire*:

Munro took the alchemist in his arms and felt the anger and the lust for power which had corrupted the old man's soul. He placed his palms together around the other's neck and stepped back. The white wall now completely enclosed Oien, and as it brightened in intensity it hid him from view. Flashes of red seemed to bounce around inside the wall and then began to fade away. The wall became a shimmering wave, like a mirage in the desert. Gradually that too vanished, and all that remained where Oien had been was a large piece of dull red rock.

The piece of dull red rock that Audun had stolen from the dungeon in Aldene, the bright red orb that was resting in its casket back in the cottage, was the thing Audun knew to be either the heart or the soul, or maybe simply the essence, of the old alchemist. Then Audun reflected on the final phase of the history of the early fourteenth century, *The History of Dewar the Third – The Peacemaker,* the king who had brought fifty years of peace and prosperity to the lands, the peace and prosperity that had lasted almost two hundred years.

Audun sat back in his chair and closed his eyes. He needed to think. History was an account of the past, or the stories that were rooted in the past, and they could not be changed. Could history inform the future? Should history inform his future? He needed time to think. He finished his jug of ale and left the Golden Fleece. Maybe a walk in the sunshine would help clear his mind.

Deep in thought, Audun wandered down through the bustling main street and left Mora by the southern gate. As always the dock area was a hubbub of activity as sailors and dockhands shouted instructions to each other. Oblivious to the noise and the activity, he crossed one of the swing bridges over the river Morel and walked out onto the Kermin Plain. The spring grass was lush green and the scent of the early summer flowers perfumed the air.

Taking deep breaths and inhaling the peace of the Plain, Audun sat on a small knoll that lifted his view over the port. Dominating his vista were the golden turrets of Mora Castle. That castle should have been his home, his inheritance. If it had been so, his mother would still be alive, and so would his grandparents. It was his right and his destiny. He had to avenge his family.

He paused and listed the guilty parties in his head: his father Alberon, the Emperor, the Empress Sylva, the Dowager Queen Ingrid and Bertalan, Sylva's brother, the King of Amina. All were guilty of the crime, the elimination of his family. That made four who were responsible, and then he remembered his stepbrothers, Aaron and Elrik. The two were still just boys and if he was correct, Aaron, the elder, was perhaps eleven and his brother maybe nine. The two boys could not be guilty, but if Audun was to assert his right to the Kermin throne then the boys would, in time, be his competitors.

He recalled the chance meeting with Aaron on the dock at Tufle when he had given the boy the letter for Alberon that had first alerted the Emperor to his existence. It would only have taken a second to remove one son by pushing the lad over the dockside. Audun was glad he had resisted the impulse.

In a short time thinking became daydreaming, and as the sun warmed him, Audun dozed.

The return to reality was sudden and disconcerting. Taking deep breaths of the perfumed air, he slowly opened his eyes. With a shudder of relief he saw that Mora remained real and solid in front of him.

He knew he could only have drifted into sleep for a few moments, but those moments had again been filled with red fire. Rather than try to shake the horror-filled images from his mind as he had done on the earlier occasions, he tried to focus on the details of the dream. He had been standing on this very knoll looking over Mora as the city burned. As in the nightmares of the previous two nights he was holding the old staff by the hilt, which was crowned with the red orb, and as he lifted the staff the red fire erupted from the tip. In contrast to the earlier dreams, it was clear that the city he was destroying was Mora. He was laughing like a madman as the fire from the staff grew more and more intense. First the ships in the harbour were consumed, and then as his laughter became more hysterical he could feel himself lifting the tip of the staff and pointing it directly at the castle. Initially the fire reflected from the golden turrets, causing violent explosions across the city. Slowly the gold seemed to surrender to the fire and golden waterfalls cascaded down from the castle roof tops as the castle itself was consumed. In the midst of all the destruction Audun could hear himself wildly screaming, "I will have my revenge!"

Audun sat up slowly, gradually controlling the tremors of fear that shook his body as the images of fire and destruction replayed in his mind. He rubbed his eyes to make sure his sight really was telling him that the city below still remained intact. Standing, up he realised he was now positioned exactly as he had been in the dream. Across the city the golden turrets glinted, as if laughing at his stupidity, whilst inside, he could recall his madness in the moment and his shout of "I will have my revenge" continued to echo in his mind.

Shaking himself in an attempt to disperse the tension, Audun walked away from the knoll and went a little further out onto the plain. As he walked, he thought. He had a right to take his revenge, an eye for an eye, Lex Talionis, but he could not hold all the citizens of Mora responsible or guilty. If Mora burned to satisfy his revenge then what next, would Tamin also have to burn? The stone was setting his compass and its desire was for ultimate power, complete power.

As he continued walking, the contradictions seemed to crystallise. He needed the power of the stone to claim his inheritance, his right to a throne. The stone, or whatever or whoever was encapsulated in the rock, wanted him to take the throne for its power and wealth and the wider opportunities it presented. He thought he could control the stone, but it was the red orb that was controlling him.

Audun was so engrossed in his own ponderings that he didn't hear the horsemen until they were almost on top of him. It was a troop of fast-moving cavalry riding under the golden eagle flag, the Kermin royal banner. Mounted on a white stallion, the lead rider wore a jewelled crown on his head, Audun recognised the rider immediately – it was his father. Crystals of resolution shattered to dust, hatred filled the void, and his cold blue eyes followed the riders: *I will avenge my family.*

Alberon didn't notice the lone walker as he and his troop thundered across the plain and then over the Morel Bridge before slowing to a canter as they followed the main street up to the castle. He had enjoyed the return journey from Iskala. He was pleased with the progress being made on his cannons, and the white stallion was a fine companion for the ride through the Doran passes, where the snow-capped peaks cooled the wind and refreshed the riders. The gallop had been exhilarating, and the grazing sheep and cattle had scattered in panic as the fast-moving riders had approached. The sun was warm, the grass a lush green and the Emperor was happy, for now.

Alberon was still smiling as he entered his private chambers, but the smile slipped when he found his mother waiting for him. Ingrid, the Queen Mother, had been widowed in 1495 when her husband Elrik, Alberon's father, had been killed as a result of a cannon jamming and exploding next to him. It was on his father's death that Alberon had ascended to the Doran throne.

Ingrid was now in her early sixties and largely kept to her own chambers, but she remained well informed and was still a shrewd politician. Alberon knew his mother seldom made social visits, so she must be here for some particular reason. He had always felt somewhat inferior in the presence of his mother, particularly as she somehow always seemed to know more about events than he would have thought possible considering her closeted existence.

Resetting his smile, Alberon greeted Ingrid. "Well mother, how nice to have you here to greet me on my return from my travels. I presume you are here to welcome me home?"

Ingrid considered her son for a long moment before replying. "I am of course pleased to see you safely returned home, but I am here to understand what you are up to."

Alberon tried to be nonchalant. "I am simply fulfilling my duties as King of Doran, and with the passes closed through the winter this was my first opportunity to visit Iskala this year. Also you know what Duke Morserat is like. He may be a good commander of light cavalry, but he is no administrator and there were a number of things I needed to attend to whilst I was in Iskala."

Ingrid held her son in a stare that made him look away as he took the seat opposite her. "So did you check on the progress of your cannons whilst you were in Iskala?" she asked.

Alberon was stunned. How did she know about these things? *Lex Talionis* had been docked at Mora for less than thirty-six hours and the metalwork had been on its way north to the Doran Mountain passes in an even shorter time. He tried to look innocent. "Mother, I have no idea what you are talking about. You know the 1508 treaties forbid Kermin from importing cannons, and if I had done, why would I transport them to Iskala? They would be far removed from where they would need to be deployed at the Kermin Alol."

The Queen smiled a rueful smile. "Alberon, you are cunning and devious. I have read the treaties, and whilst we cannot import weapons from Ackar they say nothing that prohibits us from building our own. I presume that is what Master Wayland Henry is currently doing somewhere out on the Doran Plain?"

Alberon was about to respond, but before a word got out his mother continued. "Alberon you think you are very clever, but going to war again with Amina would be simply stupid. Have you learnt nothing from the disasters of two years ago? There is no rationale for an invasion of Amina other than to satisfy your pride, your vanity and your ego. This desire of yours to be a glorious Emperor should be consigned to the history books on pages that should not be reopened. I have other questions for you that I suspect you will also try to deflect, deny or simply lie about, so I will leave those for another day."

With that the Dowager Queen rose and left her son still puzzling. How could she know all this, and what else did she know? He didn't know about the huntsmen,

Valdin and Vidur, who were retained by the Queen. They were her eyes and ears to the wider world.

Two hours later Ingrid was settled again in her own chambers when a polite knock on the door announced the arrival of the expected visitor. "Enter, Valdin" was the command. The huntsman was in his early thirties, tall and well-built with thick black hair, but his most distinctive feature was the strange tattoo on his palm, an open viper's mouth ready to strike.

The Queen indicated a seat and poured a glass of wine for her visitor. "Valdin, I have asked my son about the cannons and naturally he denies any knowledge of them. He is of course lying, and that makes me wonder what else he is concealing from me. Please tell me again about your journey to Boretar, and I want all the details."

Valdin had now told his story to the Queen several times, but as she was his paymaster he was happy to tell it again. The Queen let him finish before asking her questions.

"Do you know who this Duke of Alol is?"

Valdin shook his head. "My brother hadn't heard of him either."

The Queen smiled. Vidur was good with secrets; under orders from the Queen he had killed the Duke of Alol in the battle at the Kermin Alol in 1507. "Do you know why the Duke's instructions were insistent that the metal goods be carried on a caravel called the *Swan*?"

she asked. "To me it shows how little he understands about the sea."

Again the huntsman shook his head.

The Queen continued, "Now once more, describe the young Captain of the *Swan*."

Valdin had described Audun to the Queen before but on this occasion she stopped him part way through. "You describe his eyes as ice blue, which is unusual. Did they remind you of anyone?"

Valdin paused to think. "I was only nineteen when your husband was tragically killed so I only met him in passing once, as Vidur and I were coming to meet you to discuss a mission. What struck me were the King's eyes. I have only seen your son, the Emperor, from a distance, but he seems to have pale blue eyes. The only other time I have seen similar eyes was when I saw the young captain."

A mixture of emotions crossed the Queen's face. "Tell me again what else you know about the young man."

Valdin did as requested, but ended with a suggestion. "You could learn far more by talking to his stepfather, Ramon, who is being held by your son as a house guest here in the castle."

Ingrid had seen the man several times when he was walking the castle grounds and she cursed herself for not making the connection. "Thank you Valdin, you may leave me now." Ingrid sat alone for some time remembering the past and contemplating the present. The only other person she knew with such distinctive eyes was her eldest grandson, Aaron.

The Queen Mother was not to know it, but the man whose image she was trying to conjure in her mind was not very far away. Having watched the Emperor and his entourage gallop past, Audun had renewed his vow to have his revenge, but in his mind's eye he could also still see the images of destruction as Mora burned.

Walking back from the Plain over the Morel Bridge, the contradictions competed for prevalence. Audun wanted revenge for the wrongs done to his mother and his grandparents, and he knew who the guilty parties were, but did he also really seek the inheritance and the power that went with it? He was a sailor and he had his freedom. If he were to become a king, he would have power and no freedom. Oien, or whatever remained of him in the red stone, wanted power, and that power would only wreak terrible destruction if it were released. This much he knew from history. Should he have left the stone in the dungeon at Aldene? Maybe now he should return it, but without the stone's power how could he get his revenge? The contradictions twisted and turned but none seemed to provide an answer, or a solution, or even a way forward.

Audun paused at the turning from the main street into the tradesmen's quarter. He could see the cottage a short distance away and stood still for a long moment considering his options. Maybe he should just walk away, leave all this behind here, and return to the sea. A contrary voice replied. *What then about your revenge?* The first voice countered, *My revenge is not worth the destruction I have been shown.* The second voice would not be silenced. *If you leave the stone and the staff here it may well be found by your father and he would not hesitate to deliver the destruction you so fear.*

Audun spoke out loud, cutting through the internal debate. "I set myself on this path when I removed the stone from the cave at Aldene Castle, I must see where it leads me but I will not allow my visions of destruction to become reality."

Audun entered the cottage warily, unsure of what he might find inside. Nothing had changed since he had left that morning. The casket holding the stone glowed softly red whilst the staff simply lay against the stone wall, a piece of old wood notched with strange carvings. Audun then remembered the words he had heard a few days earlier when he had first found the staff at his front door: *The staff and I are one, now you have the power.*

Recalling the words brought back the images he had seen whilst dozing on the Plain. He shuddered as he remembered the madness that had possessed him in his dream as he screamed wildly, "I will have my revenge!" He could almost feel again the power of the orb and the staff in his hand. It was this feeling that suddenly posed the question, how had the staff and the stone become one?

When he picked up the staff to inspect it more closely it seemed to come to life again. Amber sparks ran over the notched carvings and flashed from the thin tip. The hilt of the staff was flat and carved into the surface was a capital "O" superimposed by a capital "I", Φ. The first two letters of the alchemists name.

As Audun considered the carving, the casket on the table started to shine with a deeper, brighter red, as if calling for his attention. With his heart pounding and fear flooding his veins, Audun tried to resist the call, but the stone's demand was too strong. Opening the casket he lifted the red orb out and placed it on the hilt of the staff, where it stuck fast to the Φ symbol. Immediately the amber sparks on the shaft coalesced and red flames licked the surface of the wood. Then the orb seemed to shout the words, *Now you have the power.*

CHAPTER 4

Questions and Answers

❖ ❖ ❖ ❖

Audun threw the staff to the floor as though he had suddenly realised he was holding a poisonous snake. Indeed with red flames cascading down the length of the wood from the red orb, and sparks spitting from the tip, the staff almost looked like a snake. He knew the object lying at his feet was far more dangerous than any snake, and to release his fear and tension he shouted out loud: "I want my revenge, but I am not seeking power!"

The orb seemed to understand and a voice replied more softly, *Now you have power*. Gradually the flames diminished and only the amber sparks remained, spitting from the tip of the staff and from the surface of the red orb. Audun spoke to himself. "I am not ready and I may never want this power, I need to separate them again."

Taking the staff in one hand, he grasped the orb and pulled. It responded violently. Red fire engulfed his hand, and he screamed in pain. The orb and the staff remained tightly bound together. When he pulled his hand free the pain instantly vanished, and to his amazement, when he examined his hand, it was unmarked.

Audun retained a grip on the staff with his left hand and the amber sparks danced through and over his clenched fingers. The words from moments earlier sprang back into his mind: *Now you have power.* Taking deep calming breaths and ignoring the strangeness of the moment, Audun addressed the orb directly: "If I have the power then you will separate again when I demand it." Again the right hand grasped the orb and again the red flames and the pain erupted.

He tried again, this time with a threat. "Oien, I don't understand what part of you remains locked in the stone but you are locked in and you are now in my power. You will release yourself from the staff or I will return you to the underground and bury you in a deep hole, and that is where you shall remain for another two hundred years."

There was silence. Now on this third attempt the orb and the staff separated and Audun saw that the engraved symbol Φ on the hilt of the staff was burning bright red. The power of the old alchemist was locked in the stone, and it seemed therefore that it had to be subservient to his wishes.

Then the question that had eluded Audun's thinking once more presented itself. If the alchemist was locked in the stone, who had delivered the ancient staff?

Ramon was walking the castle walls and looking longingly at the ships moving in and out of Mora's port. He had now been the Emperor's 'guest' for almost three months, and whilst he was being well treated, the time was beginning to drag and he was still no nearer to understanding the real reason for his detention. The claim that *Lex Talionis* had been transporting weapons for some fictitious Duke of Alol was clearly nonsense, but was it possible that Audun had run contraband in 1507-1508? That was the winter after the 1507 war when the Amina king had blocked all access to Mora, and whilst the poor died of starvation the rich survived on black market supplies. Would Audun have been tempted to take such risks with the *Swan*? It was possible, but it seemed unlikely that the Emperor would know about the culprit in such detail. And how did that link to the request that the *Swan* deliver the ironwork which in the end had been transported on *Lex Talionis*? The pieces of the jigsaw would not join together in his head to form any clear picture.

Deep in thought Ramon, did not hear the maid

approach him until she gave a quiet cough. As he turned the maid gave a curtsey. "I am sorry to disturb your walk, Captain, but my mistress would like to talk with you. Would you be kind enough to follow me please?"

The maid guided Ramon to some buildings clustered close to the western castle wall. They were separated from the main castle by a small courtyard which was decorated with summer flowers. Ramon had at times sat in this courtyard enjoying the solitude, but he had never entered the building. He knew these were the oldest structures within the castle walls, having been constructed in the thirteenth century. He also knew that they were the private quarters of the Dowager Queen, Ingrid. The exterior façade of the buildings might have been old, but the interior was richly decorated with tapestries and paintings.

The maid led Ramon along some corridors and up a flight of stairs and knocked on the door of what Ramon guessed was a turret room. On hearing an instruction, the maid opened the door and indicated to Ramon that he should enter.

His guess was correct. The turret room was bright with sunlight shining through the windows, some of which were of stained glass. Sitting on a chair looking out of one of the windows that overlooked the city was a lady. Her dress looked fabulously expensive with intricate designs picked out in gold thread. Her light brown hair was specked with grey and her hazel eyes sparkled with intelligence. This then was the Queen Mother.

Ingrid motioned Ramon forward. "Thank you for coming Captain, and please take a seat. I hope you will join me in a glass of wine."

For a moment the Queen said nothing more; she seemed to be taking the measure of her visitor. Ramon recognised that this was a woman who was used to power and politics, and above all, someone who expected to be obeyed.

"Captain, may I call you Ramon?" said the Queen. "I am not one for too much formality."

Ramon nodded. "Of course, Your Majesty." The Queen's voice was remarkably soft, but Ramon guessed that it could, when necessary, acquire a sharp edge.

She smiled. "No formality, please call me Ingrid. Now I have heard at second hand about your voyage from Boretar and the cargo you carried. I would like to hear your version, and I would also like to learn more about your stepson."

Ramon was taken aback for a moment. First the Emperor and now his mother; why did they have such an interest in Audun? Alberon had claimed the reason was to punish him for smuggling, but the Queen could not possibly be interested in such transgressions.

Ingrid immediately noted Ramon's discomfort. Although she really wanted to know about the son, it would be easier to start with the transported cargo.

"I know that the equipment that you carried from Boretar is said to have been at the instruction of the Duke of Alol. I know you doubt this, and I can confirm it as fiction. The Duke was killed in the 1507 war, and unless his ghost managed to sign the documents, the story is make-believe. I know you were paid by Chancellor Aracir, and without question the cargo was for my son. My sources tell me that the metal components you transported were most likely the raw materials necessary to build cannons. Is that also your opinion?"

Ramon recognised that he might now be on dangerous ground, but he had always believed that truth was the best defence. "Yes, Your Majesty," he replied. The Queen gave a slight frown and Ramon corrected himself. "Sorry, Ingrid. Yes we collected a large number of metal components from the ironworks in Ackar, including ten long metal tubes. I cannot think of another purpose for these other than for them to be fabricated into culverins in forges somewhere here in Kermin."

The Queen looked directly into Ramon's eyes. "You were taking quite a risk with such a cargo, Captain Ramon."

He nodded noting the slight return to formality. "Yes Ma'am, but I was going to be very well paid and I wrongly persuaded myself that the shipment might have been authorised as part of the treaties signed last year."

"Please tell me all the rest of the story."

Ramon did as requested, describing his arrival in port at Mora, the fabricated story about some sort of sickness on board *Lex Talionis* and his consequent arrest and the link to his stepson. At the mention of Audun the Queen leant forward, much as her son had done a couple of months earlier, but she held back the questions she really wanted to ask.

"Assuming my son commissioned the goods, and your voyage, do you know why he insisted that it be shipped on the *Swan*, the caravel captained by your stepson?"

Ramon shook his head. "No I don't, and that specific request has puzzled me ever since. A load of that size and weight could not have been transported by a caravel, even in light seas. In winter seas I doubt such a vessel would have got beyond the shelter of a harbour before it capsized. I can only assume that the Emperor has little knowledge of the sea."

Ingrid smiled. "That is certainly a correct assumption, but it is therefore even stranger that Alberon should specify the *Swan*."

Ramon shrugged his shoulders. "As I say, it remains a puzzle to me."

Suddenly the Queen's questions changed tack. "So tell me more about your stepson. His name is Audun, I believe. It is an unusual name and coincidently the same name as one of my son's forefathers. Audun was the name of the first king of Doran. How did he become your stepson?"

Ramon was taken by surprise with the change in direction. Why would both the Emperor and his mother be interested in Audun? It made no sense. The jigsaw pieces kept forming, but none seemed to join together.

Ramon went on to tell the Queen the same story that he had told her son, but Ingrid had more questions than he had asked. "The mother's name was Ragna you say, do you know what she did in Tamin or what her parents did?"

Ramon hesitated for a moment. "Neither Ragna nor the boy said much about their previous life. My only recollection is that once she mentioned that her father was a painter and Audun was learning the trade of an artist's apprentice. Audun has never shown any interest in painting so I don't know if the story was true or concocted. Ragna's skin was somewhat pigmented, so it is possible she assisted her father, although when I first met her she claimed to be a cook in some of Tamin's great houses. She was an excellent cook and housekeeper."

Ingrid asked several more questions about Audun's appearance, the colour of his eyes, how tall he was, and what colour his hair was. It seemed as though she was trying to build a solid picture of him.

Finally she asked her most important question. "How old is your stepson?"

Ramon had to think for a second. "I think he will be twenty-two this month."

Ingrid paled slightly at the answer but quickly regained her composure. She was close to drawing a conclusion, but knew Audun's age could still be a coincidence.

"Thank you Captain Ramon, I appreciate you sharing all of this with me. We will talk again soon."

Ramon had opened the turret room door to leave when a final question occurred to him, and he turned back to the Queen. "If the messages carried by Valdin came from your son, why would he address a book of poems specifically to Audun? A book of poems written two hundred years ago by a warrior poet named Angus Ferguson."

The Queen shook her head. "I have no idea."

Ingrid sat for a long while looking out over the city to the docks and thinking about a young sailor. Maybe it was just a string of coincidences, but there were too many of them. She needed to speak again with Alberon and get the truth, but first Sylva.

Over the years Ingrid had become very fond of her daughter-in-law. She admired Sylva's sharp intellect, her wisdom on matters of trade and politics and the way she usually seemed to be able to provide a calming counterpoint to her son's tempestuousness.

The Empress was in her own rooms when Ingrid was ushered in. Sylva gave her mother-in-law a warm hug. "Ingrid, what a nice surprise. Come and sit with me. To what do I owe this surprise visit?"

The Queen settled in her seat. "Sylva, I called by to see how you felt Alberon was. I visited him a few days ago and he seemed very contented, which is unusual for my son."

Sylva smiled. "Yes, he seemed to enjoy his trip to Iskala."

"Do you know exactly what he was doing in Doran?"

Sylva shook her head. "Only what he told me and that was that he was going to Iskala to sort out some administrative problems."

The two chatted for half an hour. As the Queen rose to leave, she asked an unexpected question. "Sylva, do you know if Alberon owns a book of poems by a 14th century poet called Angus Ferguson?"

Sylva paled slightly. She had her own secrets to keep. "He has so many poetry books I am afraid I wouldn't know one from another," she replied.

Alberon was in a tetchy mood as he walked through the castle from the council rooms. All morning he had been at a meeting with some of the nobles and members of the City Guilds who were demanding that recent tax increases should be rescinded. Aracir, Kermin's Chancellor, was his normal wily self, sympathising with the complaints whilst at the same time reminding the council of the depletion of Kermin's funds since the disasters of the war and the blockades of the previous years. He also reminded the merchants that it was at their request that the number of city guards should be increased to combat crime in the city.

Alberon sat through the discussions and the arguments, bored and trying to control his temper. Aracir was a master at manipulating the council, and when Alberon lost control of his temper it generally made things worse. He was glad the meeting was over and he could return to his rooms and enjoy his midday meal. He was not expecting company.

Ingrid was sitting at the table picking at some bits of bread and meat. "Mother, as always I am delighted to see you, but I have been in a council meeting all morning and I want to eat my meal in peace," he said. "Please leave and come back later."

The Emperor might have been all powerful, but he did not rule over his mother. Ingrid glared at her son. Her hazel eyes took on a steely glint and her voice sharpened.

"You will not give me orders, Alberon. I am here to get the truth from you, now sit down."

Alberon tried again. "You will cause me to have indigestion if I talk whilst I eat."

Ingrid's voice now took on a dangerous edge. "Then don't eat! Sit and answer my questions."

Alberon sat trying to control his rising impatience, knowing that if his temper slipped his mother would scold him as if he was still a child and he would soon have to submit to her will.

Pushing his plate to the side, Alberon responded. "Yes mother, what is it you want to ask me?"

"I have been speaking to Captain Ramon, and he confirms the reports I have had from my other sources that the cargo he carried from Ackar was components for cannons. As I suspected, you were lying to me when we spoke on this a couple of days ago, although why you would try to cover this up by using the dead Duke of Alol as the contractor is a mystery to me."

Alberon shrugged. "In truth I am rearming Kermin for our defence against any attack from Amina."

The hazel eyes hardened, and Ingrid lowered her voice. "Don't keep lying to me Alberon. If Bertalan had wanted to conquer Kermin it would have been very easy for him to do so two years ago. Indeed it might have been for the best."

Alberon struggled to keep his voice calm. "I am the Emperor and Amina must swear fealty to its Emperor. This time, when my cannons are ready, I will teach Bertalan the price of defiance of the Empire."

Ingrid's tone hardened further. "You may call yourself an Emperor, but you behave like a spoilt child, although at least now you are telling me the truth. There will be no war with Amina. This time, I will not allow it."

Alberon laughed. "Mother, you have been closeted in your own rooms for too long. You do not understand the current world and its politics. Besides, what could you do to stop me? Indeed, from anyone else I would consider what you have just said to be treason."

Ingrid's voice dropped almost to a whisper and her hazel eyes held his ice-blue ones in a threatening stare. "And you would have me executed as you have done to others? Alberon, I may be getting old but you would be making a very serious mistake to underestimate the power I still have and the influence I can still exert. You forget, or maybe you are too self-centred to realise, how much the people of Kermin despise you. They have not forgotten the stupid war you engaged in two years ago or the winter of starvation that followed."

The intensity in the hazel eyes was too much, and Alberon looked away. "What would you do, mother? Lead the people in a rebellion?"

Ingrid leant forward over the table, and involuntarily Alberon sat back.

"Maybe the people, maybe the King of Amina, or more likely I would demand that you step down and pass the throne to your son," she said.

At this Alberon laughed loudly. "How ridiculous, mother! Aaron is only eleven years old."

Ingrid took a moment before responding "No I was thinking about your elder son, Audun."

CHAPTER 5

Sparsholt

❖ ❖ ❖ ❖

Alberon's face turned from angry red to purple. He stood up from the table and pointed at his mother, all control gone. "You have lost your mind!" he roared. "Guards!"

The two guardsmen entered the room. "Escort my mother to her rooms and make sure she stays there until I come for her."

Ingrid remained sitting. She turned to the two guardsmen as they approached, her voice now like a whip. "Leave us." The men hesitated for a moment, and there came another crack of the whip. "Now!"

The guards stood to attention. "Yes Ma'am," they said together, and left.

Ingrid turned to her son. "Calm yourself Alberon and sit down. We need to talk about this. And please take note: if the guards follow my commands, be sure that your nobles and council will also."

Alberon ignored the instruction and started pacing around the room, smashing his right fist into his left palm in an attempt to disperse his anger. Once more he turned to his mother and pointed an accusing finger at her. "It's that bloody captain spreading his lies! I should have had him executed on his arrival rather than treat him as my guest."

Ingrid's reply was simple. "The captain is now under my protection and you will not do him any harm. Now sit down before I order the guards in and get them to make you sit." Reluctantly Alberon returned to his seat.

Ingrid nodded. "That's better, now let's discuss this sensibly. You are correct in saying that for many years I have kept away from public involvement in politics, but I have still kept my eyes and ears open. I should have intervened when you declared war on Amina two years ago, but back then I thought you might have succeeded. As I have already said, I will not allow you to travel that path again. However for now, let us talk about Audun."

Alberon's voice rose again. "I don't know anyone called Audun."

The Queen smiled. "You don't know about cannons in Doran? You don't know why you tried to commission a caravel called the *Swan* to deliver the cannons to

Mora, however impossible that would be? You didn't know that the *Swan*'s captain was Ramon's stepson, and his name was Audun? You don't know why you put Ramon under house arrest? You don't remember a maid called Ragna? You don't know that Audun happens to be twenty-two years old this month? You don't possess a book of poems written in the 14th century by Angus Ferguson? You don't seem to know much, and you seem to have forgotten a lot. Maybe I should have the guards put you under house arrest for the good of the kingdom."

"Are you threatening me again, mother?"

Ingrid smiled. "You can interpret it that way if you wish, but I am really pointing out to you that I know much more than you think I do. What game are you playing, Alberon?"

Alberon stood and paced the room again for a minute, then turned to his desk and took out a thin roll of paper. He handed the roll over to his mother and explained. "The first I knew about Audun was twelve months ago when the *Eagle* was moored at Tufle and Bertalan and I were negotiating the treaties. One evening on returning to the ship, these papers were waiting for me. I managed to learn that they had been delivered by Audun, a young Captain of a caravel named the *Swan*."

Ingrid unrolled the sheet and read the first page.

We met in the north on a spring day

I am sure now it was our destiny
Tender moments in the Nath
With the sand at our backs
Somehow fate set our path
A love that would last
Now in our winter years
Smile Elbeth my love
Shed no tears
White gold our rings
United we were
United we will always be
My love for you
Is for all of eternity

"I had long forgotten about this poem but I instantly remembered reading it out loud to Ragna when we first managed to steal some time alone," Alberon went on. "Now read the second page. I had never seen this letter before, but you will recognise it I am sure."

At our command the maid Ragna and her child are permanently banished from the Kingdoms of Kermin and Doran. Whilst our law is clear that a child born out of wedlock is the responsibility of the father, our law is also clear that if the mother used sorcery to bewitch the father then both mother and child will be sentenced to death. We have proof that the maid Ragna used potions and spells to bewitch our son. Prince Alberon has provided the evidence to support this claim. Whilst the death sentence was in our power to command, the Prince has pleaded for mercy. Reluctantly we have heard the Prince's plea and decided to be lenient. However if the maid or her child is apprehended anywhere within our territories the maid Ragna will be condemned as a witch and her child a sorcerer. The penalty for witchcraft is death.

King Elrik and Queen Ingrid, Regents of Kermin.

Ingrid nodded. "It had to be done. You were betrothed to Sylva and there was no possibility of you marrying the maid, despite the fact that you should have been obliged to by our laws. The accusation that she was a witch was of course false, but it allowed your father and me to order the banishment of her and the unborn child."

"Now read the third page," said Alberon. The third sheet contained only one word, *"REVENGE"*. Ingrid looked up from the papers, but before she could pose her question, Alberon asked one. "Did Captain Ramon tell you the name of the carrack he commanded?" The Queen shook her head. Alberon smiled. "Well I am pleased that there are some things you don't know! The ship was called *Lex Talionis*. Do you know what that means?" The Queen shrugged. "Well let me tell you, loosely translated it means 'an eye for an eye' or in one word 'revenge'. Ramon told me that Audun had insisted that this was what the carrack was to be named. I was already intrigued by the bravado shown by this forgotten son. His insistence on the name of the carrack further amused me. A ship's captain threatening the Emperor of the North? How absurd and how fascinating."

Ingrid looked up from the papers. "So you wanted to lure the young man here, to Mora?"

Again Alberon smiled. "I thought it might be interesting to meet him, and I am hoping that by holding his stepfather here I might still entice him to enter Kermin. I could have had him eliminated by now, that would have been easy. The messenger Aracir sent to Boretar was capable of delivering that mission, I believe."

Ingrid thought of Valdin, who she knew was perfectly capable of carrying out an assassination. She asked the obvious question. "So why didn't you do it?"

Alberon paused and returned to his seat. "Partly out of interest. As I said, I am intrigued to meet this son, but as importantly he is obviously intelligent. If I were him I would have copies of the papers that you have just read carefully stored somewhere with an explanation of who the guilty party was if he were to die under suspicious circumstances. "You remember of course how I used Berin's claims to manoeuvre my threat to the Amina throne two years ago? The murder of a pretender to my crowns could provide a similar opportunity for some other lord or king. So it is better to have Audun come to Kermin, where he can be disposed of legally. He is guilty of being a sorcerer, having been born of a witch, as you so nicely define it in your letter."

It was Ingrid's turn to be caught off guard. "You would have your own son executed here in Mora?"

Alberon smiled. "Mother, I only have two sons, Aaron and Elrik, and they in time will inherit my thrones and possibly also the Amina crown. I have the proof in my parents' own words that I was seduced by a witch, so I have no connection to this bastard son."

Ingrid looked long at him. "But you know the letter is a lie designed to keep the mother and child away from you and prohibit their return to Mora. I never expected that the threat of the sentence would be carried out. And that raises another question. Why did the mother and the boy have to flee Tamin ten years ago?"

Alberon paused, considering another lie, but he decided to confess what he knew. "I am not entirely sure, mother. Nine or so years ago, shortly after Elrik was born, Sylva happened to pick up the book of poems you referred to, the poems written by Angus Ferguson. I hadn't looked at the book since Ragna was banished and I had completely forgotten that I had written a letter to her. It was never sent, but was folded into the last page of the book. Sylva found the letter and demanded to know where Ragna and the child had been sent. I didn't know, and you may remember me asking you the question. I suspect Sylva instructed her brother to search for the family in Tamin and have them disposed of. Clearly Sylva's brother never found them."

Ingrid pushed back her chair and stood up. She had other questions, but these were more likely to be answered by Ramon, who knew more about the details of the story after the family's flight from Tamin. Thinking about the captain, she made a decision. "Ramon, the stepfather, is your bait, and as I said earlier he is now under my protection. I will not allow him to be present when you find the son and execute him. I have more questions for the Captain, but once I have my answers, I will release him." Alberon was about to protest, but the Queen held up her hand. "There will be no discussion on this. All this talk has made me weary. I am going to return to my rooms to rest. Enjoy your meal."

All Alberon could manage as his mother moved to the door was, "I seem to have lost my appetite."

It had taken the lone traveller two days to climb from the Kermin Plain up to the high passes that were the only known routes across the Doran Mountains. The early July sunshine was hot on the Plain and an occasional passing farm wagon had provided some rest and respite on the journey. Now, with the mountain peaks still snow-capped, the man had to pull the black cloak more tightly around his shoulders. The wind at times picked up ice crystals from the peaks and he smiled at the dance of light as the sun reflected from the frozen particles swirling around him.

Few merchants' wagons crossed between Kermin and Doran and the only people the traveller saw were the troops of Doran Light Cavalry as they criss-crossed the mountain from their bases in Doran to patrol on the Kermin Plain. The riders paid no attention to the lone traveller. Fully dressed in black with the hood of his cloak pulled over his head, he could have been a pilgrim travelling to Iskala or a beggar seeking a new summer territory in the Doran capital. Had the riders looked more closely at the staff that the man seemed to rely on to aid his step, they might have paid more attention.

The traveller knew he needed to reach the Doran side of the pass before nightfall. At the summit the temperatures would still drop to below freezing. It was early afternoon when he reached the far side of the pass and looked out over the Doran Plain. Iskala was not visible from this vantage point as it sat on its rocky promontory east of the pass and was hidden by the mountain. In the distance on the Plain he could see smoke rising from a settlement and smiled; he hoped that was his destination.

Two hours later, he had reached the highest of the summer pastures. Here, an abandoned shepherd's cottage would provide shelter for the night.

It was several days since Audun had had his battle of wills with the staff and the red orb, finally getting the orb to submit, at least partly, to his control. His nights, however, continued to be tormented by dreams of red fire and destruction, and in all the dreams he stood holding the staff by the orb with the red fire erupting from the tip. As the images played out in his dreams, so his resolve hardened.

On the third night he once again woke dripping with sweat. Crossing the main room of the cottage, he saw that the casket holding the orb was shedding red sparks and the staff seemed to be joining in the dance, with amber fire running down over the notched carvings.

Audun concentrated his thoughts and focused them on the casket. Maybe he should be done with this and simply bury this evil in the garden. At this thought the casket burned brighter and again he heard the words echo in his head: *Now you have power.*

Audun reached deep inside and found his own strength. Now he spoke out loud. "If I have the power, then you are mine to control and you will obey me." The red flames emanating from the casket grew more intense. "I will still seek to avenge my family, but I will not allow these dreams of mass destruction to become reality. Remember, I am a sailor. Maybe I should join a ship and deposit you deep in the Greater Sea." Audun staggered backwards as the fire burst forth from the casket and seemed about to totally consume the inside of the cottage. "Stop!" he shouted. Audun forced his will through the casket and over the red orb. Gradually the conflagration subsided and a quiet calm settled over the cottage.

With the afternoon sun warming his back, the traveller wound his way down towards the Doran Plain. These were unfamiliar lands, and it was only a hunch that his destination lay across the Plain where the columns of smoke drifted up into the clear sky. The sun was beginning to set behind the Doran Mountains before he was able to look back and clearly see Iskala on its rocky promontory.

The Doran Plain was sparsely populated with small farmsteads, and the traveller met few people as he walked the dusty paths towards the distant settlement. When an occasional farmhand passed by, he hunched over his staff and pulled his hood firmly over his head. No one would pay any attention to an old beggar.

With dusk falling, he approached the cluster of houses that he thought must be Sparsholt, a name he had first come across in an overheard conversation only a few days earlier. A disused barn sat a short distance from the settlement, and he would rest there until night settled in and he could move on undetected.

It was a moonless night, and a myriad stars glittered in the midnight sky as the traveller moved cautiously round the edge of Sparsholt. The only signs of life were the occasional glow of a candle from a bedroom window. Sparsholt was fast asleep. A black shadow in the night, the man moved north from the settlement. About a mile away he could see the orange glow from the fires in the furnaces. If his hunch was correct, this was the ironworks. This was his destination.

As he moved closer the light from the fires illuminated the buildings. The four smithies were damped-down for the night with the orange coals glowing gently in their hearths, ready to be woken when the smiths returned to their forges in the morning. Lying around the smithies was a multitude of metal implements, and at the furthest end of the compound, facing out to the plain, was the cannon. Intrigued, the traveller examined the weapon and marvelled at the intricate designs of the wild animals and the fire spitting dragon. How apt, he thought to himself.

When the Duke of Doran arrived on the scene the next morning at the head of a cohort of cavalry, it seemed that each of Sparsholt's residents had a slightly different version of events. All agreed that they had been woken deep in the night by multiple cracks of thunder, but after that the eye witnesses' stories diverged. Some swore that they had seen multiple flashes of lightning follow the thunder and strike the forges. Others pointed out that lightning preceded thunder, and what they had seen was fire erupting from deep within the earth, consuming the smithies. These observers swore that the ground had parted and an earthquake had struck the area. They had seen the damped coals from the furnaces being spread across the ground under the onslaught of flames rising from the depths of the earth. The less inventive simply explained it away as one of the furnaces exploding and spreading fire to the others. A few told a different tale; the fire seemed unnatural, a deep red with amber sparks, and it appeared to travel over the plain to strike the forges.

Morserat had been woken from his bed as soon as the conflagration had appeared on the horizon. He saw only the final flash of the fire, and he too thought the flames had seemed to leap across the plain to devour the last smithy, which erupted in a violent blast.

Morserat rode on out to examine the destruction more closely. The ground was still smoking and the smithies were charred carcases. Whatever had generated the fire, it was clear that it had not simply come from an exploding furnace, as in places the very stones had been melted. With such heat Morserat knew that little of the precious ironwork would have remained intact.

At the northern end of the enclosure the cannon had been reduced to a melted lump of metal lying beside the charred remains of its gun carriage. It looked as though the cannon had taken the full force of one of the fiery blasts. Morserat smiled wryly; maybe the dragon had come to life and consumed its own creation. Wildfire would not be going to war any time soon.

With all the excitement no one paid any heed to the old beggar in black, leaning heavily on his staff as he picked his way slowly south towards the Doran Mountains.

CHAPTER 6

The Dragon's Message

❖ ❖ ❖ ❖

The news of the destruction of the forges travelled quickly across the Doran Mountains, and just two days after the fire a travel-stained messenger arrived at Mora Castle's gates. Holger was at the gate as the rider dismounted. "Soren, you have been riding hard, what is so urgent?"

Soren nodded to the Captain of the Guard. "I have no time to chat, Holger. I need to see the Emperor now."

Holger shrugged. "That is not possible. The Emperor is in the Council Room discussing finances with the Chancellor and has asked not to be disturbed."

Soren pushed past him. "Sorry, I have no time to explain."

He ignored the two guards at the Council Room door and knocked.

"I have left orders not to be disturbed," said Alberon, who was sitting in discussion with Aracir, but Soren had already entered the room. Alberon rose from his seat in anger. "How dare you ignore my orders?"

Soren looked down at his feet. "I apologise, my lord, but I have the most urgent news from Doran and my uncle instructed me to deliver my message with haste."

Alberon looked the young man up and down. "It had better be urgent, messenger, or you will be resting the night in the dungeon."

Soren winced. The thought of a night in the dungeon was worrying, but the fact that the Emperor continued to treat him like a raw youth and insisted on referring to him as "messenger" was annoying.

"Well, stop admiring your toes and get on with it messenger!" snapped Alberon.

Soren knew there was no easy way to deliver his news. "The ironworks on the Doran Plain have been destroyed by fire."

Alberon stepped forward and grabbed the young man by the collar. "What do you mean, destroyed by fire?"

Soren went on to explain. Alberon leapt to the obvious conclusion and turned to Aracir, who had remained sitting and listening. "Bertalan must have found out about my intention to rearm and sent a troop from Amina to destroy the forges and the cannons."

Aracir remained calm, and as his Emperor grew ever angrier, he spoke quietly. "Sit down Soren and take your time. Tell us all that you know."

Soren did as instructed. "My lords, there was no sign of any Amina troops in the area. Indeed any large company would have great difficulty crossing the mountains undetected. Doran cavalry units ride through the mountain passes twice a day to relieve our troops who are patrolling on the Kermin Plain between here and the Alol."

Fighting to control his temper, Alberon snapped, "Then who did this?"

"My lord, we don't know if it was a someone. From the best descriptions we have from the people of Sparsholt, it seems most likely to have been a natural disaster. Most reports describe the fire emanating from cracks in the earth, either an earthquake or some other form of underground eruption or explosion. The heat must have been beyond anything we can imagine, as even some of the stones of the furnaces had melted."

Alberon was struggling to take it all in. "What about the metalwork? What about the cannons?"

Soren once again took great interest in his feet. "It is all destroyed, my lord."

Alberon collapsed into his chair. "All *destroyed?*"

Soren could only nod in agreement.

Alberon turned to Aracir. "Get Holger, and bring him here now."

It was a rather flustered Captain of the Guard who arrived a few minutes later knowing nothing about what had transpired. Alberon did not intend to enlighten his captain, and simply issued the order. "Holger, I want a troop of fifty guardsmen ready to leave for Iskala first thing tomorrow morning. Messenger, you will ride with us. Now leave me, all of you."

Alberon sat for some time with his head in his hands. It all seemed like some sort of bad dream. His cannons should have been close to completion and the plan had been to bring them secretly to Mora before the winter snows closed the passes through the mountains. From Mora they could have been deployed quickly to the Kermin Alol in the spring to spearhead his planned invasion of Amina. Now he was back where he started, back where he had been in 1507, denied the weapons he needed for war.

His thoughts turned to his mother and her promise to prohibit any future aggression against Amina. She knew about the ironworks and the weapons; could she have somehow ordered their destruction? He dismissed the thought immediately. From Soren's description, the fires that had melted stone near Sparsholt were beyond man's control. His mother was powerful, but as far as he knew she could not influence the gods. Nonetheless, with his plans in molten ruins, he would need to talk with her once he returned from Iskala.

The rain was sweeping across the Kermin Plain as the troop galloped along the road that led up to the Doran Mountains. Mounted on his white stallion, the Emperor was at the fore, and just behind him flew the Golden Eagle banner. The riders ignored the old beggar in black leaning on his staff by the roadside to stay clear of the mud thrown up by the pounding hooves. As the road started its climb towards the mountain passes it took a sharp left turn and the horsemen disappeared from sight.

Wiping a splash of mud from his cloak, the 'beggar' threw back his hood and laughed. Knowing no one could hear him now, he pointed his staff towards the bend in the road and shouted after the riders, "Lex Talionis can come in many different forms father!"

It was two weeks since Audun had finally won his battle of wills with Oien, and the red orb had at last seemed to submit to his commands. It was time to plan for his revenge, but on his own terms, not those driven by the hate and anger of the old alchemist.

Audun knew he now had some control over the power of the red fire, but how could he use this for his revenge whilst avoiding the horrors presented to him in his dreams and nightmares? For some reason his thoughts drifted back to fourteenth century history and the story of the young Prince Garan. He had been completely unprepared for the kinghood that was suddenly thrust upon him, but he had brought peace and prosperity to the lands, and earned the name history would remember him by – "The Peacemaker". Audun had always been enthralled by Garan's story and how the Prince had been transformed by a blessing from a man dressed in shimmering light blue clothing.

Audun's thoughts turned to his last visit to Aldene, two years earlier, when the man known as The Eldest had blessed the crowd in the castle courtyard and a white cloud had descended over everyone, bringing with it a deep sense of peace. The germ of an idea took root in his mind. Could he use the power of the red fire for good, rather than for destruction and conquest, yet still avenge his family?

Over the next few days Audun wrestled with various possibilities, until at last an idea developed. He knew that Ramon had almost certainly transported components for cannons on *Lex Talionis* and so his father, The Emperor, was once again preparing for war. Maybe one way to get his revenge was to destroy his father's plans, but he needed information. He knew the ship had unloaded her cargo at Mora, but he also knew that no significant ironworks were located close to the city. *Lex Talionis'* cargo must have been transported to another location.

The answer, when it came, was from an unexpected source. Audun was sitting lost in his own thoughts at a corner table in the Golden Fleece when the conversation at a neighbouring table caught his attention. The large man at the centre of the group seemed to be holding court and appeared to have sufficient coins to buy all his cronies their ale.

It was the man's boast that first caught Audun's attention, "I am only here for a day or two to report to the Emperor." One of his cronies laughed. "Master Wayland Henry getting an audience with the Emperor? Next you'll be telling us you've shared a bed with the Empress." The group joined the laughter, but the big man took on a serious expression. "You may laugh, but it's the Emperor's gold that's buying all your drinks."

As the laughter died down it was replaced by a hubbub of conversation and questions fired at Master Henry. Audun only caught snippets – Ackar, Doran, Sparsholt – before Master Henry held up his hand. "I have had too much ale and said too much already. Enough questions. Who wants another drink?"

Audun waited until the men had finished their drinks and staggered off on their separate ways before he called the serving girl over to his table. "Who was the big man who was sitting at the table there and has just left?" he asked. The sight of two shining coins encouraged her to respond.

The girl leaned over and lowered her voice. "That

would be Master Wayland Henry, he's a master smith. He used to be a regular here but two years ago he stopped coming. I know his wife and she told me he had been sent to Ackar on some secret assignment. He arrived back in Mora a couple of months ago, but he only stayed in the city for a day or two. It might be a coincidence, but at around the same time my father, who is a wagon master, returned from a very well-paid contract. He wouldn't say what he had been paid to do other than it had involved transporting a load of iron equipment over the Doran Mountains."

Audun thanked the girl and passed over the coins. The snippets of information coalesced in his mind. A master smith, a wagon transporting metal goods across the mountains to Doran, maybe a place called Sparsholt... It wasn't much, but together, the pieces made some sense. If his father was rearming then it would need to be done well away from Kermin, where travellers, or spies, would notice the activity and the information would be likely to soon arrive at Tamin and King Bertalan. Doran, hidden as it was behind its vast mountain range and inaccessible for four months in the year, could easily conceal a secret ironworks.

Audun was still laughing as he lowered the staff. Looking up towards the mountain peaks in the distance, he could see the Golden Eagle banner. He knew that the riders were following the final twists in the road before it would open up at the pass and they would cross over to Doran. He sat down on the grass at the side of the road and let the rain wash the remaining mud stains from his clothes. "I hope you have an interesting visit to your ironworks, father," he murmured. Then a great weariness overcame him, and ignoring the rain he drew his black cloak tight round him and pulled the hood over his head.

Dusk was falling when Audun woke. He was wet and cold, but he also felt surprisingly refreshed. He hadn't realised how his actions at Sparsholt had drained his energy. With the rain dripping from his hood he sat on the grass for a few moments longer, remembering. Closing his eyes, he could see in his mind's eye the forges with the orange glow from their furnaces warm and peaceful in the night. He could feel again the damp grass under his feet as he moved a safe distance away from his targets. Frustration was the first emotion he remembered, because nothing had happened when he had initially taken the red orb from his bag and located it on the Φ symbol at the hilt of the staff. The orb and the staff were now one, but they showed no sign of the power he needed to execute his plan.

As his frustration grew he spoke to the orb. "I have the power, and you will obey me." A few orange sparks danced down the staff and fizzed out as they hit the wet grass. Frustration turned to anger, and Audun slammed the tip of the staff against the ground and shouted. "You will obey me!"

In that moment the orb had started to glow red, and the staff became alive with amber flashes. Audun's anger seemed to burn like the fire now emanating from the tip of the staff. As he raised the tip towards the first forge, the red fire leapt across the open ground and the smithy exploded with a roar like thunder. In moments the destruction was complete, and all that remained of Sparsholt's ironworks was smoking ruins and molten iron. As Audun detached the orb from the staff he heard the old alchemist's words echo in his mind: *Your anger is good Audun, your power lies in your anger.*

Audun opened his eyes again and lay back down in the wet grass as the words repeated themselves. The thought that followed was one of concern. If the power he could wield through the staff was driven by his anger, then he could not control it, and it was treacherous, and dangerous.

As Audun walked towards Mora through the light rain that was still falling on the Kermin Plain he felt cocooned in the dark of the night. He was lost in his thoughts, and looking forward to getting to the dry warmth of his cottage.

In Iskala his father was already warm and dry in the castle's state room. The Duke of Doran had just completed his report confirming the news Alberon had already received from Soren. Alberon asked again. "What could have caused this? Have there ever been any previous reports of earthquakes on the Doran Plain? Maybe even in folk stories from the past?"

Morserat shook his head. "I can find no record of any such event, and if there had been one I'm sure it would have been noted in the annals stored in the castle's library. The archives record all the major events in the lives of the Kings of Doran and go back centuries. I have had scribes working through the chronicles and they have found no records of any such natural disturbances."

Alberon stood up and paced the room. "Then the only explanation is some accident at the forges themselves."

Morserat again shook his head. "It is possible, but the furnaces were tamped down for the night and when you visit the site tomorrow and see the destruction, I think you will come to the same conclusion that I have. The heat from the fires must have been unbelievably intense, as even the stones have melted. I cannot believe that a fire from the furnaces could have generated such heat. Nor does it seem possible that a man-made conflagration could have reached such temperatures. So I am only left with one conclusion. It was some sort of unexplainable natural disaster."

The next morning the weather matched the Emperor's

mood. The thick grey clouds blocked out any sunlight and the heavy drizzle hid Sparsholt until the riders reached the first houses.

Alberon reined in his stallion outside the house occupied by Wayland Henry. It seemed unbelievable that it was only two weeks ago that the smith had been reporting to him in Mora, proud of the progress being made on the cannons.

Henry was quickly out to greet his Emperor. "My lord, all our work is undone. I doubt that much of the iron is recoverable."

Alberon checked his temper; whatever had happened here, it did not seem that it could be blamed on the smith. "You will come now and show me, Master Henry."

When the first charred carcass of what had once been a smithy appeared out of the gloom, Alberon dismounted and walked towards the ruin. Henry walked at his side, eager to show the Emperor the evidence and anxious to prove that he and his fellow smiths could not be to blame.

As Alberon approached the remains of the smithy he started to feel the heat that still emanated from the ruin. It should have been impossible, considering several days had passed since the incident and for most of that time rain had been falling, but there in the centre of what had once been the core of the forge, the furnace bricks still glowed with a red heat. Henry pointed out the twisted bits of iron that had melted in the heat and had formed a metal river that flowed away from the forge. Even the iron had retained its heat, and the raindrops sizzled as they landed on the metal.

Henry interrupted the Emperor's thoughts. "My lord, I have worked with iron and fire all my life, but I have never seen bricks melt or rivers of iron flow once the metal has been formed." The smith pointed to a pool of solidified metal lying a short distance from the forge. "That, sire, was a cannon ball, a solid piece of iron. I cannot imagine the heat required to melt it down to the puddle you see lying there."

The remains of each smithy were the same: solidified pools where the iron had melted and then cooled again, charred timbers and scattered bricks some still hot and smoking. All round the area the very ground had been charred and scorched. As the pair passed the final ruined smithy, a short distance ahead of them lay the twisted remains of Wildfire.

Alberon found it difficult to comprehend that only just over a month before he had watched in delight as the cannon had first demonstrated its prowess by firing the cannonball far out across the plain. Little of the carefully forged structure remained intact. Alberon shook his head, trying to clear his thoughts.

It was then that he noticed a piece of iron lying on the ground a short distance from the remnants of the cannon. Leaving Henry fretting at the side of his molten masterpiece, Alberon walked over. Strangely, unlike the rest of the metalwork, it appeared to have been untouched by the fire. Alberon bent to pick the piece up.

It was a mistake. The pain was instant as the hot iron singed his fingers, but the Emperor's scream was not born of the pain, but of the shock. The fragment had been lying curved side down, but when it fell from his singed fingers it flipped over. Looking up at him was a dragon's head, and the fire emanating from the open mouth was a burnished red. Below the dragon's head two words were burning like a brand: "Lex Talionis".

Five days later Alberon was still in Iskala. The physicians were fussing around him, putting an ointment of crushed onions, salt and vinegar on his burnt fingers and regularly replacing the bandages. His return to Mora would have to wait until the burns had healed. The damaged fingers would make holding his horse's reins painful, but the real reason he remained in the Doran capital was to avoid painful discussions.

Sylva knew nothing of the ironworks at Sparsholt and he knew she would strongly disapprove of his plans to rearm and recommence hostilities with her brother. Sylva also knew nothing about the discovery of the existence of the illegitimate son. Soren had been ordered to return to Mora with a message for the Empress explaining that her husband would remain in Doran for a couple of weeks as he had ordered Aster, the King of

Soll, to travel south to Iskala to renew his vows of fealty to the Empire. Soren also carried a separate message for the Queen Mother.

Ingrid entered the royal apartments without bothering to knock. She looked at the physicians and issued her order, "Out!" Without bothering to sit, she turned to her son. It was a look Alberon had seen many times over the years and remembered even from his childhood. He knew from the furrowed brow and the narrowed hazel eyes that his mother was furious.

The Queen's voice was like subdued thunder. "I am too old to be taking summer trips over the Doran Mountains in a carriage. I told Holger as much, but he insisted that your request was urgent and it was an emergency. So here I am. Now go and find me some cushions and a comfortable chair where I can rest these weary bones."

It was then that Ingrid noticed the bandages on her son's fingers. The laugh was mirthless. "I knew that one day you would get your fingers burnt as a result of your overblown ego and stupid ambition." Alberon ignored the comment, but hurried to fulfil his mother's request.

Once she was comfortably seated and had taken some sips of the wine that had been brought to her, Ingrid turned her gaze back to her son. The cushions and the wine had not dimmed her anger. "Well, what ridiculous emergency has brought me so urgently from the comfort of my apartments in Mora?"

Alberon did not answer but passed his mother the now cooled fragment of iron with the dragon's head. Ingrid turned the piece of iron in her hand before handing it back to her son. "So you have dragged me all the way over the Doran Mountains to show me some relic you have discovered?"

Alberon sighed. "No mother, this is not some relic. It is the only whole fragment that remains of the ironworks and the cannons. Tomorrow I will take you out to Sparsholt to show you the devastation."

He went on to describe to his mother all he knew about what had transpired at Sparsholt. "At first I thought Bertalan must have discovered my plan to build the cannons here, but Doran cavalry regularly cross the mountains so no Amina force could have crossed unnoticed. Then I remembered you telling me that you would not allow a return to war with Amina, and I wondered if you could have ordered the destruction of the forges. So I travelled here to see for myself, and I could immediately see why Morserat thought the destruction was the result of some natural phenomenon like an earthquake. Then I found the fragment of iron and picked it up. This was the consequence." He held up his bandaged hand. "I presume you recognise the words burnt into the iron below the dragon's head?"

Ingrid nodded. "Yes, you told me that was the name of the carrack that Ramon captained and that the ship was named at the insistence of his stepson. You explained your understanding of what the words meant, but I don't see the connection to this piece of iron."

Alberon leant forward in his chair and held the fragment of iron out again to show his mother. Slowly he verbalised his thoughts. "I am not sure that I understand either mother, but if the disaster at Sparsholt was caused by an earthquake or some other natural phenomenon it seems highly improbable that the gods would have left this specific message."

It had also been five days since Audun had returned to his cottage in Mora's tradesmen's quarter. He had slept peacefully for the first twenty-four hours while he recovered from the exertions of his trip to Sparsholt. He knew that the journey, whilst arduous, had not in itself been enough to leave him so exhausted.

Over the next few days he replayed the destruction of the ironworks in his mind, trying to recall every small detail. He remembered again his frustration as the red orb and the staff refused to obey his commands. He knew it was his growing anger which had brought the staff to life. He could still hear the words whispered in his head: *Your anger is good Audun, your power lies in your anger.*

Gradually other memories coalesced. Not only had the staff refused to follow his commands, initially the orb had fought his will. He went through the conflict in his mind. He was intent on destroying his father's weapons, but the orb kept insisting that he would need them to extract his revenge. One day his army would want these weapons. The orb had refused to release its fire until his anger overcame its resistance.

Then he remembered the moment he had lifted the staff and pointed it towards the forges. It was then that the image of the motif on the cannon filled his mind, the dragon with its open mouth spewing fire. He remembered shouting, "Let the dragon's fire consume it all, Lex Talionis!" Audun had no idea that his very words would etch themselves under the dragon motif. The only lasting thought was the one that had first come to mind as he lay on the sodden grass at the side of the road on the Kermin Plain. If the power he could wield through the orb and the staff was driven by his anger, then he couldn't control it. It was treacherous, and dangerous.

Sylva had received her husband's message from Soren a few days earlier and thought little about it. If Alberon wanted the Soll king to renew his vows of allegiance, then it made sense to do it whilst the summer allowed travel from the north.

It was only a few days later when Sylva called to see the Queen Mother that her suspicions were aroused. Ingrid's maid told the Empress that the Queen had left a couple of days earlier to travel to Iskala on the orders of the Emperor. Sylva knew that Ingrid seldom left her own quarters and virtually never left the castle. She could think of no reason for her husband to order his mother to take the arduous journey over the Doran Mountains. It certainly wouldn't be to witness a minor event like King Aster's renewal of Soll's loyalty to the Empire.

As she walked back from the Queen's quarters, Sylva met Ramon taking his morning exercise on the castle walls. She knew that the captain was under house arrest, but she had never enquired of her husband the reason why. Something piqued her curiosity.

"Good morning – Captain Ramon, I believe."

Ramon bowed. "Yes my lady, and it is a fine morning for a walk."

"It is," she replied. "You have been held here for some months now and you must be getting bored. I have never discussed you with my husband but maybe it's time I heard your story. Would you be kind enough to visit me this afternoon for a glass of wine and explain to me why my husband has detained you?"

Ramon nodded. "I would be happy to, my lady."

"Excellent, I will see you later then." With that Sylva walked on back to her apartments.

That afternoon Ramon was sitting opposite the Empress in her private apartments. Inwardly Sylva was cursing herself for not having interviewed him earlier.

"So let me see if I understand your story so far," she said. "You are under house arrest because my husband accuses your stepson of having run black market goods from Andore during the winter of two years ago, and you are to be held here until he returns here and gives himself up?"

Ramon nodded. "That is my understanding of the situation, my lady."

"And the cargo that you shipped here earlier this year was a multitude of iron components that you believe were the core elements necessary to build cannons?"

Again Ramon replied in the affirmative. "Yes my lady, I believe the pieces would need to be further forged and could then be assembled into cannons."

Sylva frowned. "And do you know where these materials were destined for?"

Ramon shook his head. "No my lady, I don't. Wagons were waiting at the dockside and the cargo was unloaded as fast as possible, although it took a couple of nights to complete the offload. All I can tell you is that the wagons quickly left Mora and crossed over the Morel bridges. As I have said, my contract was for the Duke of Alol, but my payment came from Chancellor Aracir."

Sylva said nothing for a few moments. Berin, the

Duke of Alol, had been killed in the battle at the Kermin Alol in 1507. She would need to talk with Aracir.

Sylva suddenly changed the subject. "Tell me about your stepson. I am intrigued that my husband holds you here hoping that your stepson will come to Mora, turn himself in and admit his guilt. It seems a very minor offence to interest the Emperor. Remind me, what is your stepson's name?"

Ramon smiled. "His name is Audun, and strangely both your husband and your mother-in-law also wanted to know about him and his background. Is that a coincidence?"

Ramon once again told the story of Ragna and her son's flight from Tamin and their life in Boretar. He finished his story with Ragna's death and Audun's rise to become the Captain of the *Swan*. Sylva paused. The name Ragna was somehow familiar, but she could not recall why.

She smiled. "Thank you Captain Ramon. I wish I had talked with you a few weeks ago. Your stories are very interesting and I will probably want to talk with you again."

Ramon nodded. "Of course my lady, I will be happy to visit again any time you request."

At around the same time as Sylva was learning about Ramon's history, on the other side of the Doran Mountains, Alberon and Ingrid were sitting in the royal apartments in Iskala Castle. That morning the Queen had travelled out to the Doran Plain to see for herself the destruction at Sparsholt. Whilst Wayland Henry and his smiths had started rebuilding some of the smithies, the intense ferocity of the fires that had devastated the area was still plainly visible. What had been molten iron had solidified around bricks from some of the forges, creating grotesque statues that stood like silent witnesses to the destruction. The blackened earth was evidence of the area the fire had swept across.

"The devastation is so complete and across such a large expanse that surely the only explanation can be that it was a natural phenomenon?" said Ingrid.

Alberon looked across at his mother and replied in a tremulous voice. "That would not explain the words etched below the dragon's head."

Ingrid looked quizzically at her son. "You have some other explanation then?"

Alberon hesitated for a moment. "I don't know, but suppose the maid Ragna was a witch and beguiled me? Then her son could be a sorcerer. The words on the broken piece of iron are his words."

Ingrid laughed. "That is a preposterous suggestion. As far as I remember the maid was a pretty girl and you were young, smitten and in love. No witchcraft was used to beguile you, she didn't need any magic. The words in the letter you were given were only used to stop the girl returning to Mora to seek what was her right and marry you."

Alberon closed his eyes for a moment as though processing his mother's words. "I know it sounds ridiculous, but if Audun is a sorcerer and can harness unnatural powers, then it would explain the destruction of the ironworks and the words etched into the piece of iron."

It was Ingrid's turn to pause. "But what motive would he have to destroy the forges?"

Alberon's face paled somewhat at the thought. "Perhaps he is beginning to exact his revenge."

CHAPTER 7

The Empress

❖ ❖ ❖ ❖

The day after Sylva had met with Ramon, she was again in her private apartments waiting for a visitor. With a formal knock on the door Aracir entered the room. "My lady, you requested my presence as a matter of urgency, so here I am. What can I do for you?"

Sylva nodded to the chair opposite her. "Thank you for being so prompt, Aracir. Please take a seat."

Over the years Sylva had been in many meetings with the Chancellor. She admired his intelligence and his honesty and knew that he was her husband's most trusted advisor. She started with a direct question. "Do you know what the cargo was that Captain Ramon transported here from Ackar a few months ago? I spoke with the captain yesterday and he has his suspicions, but as I believe you were the paymaster, perhaps you could confirm for me."

Aracir nodded. "Yes, my lady. Before the war with Amina started, the Emperor despatched a small number of smiths to Ackar to learn the skills required to forge cannons. Captain Ramon's vessel transported the smiths and the components that had been forged in Ackar back here. You will remember that the 1508 treaties with Amina prohibited Kermin from importing cannons from Ackar. The Emperor signed the treaties knowing that the wording did not prohibit us from building our own weapons."

Sylva frowned. "Who knew about this? Am I the only one who has not been told?"

Aracir hesitated before replying. "I think very few people knew the details, my lady. The Emperor tasked me with finding a messenger to travel to Boretar. I was not privy to the details of the message other than that I was to pay whatever was required to get the message delivered before February's snow moon. The messenger was told his instructions were contained in the package he was carrying and should not be opened until he reached Boretar. It was only when *Lex Talionis* docked in Mora that I learnt the nature of the cargo."

Sylva raised an eyebrow. "It is a strange name for a carrack. Does it have a meaning?"

Aracir shrugged. "I am sorry my lady, I don't know."

Sylva continued. "It doesn't matter, I can ask the captain. Now back to the point of my question. Who else knew about the details of this cargo in advance of the arrival of the carrack?"

Aracir sensed that the Empress was beginning to get angry, and he knew from experience she could be quite fearsome when her temper was roused, so he quickly responded. "The only person who I think would have known in advance is the Duke of Doran."

Sylva's voice took on a sharp edge. "Why on earth would the Emperor confide in Morserat?"

Aracir flinched slightly under the Empress' stare. "I have only recently learnt that during the past winter the Duke had been tasked with erecting a number of forges on the Doran Plain. He also established a settlement there called Sparsholt. The iron components from the carrack were immediately loaded onto wagons and transferred to Doran."

Sylva spoke quietly and almost to herself. "Of course, if Alberon is rearming then it would need to be well away from any prying eyes that could report back to my brother. Doran would be an ideal location."

Sylva was about to dismiss the Chancellor, but he had not finished. "There are two other pieces of information you need to know, my lady. Firstly the Emperor was indeed concerned that the King of Amina might find out about his plan. This was why the package carried to Boretar bore the seal of the Duke of Alol. Secondly, and more importantly, we learnt a week ago that some natural disaster had struck on the Doran Plain and the ironworks have been completely destroyed."

A thought struck Sylva. "Does the Queen Mother know about any of this? Is that why she left for Iskala?"

Aracir shrugged. "I am sorry my lady, I don't know."

As soon as the Chancellor had departed Sylva called one of her ladies. She now had two people she needed to talk with urgently. The first to arrive was Ramon.

"Thank you for coming again captain, I need you to answer one more question for me," she began. "Why was your carrack called *Lex Talionis*? What does it mean?"

Ramon once again explained the meaning of the words and told her that the carrack had been named at the insistence of his stepson.

A short while later Soren was ushered into the royal apartments. Sylva interrogated the young man about what he knew of the disaster that had occurred on the Doran Plain and also what message he had delivered to her mother-in-law. Soren explained all that he knew about the fires at Sparsholt, but he was not privy to the message he had delivered to the Queen. All he could tell Sylva was that having read the message the Queen had instructed him to find Holger and have him report to her immediately.

Sylva nodded. That would explain why the Captain of the Guard was not present in Mora. He must have escorted Ingrid to Iskala. She knew it was time she also crossed the Doran Mountains and got to the truth of what was happening.

"Thank you Soren. I presume some of your countrymen are still patrolling on the Kermin Plain?"

Soren nodded. "Yes, my lady."

Sylva smiled. "Excellent. You will go and get six of your best troopers and meet me at the castle gate first thing tomorrow. You will be my escort to Iskala."

Sylva had been taught to ride almost before she had learnt to walk, so she was an excellent horsewoman. The young palfrey she was mounted on covered the ground at an easy canter. As the small troop crossed the Kermin Plain, Sylva let the aromatic smell of the summer wildflowers fill her nostrils and ease her tension. She was glad to be on the move away from Mora, and the journey gave her time to think.

The facts she had discovered mostly made sense. She knew that her husband would somehow want to rearm, and that any future attempt to invade Amina would require cannons. Doran was the ideal place to set up the required forges. Transporting the components from Boretar before the spring also made sense as she knew that the patrols at the Morel estuary had resumed in April, although they were only routine searches, not a blockade as such.

However, other facts did not quite fit the story.

Ramon had mentioned her husband's request that a caravel called the *Swan* should be used to move the cargo from Boretar. A silly request, as even she knew that a caravel would not be able to cross the Eastern Sea in late winter. The *Swan* was captained by Ramon's stepson, Audun. Why had the son insisted on calling the carrack *Lex Talionis* - Revenge? Why had Alberon held Ramon captive in Mora? Surely it was not simply to try to apprehend a black market profiteer? What did Ingrid know, and why had she been ordered to Iskala? It suddenly struck her that she had not asked Aracir who had carried the message to Boretar. She would need to find out when she returned to Mora.

The group rode on through the early evening dusk and set up camp on the high mountain pastures, a short distance below the passes that led over the mountains to Doran. A shepherd was happy to accept a gold coin and allow the Empress the luxury of his hut rather than the alternative of a military tent.

Sylva walked out from the hut as the moon rose. The view was breathtaking. In the distance the hills of the Kermin Alol were just visible. So Alberon had been planning to once again march to war, and when he did the Alol would again be the battleground. Sylva was determined not to allow it to happen, and that would be her stance tomorrow when she reached Iskala.

Sylva had only visited Iskala a few times. She found

the town rather depressing and the castle itself was grey and often cold, lacking the luxuries of her rooms back in Mora. Soren led her through the stone-walled passageways to the Emperor's private rooms. Sylva had demanded that there should be no announcement of her arrival, so her husband was completely taken by surprise when she threw open the main door and marched into the room.

"Sylva, what are you doing here?" was all he could say.

Sylva's reply was sharp. "I could ask the same about your mother," she said, pointing at the Queen, who was sitting opposite her son.

"The Queen is here to witness the ceremony to be held tomorrow with the King of Soll," Alberon blustered.

He immediately wished that he had stood when his wife entered the room, although even then he would have still had to look up to meet her gaze. As it was, the hard emerald green eyes seemed to pin him to his seat. "Liar!" Sylva spat out. Her voice was as sharp as honed steel. "Instead of lying to me, you can explain about cannons, a carrack called *Lex Talionis*, a caravel, the *Swan* whose Captain is Audun, a natural disaster on the Doran Plain and finally why your mother knows about all of this and I know nothing?"

Ingrid was quietly impressed. She knew her daughter-in-law was a strong character, but she had never seen her so angry. She also noticed how her son seemed to quail from his wife's steely gaze, and wondered why.

It was the Queen who broke the silence. "Sylva, please sit down, you are giving me a crick in the neck looking up at you. I surmise from your questions that you have been talking to Captain Ramon? I first spoke to him a couple of weeks ago and had similar questions. I had other sources of information too and put the pieces together before demanding answers from Alberon. I should have confided in you, but some parts of the story didn't make sense so I waited. I apologise for that."

Sylva made no response, but continued to gaze intensely at her husband.

Ingrid turned to her son. "You'd better explain it all, Alberon."

Sylva's gaze turned to a glare. "Yes Alberon, you better explain it *all*, and it had better be the truth. Don't dare to lie to me again."

Sylva listened intently as Alberon finally explained everything. Her only reaction came when she learnt the truth about Audun. She let out a short gasp. "Ragna! I knew the name was familiar." For a moment she closed her eyes, thinking back to nine years previously when she had found the letter addressed to the maid. Her brother had never found Ragna, or the child, and now, as she had predicted, the man had returned to seek his revenge, and perhaps his inheritance.

Once Alberon had finished, Sylva's stare turned

to her mother-in-law. "You knew about all of this and didn't think to inform me?"

Ingrid frowned. "Like you, I learnt some of this when I spoke to Captain Ramon, but also like you, I was making assumptions based on what might have been coincidences. I have really only managed to fit all the pieces together since I arrived here a few days ago."

Sylva turned back to her husband. "So you were planning to mount another invasion of Amina? Next spring, I suppose? You know I would not have allowed it. Indeed, had I found out I would have left you and travelled to Tamin to warn my brother. Besides, from what I do know, it would have been another stupid expedition, as Bertalan has the Alol lined with defensive positions and cannons."

Alberon lowered his eyes before his wife's stare. "That is of course the reason I could not confide in you."

"That at least is something we agree on, Sylva. I have told him that I would not allow Kermin to repeat the mistakes of 1507 and march against Amina again."

Sylva nodded. "I am glad to hear you say it." She addressed her husband. "And you have known about your bastard son for more than a year? Why has he not been eliminated? Instead of dealing with the situation, you have engaged in a game of words with him, hoping to tempt him to come to Mora to try to pull off some heroic rescue of his stepfather?"

Alberon said nothing. The Empress was a woman

of her time, intelligent, logical and pragmatic. "And what is this nonsense about him being a sorcerer?" she continued. "What a preposterous idea!"

Until now Alberon had not mentioned the dragon's head. He leant forward and passed his wife the piece of iron. "How else would you explain this?"

Sylva's breath caught, and for a moment a shiver of fear ran down her back, but it passed in a moment. "There must be some logical explanation. Maybe the smiths forged the words in memory of the vessel that transported them home? After the disasters with the cannons in 1507 it would be natural if the gunners wanted to announce that their new weapon would give them revenge."

Alberon waved away the suggestion. "I have questioned Master Henry and the gunners and none of them recognise these words. Remember, Lex Talionis meant nothing to any of us until Captain Ramon explained the meaning. Also, of all of the iron destroyed at Sparsholt this is the only piece that retained the initial engraving. Everything else was reduced to molten lumps of metal."

Sylva could not conceive of the concept of a sorcerer other than from the pages of fictional stories. She wanted to establish the facts. "So where is this Audun now? I suppose you have men out trying to find him and arrest him, or better still terminate him?"

Alberon nodded. "Yes, I have been trying to find

him ever since it became clear that he was not going to simply arrive in Mora to negotiate the release of his stepfather. About two months ago he was in Anelo with his ship, the *Swan*. Then he seems to have disappeared from the face of the earth."

Sylva's temper rose again. "Idiot! If what you claim is true, then Audun is either here in Iskala or he is in Mora. If the destruction at Sparsholt was his doing, which I still find hard to believe, then he could not have delivered the fire from Anelo. What do you think he wants?"

Alberon's face paled slightly. "I will repeat what I said to my mother a couple of days ago. He is here for revenge, an eye for an eye – Lex Talionis."

The subject of the royal family's discussion, as the Empress surmised, was indeed in Mora. The Golden Fleece had become a regular haunt for Audun. However he kept himself to himself, either sitting at a corner table in the tavern or in the shade out in the courtyard. The inn's regulars recognised the young man, but they respected the distance that he seemed want to keep and simply nodded a greeting when he entered the inn.

Arvid was the one exception to the respect the locals showed for Audun's privacy. The big man regularly came over and planted himself on a seat at Audun's table and attempted to start a conversation. After a minute or two, having received only monosyllabic responses,

Arvid would cross back to the bar and announce loudly to his cronies. "He's an odd one that one. No respect for someone trying to be friendly. I don't know why I bother."

One particular day Audun was sitting in the courtyard lost in thought and only occasionally sipping his ale. He deliberately ignored Arvid's approach, hoping that for once the big man would take the hint. As usual Arvid ignored the signal and pulled up a seat.

"Have you heard about the earthquake that hit the Doran Plain?" he said.

Audun immediately looked up. "No I haven't. What earthquake? Tell me about it."

Arvid leant closer and his voice took on a conspiratorial tone, as if he was sharing a well-kept secret. "I don't think it is common knowledge, but a friend of mine heard the story from a blacksmith who has just returned from Doran. He was working there on some sort of secret project for the Emperor. Apparently the smiths' forges were located near a settlement called Sparsholt, which I had never heard of, but then again, I've never visited Doran."

Audun realised that unless he intervened the story was going to be long in the telling. "So tell me what happened, Arvid?"

The other man was not going to be deflected from telling his story to the full. "Well this Sparsholt place was apparently only built last autumn and the forges were constructed during the winter. My friend's friend had spent the past year in Ackar and only arrived in Doran a few months ago. There was a lot of work to do and several other smiths were brought to work there. Each was assigned their own forge."

Audun tried to hold back his impatience, but failed. "So what did the smith say about the earthquake?"

Arvid sighed, slightly annoyed by the interruption to his monologue. "Well, apparently a few nights ago, the earth opened up near the forges and fireballs erupted from deep in the earth. The fires were so intense that all the forges were completely destroyed and apparently there were rivers of molten iron flowing over the ground. I've never heard of such a thing. You're well travelled Adun, have you ever experienced anything like this?"

Audun had never changed the name he had used in his initial introduction to Arvid, so everyone in the inn knew him as Adun. He shook his head. "No I have never witnessed the sort of event you describe." He smiled as a thought occurred to him, then added, "I have read history books that do describe similar events."

Arvid was intrigued. "What, earthquakes and balls of fire and destruction?"

Audun nodded. "Well truthfully, not actually earthquakes, but of ancient alchemists and sorcerers who could conjure up fire at will and use their power in battles to destroy enemy armies and devastate their cities."

Arvid erupted in laughter. "You live in what is supposed to be a cursed cottage and don't believe in curses, but you believe in myths and fairy stories?"

Audun smiled. "I believe what is reported in the historical records."

So it was that the rumours started to spread in Mora, and as with every whispered secret, the story took on a life of its own. Some told of a great earthquake that had been created in the Doran Plain by a wizard who had a grudge against the Emperor and had left his cave in the Doran Mountains intent on destroying Iskala. Others said that they had been told that a dragon had flown from its lair in the wastelands of Esimore, attracted by the fires he could smell burning on the Doran Plain. When the monster discovered the forges, and not the mate he was searching for, in his fury he incinerated everything in sight. A few, who like Audun had read the history books, concluded differently. Dragons were for fairy stories, but history told of the power of alchemists and sorcerers.

If the eye-witness reports from Doran were accurate, then history suggested that a sorcerer had travelled to the Doran Plain. Some said he must have been sent by a foreign power to destroy whatever the Emperor was building there. These were quick to assign the blame to the Empress' brother, the King of Amina. Others set a more worrying narrative. History maintained that sorcerers were evil and hungry for power and wealth.

Mora was powerful and wealthy. Would the fire next be targeted at the city?

As Audun picked up snippets of the rumours at the docks, in the markets and in the overheard conversations at the Golden Fleece, he smiled to himself. His father had wanted to convict him as a sorcerer, and now even the people would believe Alberon. Deep inside, however, he was still worried about the direct connection between his ability to harness the red fire and his anger.

CHAPTER 8

The Sorcerer

❖ ❖ ❖ ❖

The rain shower had just blown past and the August sunshine was sparkling on the wet grass. Audun was again crossing the Kermin Plain. This time the Doran Mountains were in the distance behind him as he made his way south towards the Kermin Alol. Once again he was dressed entirely in black, and despite the warm sunshine the hood of his cloak was pulled over his head whenever other travellers passed close by.

During the day several wagons had stopped to offer the old beggar a lift. The waggoners were always met with a shake of the head as the old man continued on his journey leaning heavily on his staff. Audun knew he was embarking on a long walk, but he had to hide behind his disguise in case, by chance, he was recognised.

Dusk was beginning to fall as another wagon halted beside Audun. The wagon master shouted down, "I don't know where you are headed to old man, but wherever it is it's a long walk." He pointed back to the wagon bed. "I'm transporting this hay to my farm which lies close to the Alol. You're welcome to lie there and rest your legs. I have lanterns and I'll be travelling through the night."

"Thank you, sir," replied Audun, feigning a croaky, brittle voice. Slowly he climbed onto the back of the wagon and lay down, hoping that the night would conceal his true identity.

Fortunately the wagon master was not much of a conversationalist and seemed happy to whistle to himself as he encouraged his horses to "Move on." Audun dozed in the rear of the wagon, resisting sleep and the nightmares that might accompany it.

Dawn was breaking in the eastern sky when Audun was jolted awake. The wagon had stopped. The master turned and shouted back, "If you are headed through the Alol old man, then this is as far as I can take you. My farm lies some miles east of here so I can't take you any further on your journey."

Audun slowly climbed from the back of the wagon and leaned heavily on his staff. "Thank you sir, you have been very kind to an old man," he croaked.

Audun watched the dust from the wagon's wheels move away east before he took in his bearings. Ahead of him the road's gradient gradually increased as it started to rise towards the hills. Audun knew that this was the main route through the Kermin Alol. He also knew that it was in the central valley that the Kermin troops had been slaughtered by the Amina cannons in 1507.

In the distance he could see smoke and sparks rising from cooking fires. His overnight travel had brought him close to the border between Kermin and Amina. If his information was correct, whilst the road through the central valley was open to travellers and merchants' wagons, Amina cannons still looked north, prepared to repel any attack from Kermin. The treaties had held, but clearly the Amina King did not trust his brother-in-law to keep the peace.

Audun smiled. "You needn't worry Bertalan, there will be no Kermin cannons approaching your border this year or next," he murmured.

Audun needed elevation, so he left the road. The hills to the west rose sharply from the entry to the central valley, and he decided to tackle them. It would be an arduous climb, but there would be no passing travellers, so he could discard the black cloak and enjoy the early morning sunshine and the wind in his hair. Indeed he could enjoy the walk; he had plenty of time. He only needed to reach his planned destination at the summit an hour or so before night fell.

The royal party had arrived back in Mora the evening before Audun set off on his journey to the Kermin Alol. Whilst there had been further discussions in Iskala, there had been no agreement on how to approach the subject of the illegitimate son, or as Alberon now termed him, "the sorcerer". All three acted according to their individual instincts and characters. Alberon ordered Holger to move Ramon from the comfort of his rooms and lock him in the castle dungeon. Ingrid sent a message to Valdin instructing him to meet her early the next morning.

Sylva continued to search for a rational answer and requested that Ianis, the Keeper of the Books, should meet with her next day. Ianis was in his seventies and still sprightly. He had looked after Mora's libraries for decades. He was also a philosopher and an historian. Sylva thought that if anyone could explain the strange events at the ironworks on the Doran Plain, it would be Ianis.

Valdin arrived at the Queen's rooms as instructed, and Ingrid waved the huntsman to a seat. "Thank you for coming Valdin, I have something I need you to do for me. It is very sensitive and you cannot discuss this with anyone, not even your brother."

Valdin nodded. "As you wish my lady. What is this task? Is it in any way related to the rumours and gossip circulating in the city?"

Having only arrived back in Mora the previous evening, the Queen was not aware of the stories that had been the topic of conversation and speculation in most of the city's inns over the previous week. She looked questioningly at the huntsman. "What rumours?" She said.

"Do you want me to find and eliminate the sorcerer?"

Ingrid was taken aback, and took a moment to regain her composure. "I don't know what you mean Valdin. You'd better explain."

Valdin went on to describe the various stories he had heard in the ale houses. "If there is any sort of truth to these rumours then I presume you want this enemy dealt with," he said.

The Queen let out a slightly strained laugh. "Valdin, I'm surprised at you! I would not have taken you as someone who paid any attention to gossip. I certainly would not have expected you to believe in wizards and sorcerers. Or maybe you expect me to send you to kill a dragon? These are characters from fictional stories. The only truth in the gossip is that there was some form of earthquake on the Doran Plain and a settlement there was destroyed. I have a much less dangerous task for you. I believe that Audun, who as you know is the captain of the *Swan*, has travelled to Mora. He has not come here on his own vessel, so I suggest you start asking questions at the docks, as I have to assume he came on another ship. When you find him I want you to bring him to me in secret, probably by night. And Valdin, to be clear, I do not want him harmed in any way."

That same afternoon Ianis was ushered into the Empress's private rooms. He bowed as he entered. "My lady, you asked to see me. How can I be of help to you?"

Sylva rose from her seat. "Thank you for coming so promptly, Ianis. Can I offer you a glass of wine?"

The old man nodded. "Thank you my lady, that would be much appreciated."

Once the Keeper was settled, Sylva came quickly to the point. "Ianis, I need you to do some research for me. I want you to check your history books for a number of different things. Firstly can you find any references to major natural catastrophes on the Doran Plain, particularly any describing earthquakes or tremors occurring on the Plain? Secondly, are there any historical references to a sorcerer able to conjure fire to his will? And thirdly I need to know more about an ancient Aramin story or myth. I think it's described in a book called 'Lex Talionis: A story of deceit, of fire and revenge'."

Ianis replied. "Of course my lady, I will have my scribes start the search right away." Then he smiled and added, "Just in case you were going to ask, my lady, there is no historical evidence that dragons ever existed in Soll."

Sylva looked quizzically at the old man. "I don't

understand. What do you mean?" Ianis explained, and so Sylva also learnt about the rumours spreading through the city.

Ramon was still forbidden from leaving the castle, but rumours and gossip have no respect for castle walls. The morning before he had been moved to the dungeon, the servant had interrupted his reading in the library. "Excuse me Captain. You are well read and also you must have visited many lands in your time, have you ever seen a dragon?"

Ramon was amused by the question and asked the servant to explain. That was how he learned about the fires.

During his first night in the dungeon, Ramon wondered if there could be any connection between the change in his accommodation and the rumours. He concluded it must be a coincidence, but he could think of no reason why the Emperor should suddenly order his imprisonment.

After spending a day and a couple of nights in the dungeon it was a rather dishevelled captain who was escorted to meet the Emperor. Alberon was in no mood to be civil, or polite. He rose from his seat as Holger led Ramon into the room and pointing his finger at the other man shouted, "Did you know your stepson is a sorcerer?"

Ramon was speechless as the Emperor raged on. "His mother was a witch and she seduced me. I find you guilty of raising and harbouring a sorcerer. My sentence is death. You will burn at the stake." Alberon turned to Holger. "Take him back to the dungeon and chain him this time."

An hour later, with his hands and feet in chains Ramon was utterly bemused as well as terrified. He had not been allowed to utter a single word as he listened to the Emperor's tirade, but he could recall every word that had been said. Suddenly it dawned on him that the Emperor had gifted him the final piece of the jigsaw: *His mother was a witch and she seduced me.* Audun was the Emperor's illegitimate son. It explained everything, the deep interest in his stepson by the Queen, the Empress and the Emperor, the naming of the carrack, *Lex Talionis*, his house arrest, and the Emperor's impossible insistence that the iron cargo should be transported on the *Swan*. As Ramon again replayed the Emperor's words he remembered his first meeting with him and those ice-blue eyes, so like Audun's.

As his stepfather was being chained in the dungeon, Audun was close to completing his climb. Initially he had walked west on the lower slopes before starting his ascent. It was unlikely that anyone in the valley would spot him, and if they did they would probably think he was a shepherd tending the sheep that roamed the grassy slopes; nonetheless he still felt the need to remain hidden from any eyes watching from the central valley.

As he came close to the crest of the hill Audun moved cautiously east and took in the vista that lay below him. His information was correct. At the mouth of the valley were the cannons. The six culverins were arrayed with three on each side of the road. Even his untrained eye could recognise the strength of the defensive formation. From their elevated position the culverins commanded an open view north across the Kermin Plain. Any Kermin army marching towards the Alol would have to cross a half-mile killing zone before they could reach the cannons.

Audun was pleased to see that there was little activity close to the culverins. The Amina camp was located a few hundred yards further back in the valley, south of the line of cannons, and he hoped that the Amina troopers patrolling what was now the border between Kermin and Amina would return to their tents come the evening.

Looking directly across the valley to the east, he suddenly realised that his choice of hill had been fortunate. Halfway up the opposite hill, on a flat area, was a small cluster of tents. The Amina lookout post would have an open view miles north across the plain. The lookouts would have plenty of time to alert their colleagues in the valley if any threat appeared from the north. This would explain the relatively small number of troopers patrolling on the valley floor.

For now though, he needed a place to rest up until night time. Moving down from his position on the crest of the hill, he noticed a wooden platform cut into the hillside fifty feet or so below him. Whatever had previously occupied this position had been moved away a long time ago, as the weeds growing through the wooden beams confirmed. It was however a perfect vantage point with a direct line of sight to the cannons below.

As he lay down on the wooden beams to rest, Audun was not to know that it was from this platform in 1507 that the Amina culverins had unleashed the fire balls that had torn apart the marching divisions of Kermin pikemen. Had he known, Audun would have considered his location eminently appropriate.

It was mid-afternoon before the Queen's message got to Holger. After escorting Ramon back to the dungeon and ensuring the Captain was locked in chains, as the Emperor had ordered, he had left the castle to take some time to think. Like Ramon, Holger had heard Alberon say, "His mother was a witch and she seduced me."

Holger had been on the Doran Plain and seen the destruction with his own eyes. He had also heard all the gossip circulating in the city. He completely discounted the dragon rumour, but a sorcerer? If the Emperor's angry words were true, Ramon's stepson was not just a sorcerer but the Emperor's illegitimate son. Was that really possible? He decided that for now he would keep his knowledge to himself.

Ingrid had not been waiting patiently, as Holger found out when he was ushered into her apartments. "Where have you been? I sent for you hours ago," she snapped.

Holger took a sudden interest in his feet as he replied, "I am sorry my lady, I had urgent business to attend to in the city. I have only just returned and received your instruction."

"So I suppose I should be grateful you are here now. Remember in future captain, when I give you an order there is no more urgent business. Now where is Captain Ramon? I need to speak to him. My maid can't find him in his rooms or anywhere in the castle grounds. I hope you know where he is?"

Holger seemed to find his feet even more interesting. "Yes my lady, I do."

Ingrid was becoming increasingly irate. "Well captain, do you want me to start guessing, or are you going to tell me?"

Holger knew his answer would not meet with approval. "The Emperor has ordered that Captain Ramon be held in chains in the dungeon. He has been sentenced to death."

Ingrid was stunned. "What! You'd better explain."

THE EMPEROR, THE SON and THE THIEF

Holger told the Queen what had happened earlier in the day, omitting the Emperor's exact words. Ingrid was furious. "You will go now and release Captain Ramon, return him to his rooms and bring him to me this evening," she said.

Holger was caught in a dilemma. If he followed the Queen's order he would be defying the Emperor, but if he did not do as instructed he would be defying the Queen.

"My lady, I can't do what you request," he said. "I would be disobeying the Emperor's direct order."

Ingrid's voice took on a threatening tone. "So you prefer to disobey my direct order? I promise you that would be a very bad, and possibly dangerous, decision. Now go and release Captain Ramon. I will deal with my son. Go and do it now."

Alberon was sitting in his office poring over some papers when his mother burst in. "Mother, you might at least knock before charging in and interrupting me," he said.

Then he paused; it was clear his mother was furious. "What's wrong?" he enquired.

Ingrid spat out the words. "You are what is wrong! I told you that Captain Ramon was under my protection, and now I hear you have dared to defy me. I am told that the captain is in chains in the dungeon."

Instantly Alberon's temper rose and he snapped

back, "His son is a sorcerer and is a threat to the Empire. His son has committed treason and I now find the father culpable of assisting the son. Therefore, by association, I have also found the father guilty of sorcery and he will burn at the stake."

The hazel eyes narrowed and the Queen's voice lowered. "His son?" She raised her voice and said it again. "His SON? You mean YOUR son! It is you who is guilty of fathering a sorcerer. If anyone is guilty it is you. I should have you burnt at the stake!" She took a deep breath to calm herself, then continued in a quieter voice. "By now I hope Holger has released the Captain and returned him to his rooms."

Alberon rose from his seat, eyes ice cold. "If Holger has acted on your instruction and reversed my order he will find himself bounced back to the ranks. How dare you contradict me?"

Ingrid stepped forward and the blow came so suddenly and unexpectedly that Alberon had no time to avoid it. Ingrid's open palm struck his cheek with a crack. "You are still the same spoilt brat that you were as a child!" she roared. "I have told you before that you would be unwise to underestimate the power I still have and the loyalty I can still command."

Alberon was stunned. A mixture of emotions welled up inside him. The child wanted to cry, while the Emperor wanted to strike back. Before either emotion won out, his mother continued. "Sit down Alberon. Sit down now!"

The child obeyed the mother, and Ingrid continued. "What did you say to Captain Ramon? Does he now know the truth about his stepson? I presume Holger was present all through this interrogation? Do you know about the rumours circulating in the city?"

Alberon shook his head. "What rumours?"

Ingrid told him about the rumours of sorcery. "Now we need to ensure that Holger and Captain Ramon are sworn to secrecy," she went on. "I will deal with that. If Mora's citizens were to build on these rumours by speculating that the sorcerer they are worried about was the Emperor's son, then that would be very unfortunate, and maybe the stake would be your destiny. Unless of course we could persuade the people that you had sired a dragon!" With those words the Queen turned and left, leaving the son slightly bewildered.

It was a moonless night and the clouds floating above the Alol kept blocking out the starlight. Audun looked out over the valley. Camp fires were burning close to the tents on the lookout post opposite him and in main Amina camp in the valley below. The culverins appeared to have been left on their own to slumber through the night. Maybe in time innocent deaths would be necessary, but not on this night.

Taking the red orb from his bag Audun located it

on the Φ symbol at the hilt of the staff, as he had done a few weeks earlier on the Doran Plain. As before the two instantly locked together, but this time a shower of amber sparks danced down the length of the staff, as if in celebration of the joining. Despite his concern about it, Audun knew that he could only conjure the red fire through his anger. Closing his eyes he forced himself to recall the images from his nightmares, the Amina King reading the Empress's letter, and his grandfather lying dead on the dungeon floor in Tamin Castle.

As the scenes replayed in his mind, Audun could feel his anger building. This was not the fiery anger he had felt in front of the forges in Doran, but a cold fury that seemed to build from deep within him, and this time he could feel the power beginning to flow through the staff. Unbeknown to him, his eyes when he opened them reflected his rage; ice blue had become glacier blue.

Raising the staff and pointing the tip down towards the sleeping culverins, Audun channelled his fury. The orb and staff seemed to respond in kind. Rather than the red fire that had incinerated the smithies, it was blue bolts of lightning that leapt from the tip of the staff and erupted around the culverins. As each bolt hit the ground, the blue turned to red and the culverins were engulfed in intense flames.

Audun had not anticipated the consequent explosions. The containers holding the balls of saltpetre, charcoal and sulphur were located close to the culverins and as the flames reached the gunpowder boxes, these in turn exploded.

With the conflagration below beginning to light up the hillside, Audun knew it was time to move on. As his fury subsided, the staff and the orb quietened. The orb resisted for only a moment before being released from the staff and returned to his bag.

Turning to leave the platform, Audun had one last look down at the destruction in the valley. "A suitable funeral pyre for my grandfather," he murmured.

CHAPTER 9

Explanations and Revelations

❖ ❖ ❖ ❖

Holger had followed the Queen's orders and released Ramon from his chains some hours earlier. Now he was escorting him to the Queen's rooms. As they walked along the castle wall, they both spotted the sudden bolts of lightning in the far distance. Holger knew the land and remarked, "Unless I am mistaken, that lightning is striking over the Kermin Alol close to where the border now is, just where the Amina cannons are positioned."

The Captain of the Guard might have known the layout of the land, but the sailor had the sharper eyes. Ramon gazed at the distant flashes. "There is something odd about that lightning," he said. "It appears to be coming from the side of the western hills rather than from the sky above."

A moment later, they saw red fire rising from below the spot where the flashes had been. Holger knew about cannons. "I think the lightning has ignited the gunpowder," he said. "We'd better move on. I have recent experience of the Queen's anger if she is kept waiting."

Holger led Ramon to the same turret room where he had first met the Queen. Ingrid rose from her seat as the pair entered. "Thank you Holger, you may leave us now, but I will want to talk with you later." Holger bowed and left.

Ramon also bowed as the Queen continued. "I apologise for the way you have been treated, Captain Ramon. My son can get a bit too emotional and overreact, and the chains in the dungeon and the sentence of death upon you are rather typical. However I now also need you to answer more questions for me. Please take a seat."

Ingrid leant forward and Ramon could see the tension behind the hazel eyes as she asked her first question. "Tell me captain, do you now know, or at least suspect you know, the true identity of your stepson?"

Ramon hesitated, then nodded. "If the Emperor's tirade earlier today held any truth, then yes, I suspect I do. My conclusion would also explain the interest you and the Empress seemed to take in Audun and why your son would want to hold me here to entice him to come to Mora. The declaration made by your son allowed all the jigsaw pieces to fall into place. Audun is the Emperor's illegitimate son."

Ingrid sighed and sat back in her seat as Ramon continued. "However, if that conclusion is the truth, I cannot believe in the additional assertions that Ragna was a witch and her son a sorcerer. That has to be pure made-up nonsense."

The Queen was silent for a moment before responding. "I don't really understand it all either but I think you deserve to know as much of the truth as I can tell you, but you need to swear to keep it secret." Ramon looked directly into the hazel eyes. "I promise I will, my lady."

Ingrid started with the most recent event before revealing the history. "You know about the rumours of an earthquake on the Doran Plain?" Ramon nodded. "The event on the Plain appeared to be a natural disaster, and it completely destroyed all the ironwork that you had transported here from Ackar. Alberon had established his ironworks in Doran near a new settlement called Sparsholt, well away from any prying eyes. It was there that he was building his cannons. Did the Emperor show you the dragon's head?"

Ramon shook his head. "No, I don't know what you're referring to."

"All the ironwork was destroyed. Melted lumps

of iron lay all round the smithies, but there was one fragment that remained whole, a motif from one of the cannons, a dragon's head. Below the mouth, two words were embossed in the metal: 'Lex Talionis'."

Ramon drew the obvious conclusion. "The words must have been added to the metal work along with the dragon motif. Calling a cannon 'revenge' is quite plausible."

The Queen nodded. "I thought the same thing, albeit a strange way to capture the word 'revenge'. However there is no indication that any of the smiths recognised the word, but I need to explain more of the history."

She went on to tell Ramon about the letter banishing Ragna and her unborn child, the accusation of witchcraft, the Empress' discovery of the illegitimate child and the request to her brother in Tamin to search out the family and eliminate them. She described what she knew about the message Audun had delivered to Alberon in Tufle a year earlier.

The jigsaw pieces in Ramon's head now all fitted perfectly, but he was still perplexed. "Audun is a smart young man, an excellent captain and sailor, but I can't imagine him having unnatural powers," he said. "He is well read and has a particular interest in early 14th century history, but much of the histories from that time are a mix of fact and fiction. I really don't understand how he could cause the destruction you describe. I also don't understand why you have told me all this."

Ingrid leant forward again. "I am telling you because I think you had already guessed about Audun's parentage and I needed to be sure that you would keep this a secret. Also, I believe he is either here in Mora or in Iskala. I want you to go and find him and bring him to me."

Ramon inclined his head questioningly. "I am under house arrest, and indeed sentenced to death. I cannot leave the castle grounds."

Ingrid smiled. "I have dealt with all that. You will be free to wander the city from tomorrow."

With a sigh of relief Ramon asked one last question. "If this is all true, why did he cause the destruction of the ironworks?"

Ingrid's look became more serious. "He is seeking revenge for the way we treated his mother."

Walking back along the castle walls towards his rooms, Ramon wondered again about the lightning he had seen in the distance and the way it had appeared to come from the hills rather than the sky. With no moon, the dark of the night hid the hills at the Kermin Alol.

James Daunt was the senior commander of the Amina forces at the Alol. He had travelled from Ackar in 1507 to train the Amina gunners and had overseen the deployment of the culverins against the Kermin forces in this very valley two years earlier. There were only a few hundred troops stationed at the border, since Daunt had persuaded the Amina Commander in Chief, Silson, that any attempted invasion from the north would be spotted long before the hills could be reached, and if the treaties had been adhered to by the Kermin king, it would be a foot army, which would be obliterated by the Amina cannon fire.

Daunt had been in his command tent when the lightning suddenly flashed. He had just pulled back the tent flap to see what was happening when the first of the gunpowder boxes had exploded. The concussion had knocked him to the ground, and from his prone position he had watched the red fire and the multiple explosions light up the night. The fires had seemed to burn for an unnatural length of time before the final sparks guttered out and the dark closed in again.

With the earth still smouldering, Daunt walked along the front line, where each culverin lay destroyed, a useless lump of twisted iron. Broken metal fragments, the remnants of the iron boxes that had held the gunpowder, were scattered across the valley floor.

James Daunt was a master gunner and he knew how much heat the smiths in the Ackar ironworks had to generate in their furnaces to work the iron and forge the cannons. It seemed inconceivable to him that lightning could generate such heat across such a wide area, even when supported by the exploding gunpowder.

He was approaching the remains of the sixth cannon on the eastern side of the valley when the trooper called out to him. "Sir, the lightning, I need to speak with you."

Daunt recognised the man as one of the troopers who was stationed at the lookout post on the hill side three hundred feet or so above him. "Yes trooper, what is it?"

The man saluted, "Sir, we saw the lightning strikes from the lookout post." The trooper pointed to the post above.

Daunt was slightly irritated. "Yes I know where the lookout post is and unless you were all asleep I would hope you did see the strikes. Is this what you have deserted your post to come and tell me?"

The trooper blanched slightly as he recognised his commander's impatience. He blurted out, "Sir the lightning flashes appeared to come from the western hills opposite us and not from the sky."

Daunt was about to rebuke the stupid trooper when he noticed a large piece of iron lying close to where the man was standing. Unlike the rest of the ammunition boxes, whose broken fragments were scattered across the valley floor, the lid of this last box appeared to have remained intact. Daunt approached the lid and saw two words etched in the metal, still glowing red: *'For Arin'*.

Cloaked in the black of the night, Audun had made his way west from his hill top platform and had descended to the drover road that ran alongside the Mina River. As had been the case a few weeks earlier on the Doran

Plain, the force of will required to control the orb had taken its toll, and after splashing his face in the cold river water, a nearby copse provided a cover for rest.

Lying down and using a tree root as a pillow, Audun looked up through the leafy canopy and contemplated the stars twinkling in the infinite black sky. After a moment he closed his eyes, searching for sleep, but the glinting blue-white of the celestial bodies continued to flicker on his closed eye lids, and suddenly he was wide awake. He had suddenly remembered that the orb and staff had responded to his cold fury with blue bolts of lightning, in stark contrast to the red fire that had been fuelled by his raging temper on the Doran Plain.

Audun sat up; it was time to think, not to sleep. He knew that the power he could wield through the orb and the staff responded to his anger, but it now also seemed that the power could be controlled if he focused his wrath. A violent rage was uncontrollable and dangerous but a cold fury, that was a different matter altogether.

He smiled and whispered to himself, "So be it. My revenge must be taken cold." The myriad tiny lights in the vast blackness above him seemed to shine brighter in agreement.

Two days had passed since Sylva had set Ianis his task, and she was beginning to wonder if the librarian had failed to find anything and had forgotten to report back to her. She was about to call for her maid to go and get the old man when there was a knock on the door and the maid came in. "My lady, the Keeper of the Books is requesting an audience with you, shall I bring him in?" she said.

Sylva rose from her seat. "Yes bring him in, and then bring us something to drink."

Sylva waited as Ianis settled himself in the offered chair and shuffled with the papers he had brought with him. Eventually he appeared to be ready to report. The Empress's patience was beginning to run out, and she was not prepared to wait for more paper shuffling. "Well Ianis, with so many notes I have to presume you have a lot to tell me, so please begin."

The old man was slightly flustered by the Empress' curt tone. "My lady, I need to be sure to report back to you in an orderly manner and these notes have been written by several different scribes."

"Ianis, please just get on with it and tell me what you have found out."

"Well my lady I can confirm what I said when we met a couple of days ago, that there is no historical evidence for dragons existing in the real world."

Sylva was now beginning to get irritated. "I didn't ask you about dragons! Now tell me what you have found out about the specific questions that I asked you to research."

Ianis realised that the little joke he had made to try to settle his nerves had backfired. "My apologies, my lady." He continued in a more serious voice. "Firstly I can confirm that the scribes cannot find any documented reports of earthquakes or volcanic eruptions occurring in Doran, or indeed in the Doran Mountains. There are some questionable histories that report flames erupting in the Inger Mountains which lie in the far north of Andore. I will return to this later."

The old man paused to take a sip of wine and moved to the second page of his notes. "You asked about a book that was possibly called *'Lex Talionis: A story of deceit, of fire and revenge'*. Such a book does exist and we have a copy in the library."

Ianis went on to explain the origin of the book and to state it was a translation of ancient scripts that had been found in the Kermin Alol a few years earlier. Sylva knew how the ballad ended, but this was the first time she had been given this detail.

Two points particularly caught her attention, and she wanted to be sure. "Did you say that the child in the ballad was called Adun and that the golden city of the Aramin was destroyed by red fire?"

Ianis nodded. "Yes, my lady."

Sylva paused for a moment to compose her thoughts and then invited the librarian to continue. Ianis again shuffled his notes before responding.

"We have found some evidence for a sorcerer who could conjure fire at will. Very few texts have been recovered from the second age and these are more likely to be recording myth than factual history, but there are references to an alchemist who could harness the power of a mineral called othium. Strangely an early 14th century book titled "White Light Red Fire" by an author called Angus Ferguson describes a similar character and the red fire that this individual could conjure up at will. The book also describes the spontaneous eruptions of red fire from cracks in the Inger Mountains that I referred to earlier."

Sylva held up her hand to stop the librarian. "Did this Angus Ferguson also write a book of poetry in the same period?"

Ianis looked back at his notes. "Yes, that is correct, my lady."

Sylva again stopped the old man. She didn't need more information; right now, she needed to compose her thoughts. She also needed a copy of the book "White Light Red Fire".

"Ianis, is it possible for me to borrow this book or does my husband already own a copy? I presume it is a rare object?"

Ianis smiled. "I can get you a copy within the hour, my lady. The library has several modern copies of the book as it was printed in Aldene, the capital of Bala, a few years ago. Bala was Angus Ferguson's home land. However I would suggest you read it with a degree of cautious perspective. Whilst the story probably does in some ways accurately record the wars of the early

14th century, it is almost certainly also a mix of fact and fiction."

Once the Keeper of the Books had left, Sylva gave instructions that she was only to be disturbed if there was a delivery of a package from him. If Ianis was as good as his word, she had a little time to reflect on the old man's reports. A child called Adun seeking revenge, 'Lex Talionis', a city destroyed by red fire and an alchemist who seemed to be able to conquer time and space and could conjure red fire at will. It seemed like a mix of myth, fantasy and fiction but there were also strange coincidences. A disinherited child called Audun, a poem written by the author of the book she was now waiting for and red fire destroying the ironworks at Sparsholt. Simply coincidences? She wondered.

Audun had spent the morning resting in the copse close to the Mina River. The early August sun was hot and the shade of the trees, together with an occasional trip to the river to splash his face with cool water, had helped him to recover from the weariness he had felt after the exertions of the night before. It was also a time to think and to plan.

In destroying the Amina cannons he had tried to hold to his promise to avoid killing innocent bystanders if at all possible. He had waited until the Amina troops patrolling the border had returned to their tents before unleashing the fire from the staff, and he hoped that none of the troopers had been injured in the resulting unexpected explosions.

Lying back against the tree root, he considered what to do next. He had resolved to use his power to follow the path taken by Garan, the King whom history had called the Peacemaker. He felt that the destruction of the weapons of war on the Doran Plain and at the Kermin Alol would have been approved of by the Peacemaker, but were these actions really fulfilling his desire to avenge his family?

When he closed his eyes for a moment, images from his earlier nightmares flashed in front of him, images of red fire consuming cities and citizens, and there he was, always at the heart of the destruction, with red fire spewing forth from the orb and staff.

Jolted back to the present, Audun looked up through the tree canopy to the clear blue sky and renewed his vow that he would never use the power of the staff for wanton destruction. He felt as though he could hear the laughter and ridicule emanating from the orb lying in the bag at his side. To strengthen his resolve, he addressed it directly.

"You are subservient to my will and your power is mine. I am sworn to use it for peace, and you will obey me." The laughter continued to echo round the trees.

What Audun did not know was that he had left his fingerprints behind; in Doran below a dragon's mouth and in the Alol on an iron box lid. He also didn't realise that his actions in destroying the Amina cannons might have the opposite effect to that which he had intended.

CHAPTER 10

Fields of Fire

❖ ❖ ❖ ❖

Rumours and gossip travel quickly along trade routes, and Bertalan, King of Amina, already knew that some sort of disaster had struck the Doran Plain. As a pragmatist, he discounted the stories of wizards, sorcerers and dragons as nonsense, but his own historians could find no reference to natural disasters occurring in the northern country. Worse still, his spies in Mora could not find out what had been destroyed in Doran other than that it was near some sort of settlement called Sparsholt. Had his enquiries not been interrupted, Bertalan might have followed his sister's approach and searched more deeply into history.

Silson did not bother to knock before interrupting

his king. Bertalan was about to reprimand the Duke until he saw the concern in the other man's eyes.

Silson went straight to the point. "My lord, our defences at the Alol have been destroyed. A trooper has just arrived from the border and apparently a freak lightning storm struck last night and all of the culverins were consumed in the resulting fires."

Bertalan rose from his desk. "What? The border is undefended? What sort of storm was it? I can't imagine a lightning storm causing such destruction. Is it a coincidence that some sort of natural eruptions are also rumoured to have destroyed a settlement on the Doran Plain? Is this some sort of plan by Alberon to drive us back to war? Get Bartos and have a troop of my guardsmen ready to ride to the Alol first thing tomorrow morning."

News of the destruction at the Alol did not get to Mora as quickly as it had reached Tamin. Doran and Kermin cavalry under the command of Orran, the Duke of Doran's brother, patrolled the plain north of the border but kept their distance from the Amina cannons. From their night camp Orran and his cavalrymen had witnessed the lightning strikes and the resultant fires, but they were too far away to see what had happened on the ground.

At the border, James Daunt had acted quickly. He

realised that without the cannons as defence there was a possibility that the Kermin cavalry might attempt a raid on his force and try to capture the border. He had four hundred troops guarding the border crossing, a mixture of gunners, archers and halberdiers along with fifty light cavalry.

Most of the gunners were also trained arquebusiers. The arquebus had been invented in Ackar a decade earlier. The long barrel was either held at the shoulder or supported on a tripod and could shoot a one-ounce iron or lead ball over three hundred yards, although accurate fire was limited to fifty yards. The arquebusiers, along with the culverins, had first been deployed in battle at the Alol in 1507.

Daunt quickly deployed these men to close the border. The merchant's wagons travelling south from Mora were stopped a mile from the Kermin Alol. Similarly, those travelling north from Tamin were held before entering the open valley. The wagon masters were told that a lightning storm had damaged the main road through the valley and it might be some time before it would open again.

Orran watched the queue of wagons lengthen during the morning and decided he had better find out what was happening. One of his troopers was sent to the wagon train to question the wagon masters. The trooper kept some distance from the arquebusiers guarding the road. Since the signing of the peace treaties in 1508 there had only been occasional clashes between the cavalry units patrolling close to the border at the Kermin Alol; these had usually been minor incidents when one side or the other had approached too close to the other side's lines. The trooper returned with the information that the storm during the night had damaged the road and it was closed.

Orran had also sent two other troopers on a more dangerous task. He needed to know what had happened in the Alol. With the Amina lookout post on the eastern hills, the two men moved through the wagons and on towards the west. Keeping the hill between themselves and the Amina troops, the two cavalrymen passed close to the copse where Audun was preparing to restart his journey.

Audun remained hidden, but wondered what two Doran cavalrymen were doing on foot following the route he had taken the previous afternoon to climb the western hill. He decided to stay in the copse for another night before starting out again. In the morning his destination would be the Tamin Plain.

It was early evening before the two troopers reported back to Orran. Their report was difficult to understand without seeing the ground in person. They described a large swathe of the valley floor which was now blackened, scorched earth. More surprisingly, the cannons that had looked out threateningly over the

Kermin Plain for the previous twelve months appeared to have been destroyed by the lightning. Orran was stunned. He realised that if the report was correct, then the balance of power at the border had changed. It was time to report to his brother, Morserat.

Another glorious August day greeted Audun as he left the sparkling waters of the Mina River and walked back towards the main road that led through the Alol to the Tamin Plain. During his time sheltering in the copse he had had plenty of time to reflect on his actions and plan what to do next. The destruction of the cannons reaffirmed his belief that his power could be used for peace. In addition the treasuries of his father and the Amina King would suffer as a result. Buying new military equipment would be expensive. It was this thought that informed his plan. He would take his revenge by destroying Alberon and Bertalan's sources of wealth.

Rounding the foot of the hill, Audun saw the queue of wagons and the line of Amina soldiers. He had hoped to beg a lift through the Alol on a wagon, but the way was closed and he guessed he knew why. Doubling back on himself, he returned to the drover road that followed the Mina River south. The path was not wide enough for wagons, so the only company he encountered on his way were a few shepherds and their sheep making their way to the markets in Kermin or Amina. None of the shepherds knew why the main road was closed.

After a couple of miles, Audun reached a junction. The drover road continued following the river south, whilst a side path cut south east, climbing up to a gap in the hills. He decided that the side path was the best option. Maybe he could join the main road south of the valley and still find a wagon travelling towards Tamin.

As he reached the summit of the pass, he looked down onto the main road; another queue of wagons, another line of Amina troopers and in the far distance, to the north, the blackened earth.

He sat for a moment to admire the view and survey his handiwork in the distance. Above him, swallows darted through the sky chasing their next meal. In the distance, over the eastern hills, a golden eagle soared effortlessly; his father's royal symbol and a reminder of his mission.

His ponderings were suddenly disturbed by the noise of horsemen approaching from the south. It was a large, fast-moving troop of cavalry, Audun guessed about two hundred strong. At the head of the riders flew the red, white and blue colours of Amina alongside the grey wolf banner of the Amina king. Bertalan was coming in person to inspect the damage at the border.

Morserat had arrived in Mora a week earlier, so Orran knew that his brother was in the Kermin capital and not in Iskala. Alberon had ordered the Duke to come and report on the progress in rebuilding the smithies at Sparsholt. Despite the comfort of the palatial residence he occupied in Mora, the Duke hated being in the city and being at the beck and call of his nephew, the Emperor. He had now been waiting several days for Alberon to demand his presence, and he was getting bored. He also knew that his report would not please the Emperor.

The command from Alberon was delivered simultaneously with the arrival of the Doran cavalryman. Morserat looked at the note first; he was ordered to go to the council room in the castle immediately.

He turned to the Doran trooper. "I need to report to the Emperor so I will hear my brother's news when I return," he said.

The trooper bowed. "Apologies my lord, but my message is urgent and I think you might want to hear what has happened at the border before you meet with the Emperor." Morserat hesitated. "Well, it had better be very important. Get on with it, and be quick!"

Alberon was not a patient man, and he had now been waiting for thirty minutes. Why was the Duke not here on time as he had commanded? The ice-blue eyes glared at the Duke as he entered the council room. "Did you get lost on the way here my Lord Duke, or do you just enjoy keeping your Emperor waiting?"

Strictly, the treaties signed in 1508 required Alberon to relinquish the title "Emperor", but his brother-in-law was a long way to the south and Alberon had decided to ignore this clause of the treaties, much as he planned to disregard others.

Morserat bowed. "My apologies sire. I received news from the Alol just as I was coming here, and that delayed me."

"Well at least you are here now. What progress is being made at Sparsholt?"

Morserat knew that his reply would not be well received. "Work is progressing sire, but the forges will not be functioning before winter sets in and with all the components that were shipped from Ackar destroyed, the smiths will need to start all over again. Master Henry estimates that it will be at least nine months before the forges are able to start working on the cannons. It will be several more months before the components can all be assembled."

Alberon stood up, raising his voice and pointing furiously at the other man. "I want my weapons over the Doran Mountains by next spring at the latest, and I want to hear no excuses. I will hold you personally responsible for any failure to meet my command."

Morserat bowed. "Yes sire." He had never liked his nephew, and the other man's irrational demands were among the reasons. Unfortunately he had other news that would probably draw a further rebuke. He continued nonetheless.

"Sire, I also have news from Soll, or perhaps it is best to describe it as rumours. King Aster is getting old and has apparently been bedridden for the past few months. He has announced that his grandson, William, is to be heir to his throne. Rumours have it that the young man has been stirring up revolt in Soll. He has announced that he will stop paying the tithe that Soll pays to the Empire each year."

Alberon laughed. He had paid no attention to the dynastic line of the King of Soll. "Revolt in Soll? It is a land populated by peasants, and as for the tithe, it is a pittance, merely a token to reinforce their subservience to the Empire. Take a troop of your Doran cavalry to Soll and arrest this grandson. Bring him to Iskala, where he will swear fealty to me or be found guilty of treason and executed. You may leave now, Duke. Go and get the forges producing my cannons."

Morserat bowed. "Sire, I have one last piece of news which I have only just received from my brother, who is patrolling on the plain close to the Alol."

Alberon held the Duke in a long, cold stare before responding. "I hope this news is more interesting than the rest."

Morserat went on to describe as best he could the destruction of the cannons at the Amina border.

At the same time as Alberon was trying to take in Morserat's news, his brother-in-law was at the Alol inspecting the destruction himself. Bertalan shook his head and turned to James Daunt. "It's hard to believe that lightning could deliver enough heat to melt six cannons. Have you ever witnessed anything like this before?"

The master gunner paused before replying. "No my lord, I have not. I know the amount of heat that is needed to forge the iron in the first place and whilst I can imagine that a lightning strike could destroy one cannon, I have never seen lightning create fires with such intensity over such a large area. There is also something odd about these fires. If we go back to my tent I will try to explain."

Sitting in the command tent, Bertalan asked, "Well Master Daunt, what can be odder than lightning randomly destroying all of our cannons?"

Daunt beckoned the trooper who had spoken to him into the tent. "Please explain to the King what you thought you saw from the lookout post," he said.

The man was overawed to be in the presence of his King and struggled over his words. "I, er. I…"

Bertalan snapped, "Get on with it man what did you see?"

The man repeated what he had told Daunt. Bertalan was staggered. "You are certain that the lightning strikes originated from the hillside? How could that be possible?"

The trooper haltingly replied, "I can only report what we saw, sire."

Daunt dismissed the trooper and walked to the back of the tent. "There is something else, my lord, that cannot be easily explained." He returned and passed Bertalan the lid of the ammunition box. The words still stood out, ochre red, against the black of the iron: *'For Arin'*.

Bertalan looked quizzically at the other man. "What does this mean?"

Daunt sat down. "I don't know my lord, but the lid was one of the few intact pieces left after the lightning storm. The letters were still burning red when I found the piece. It's as if the lightning left a message."

Bertalan snorted. "Ridiculous! There must be a simpler explanation." He turned to his cousin. "Bartos, does this name 'Arin' mean anything to you?"

The commander shook his head. "No my lord, it does not, although it is not an uncommon name in Amina."

Audun made his way down from his hilltop perch to the valley floor and started to follow the road south towards Tamin. He was fortunate to be overtaken by a wagon from Mora which had crossed the border before it had been closed but had then had to stop to repair a loose wheel. The wagon master was happy to have some company as he continued the journey towards Tamin.

It was early evening before the road through the Alol started to open up and Audun could look down over the Tamin Plain. Leaving the wagon to continue its journey south, Audun struck out east. He only vaguely knew what he was looking for and hoped that a wider view across the Plain would guide him. Having often transported Amina's exports from Tufle on the *Swan*, he knew that much of the country's wealth was generated from its exports of wine and linen. The taxes on these products helped fill the Amina King's coffers.

It was a relatively short and pleasant climb to the crest of the last of the south eastern Alol hills. In the far distance the sun was setting over the Middle Sea, bathing the distant Tamin Castle in an orange glow. Below him the Amin River was flowing sedately westwards, separating the Tamin Plain from the Vale of Tember. Looking out over the vista, Audun realised that his choice of direction had been fortunate. As the nearby Alol hills rolled down towards the Tamin Plain, their southern slopes were covered with vines, their ripe grapes waiting to be harvested. On the Plain itself bundles of flax were stacked, the stooks left to dry in the August sun before going on to be threshed.

As dusk settled in with purple and orange hues, Audun took the orb from his bag. The stone instantly burned with a deep red, shedding sparks as if in annoyance. Audun heard the voice ring in his head: *This will not deliver you your throne.* He laughed and as before addressed the orb directly. "I will have my revenge my way, and you will obey me." The sparks increased in intensity and the orb burnt an angrier red.

Enclosing the orb in his hand, Audun called up his own will and once again drew on the image of his grandfather lying dead in Tamin Castle's dungeon. Slowly the orb seemed to submit and the red cooled. As he placed it on the hilt of the staff, Audun could feel his fury grow, ice cold like his eyes. Raising the staff and sweeping the tip across the vista below him, he released his fury. Bolts of blue tore through the vineyards shredding the vines. He pointed the tip further south, to the Plain, and the stooks of flax burst into flames, creating fields of fire.

Silson, Duke of Amina, was standing on Tamin's castle walls admiring the twilight colours of the evening sky when the flashes of blue light from the Alol caught his attention. Initially the Duke was taken by the beauty of it, the flashes of lightning against the twilight colours of the evening sky. A moment later, horror replaced the beauty. From his distant viewing point it appeared to the Duke that the very earth of the Alol was being consumed by red fire as the flames leapt in an evil dance high into the night sky.

Miles further north, on the other side of the Kermin Alol, Bertalan noticed the strange orange glow that appeared to be reflecting in the sky over the distant southern Alol hills. A strange trick of the setting sun he thought, and dismissed it; he had other things to think about. With the cannon defence at the border destroyed, he was concerned that his brother-in-law might make an opportunistic attack on the border. Bertalan's spies had kept him well informed, and to the best of his knowledge the 1508 treaties had held. Alberon had not imported new weapons from Ackar, and although the Doran Cavalry patrolled the Kermin Plain in small units, most of the Cavalry seemed to have remained stationed on the far side of the Doran Mountains at Iskala.

Audun looked out over the destruction that he had inflicted and smiled. "Revenge taken cold rather than in uncontrolled fury. This must be my way."
The red fury seemed to be reserved for the orb, which burned with anger and refused to be released from the staff. Audun was tired, weary to his bones, and again it seemed that the willpower it took to control the orb had soaked up all of his strength.

Summoning up his remaining resolve and delivering a sharp instruction, he separated the orb from the staff; it was still spitting angry red sparks as he placed it beside his bag. As he lay down on the grass a gentle rain started to fall. It seemed as if nature had recognised his lightning, and as is the way with nature, it did what it always did and sent in the rain clouds. On the Plain the smouldering sheaves of flax spat and hissed as clouds of steam rose into the air.

CHAPTER 11
Unforeseen Consequences

❖ ❖ ❖ ❖

The sun poked its head over the eastern Alol and the morning dew sparkled on the waking grass as Audun stirred. Shaking the wet from his cloak he sat up, feeling refreshed. A dream-free night had cleared his head, but it took him a moment to take in his surroundings. Then he remembered; cold fury and lightning bolts. Looking out to the south, he saw the fields he had destroyed. The vineyards lay wrecked as if a great hand had torn through the vines, ripping the plants from the ground by their roots. Below the vineyards all that remained was blackened ground and the still-smoking remains of the flax stooks.

Audun was taken aback for a moment by the scale of

the destruction he had wrought and hoped that the field workers had remained safe in their village, which sat to the west on the banks of the river Mina, close to the main road. Then something caught his attention in the furthest of the flax fields. Initially it was indistinct, but as the sun rose, the air cleared, and there in the distance the charred ground held its message scorched into the earth: *'For Arin, Lex Talionis'*.

Audun was stunned. He had no recollection of commanding the staff to deliver such a message. It made him pause for a moment. What other evidence had he left behind him in the wake of his destruction on the Doran Plain and at the Amina border? Was the orb now playing a word game with him? He sensed amusement gurgling from the red stone lying beside his bag, much like the laughter and ridicule he had heard in the copse by the river Mina two days earlier.

Looking back out over the plain towards Tamin, he saw the horsemen in the distance and knew it was time for him to move on. Stuffing the now silent orb into his bag, he headed north, and with the hill behind him he kept out of the sight of the approaching riders.

A dozen guardsmen, led by the Duke of Amina, had ridden out from Tamin at dawn. It had been a restless night for the Duke as images of lightning and red fire had populated his dreams. On waking, one particular image haunted him: Tamin being consumed by fire.

Something else about the lightning strikes and the fires troubled him, but he could not put his finger on what it was. He needed to see more closely what had transpired the previous night on the slopes of the Alol.

When he came to the charred remains of the first of the fields of flax, Silson reined in his horse and stared in astonishment. At the edge of the field some farmhands stood in shock, their summer's work destroyed in a few moments by some sort of thunderstorm. When Silson questioned the locals it transpired that none of them had actually seen the storm; they had only witnessed the resulting fires. On further questioning there seemed to be an even stranger fact. The farmhands had not seen any lightning or heard any thunder. How could that be?

It suddenly struck Silson that he had not heard any thunder either, although he had seen the lightning. He had not thought about it at the time, assuming that he was too far away in Tamin, but these workers lived less than a mile from the centre of the storm and they had heard no thunder either. Silson racked his brain. What else was strange about the storm? He had been entranced by the initial bolts of lightning, and then horrified by the fires, but what had he missed?

Nudging his horse forward, he moved onto the blackened ground. The animal was skittish as red sparks popped out from under its hooves. It was as if the ground below was still burning. As the Duke looked out across the plain towards the river Amin, the scale of the destruction became clear. Acres and acres of flax were now no more than charred stalks, and on the southern Alol slopes not a single vine appeared to have survived. It would be a very quiet autumn for the wineries, the vintners and the linen mills.

As he started to turn his horse around to return to the village, Silson noticed strange markings in a nearby flax field. The charred remains of the stooks seemed to be less randomly scattered in this field, and as he drew nearer he realised that the scattered black remnants were indeed ordered, as if carefully positioned. From up close it took some moments to decipher the pattern, so it was only after he had ridden round the field that it became clear: *For Arin, Lex Talionis*. It made no sense to the Duke.

It had been a busy day at the border. James Daunt's gunners had moved the remnants of the culverins to the sides of the valley and had managed to assemble some of the broken bits of iron into something which, when viewed from a distance, resembled a weapon. With one construction at each side, and hoping his subterfuge would work, Daunt had allowed the border to reopen, and now the wagons were trundling over the scorched ground with the wagon masters curious observers.

Bertalan was concerned that if there were significant numbers of Kermin forces on the Kermin Plain and they learnt of the destruction of the cannons, they might make an attempt to capture the border. It had become clear in the war of 1507 that holding the northern end of the Kermin Alol was vital for Amina's defence. So as the wagons started to roll through the valley, Bartos, with one hundred cavalry, made a sweep of the southern edge of the Plain. The only Kermin force in the vicinity was Orran's twenty Doran Cavalry. Heavily outnumbered, Orran and his troop moved quickly north. Bartos' orders were to push any Kermin forces back from the border land, but only to engage if threatened.

It was late afternoon when the guardsman arrived at the northern end of the Alol to deliver Silson's report to Bertalan. The King was dumbstruck. First his cannons had been destroyed by lightning and now a similar fate had struck the rich farmlands of the Tamin Plain. Was nature, or some god, trying to punish him for some crime he had unknowingly committed? He needed time to think. Ordering Daunt to continue to build more defensive positions at the mouth of the valley, he decided he could think best whilst walking.

The late afternoon sun was pleasantly warm as the King slowly climbed the western hill. It wasn't long before he reached the platform that looked down over the valley. He smiled to himself, remembering that it was from here in 1507 that his culverins had destroyed the advancing forces of his brother-in-law. One thought led to another. Did Alberon know about the destruction of the cannons? Surely he must by now, with the wagons moving north again towards Mora. Hopefully Daunt's subterfuge would work and the wagon masters would spread the story that some, but not all, of the cannons had been destroyed. If Alberon sensed an opportunity, surely he would act.

Sitting down on the platform, Bertalan tried to order his thoughts. The trooper from the lookout post on the other hillside, now directly opposite him, thought the lightning had originated from this hill. He tried to imagine he had the power to create lightning and realised that from this position it would be easy to sweep fire across the valley below, but who could wield such power and why would they?

He then remembered that fire had also destroyed some settlement on the Doran Plain, and recalled the rumours that had circulated at the time, about a sorcerer seeking revenge for some injustice done by the Emperor. He had dismissed the stories as ridiculous nonsense, but now he wondered. Could the rumours be true? Was the sorcerer's name Arin? What did 'Lex Talionis' mean?

If he could have seen far enough to the north, Bertalan would have nodded to himself; his concerns were justified. Alberon was in the council room in Mora Castle with Morserat and Holger, and he was anxious for information and for action.

He turned first to Holger. "What have you learnt from the waggoners?" The first of the wagons that had been allowed through the Alol earlier in the day had reached Mora a short time ago.

Holger could only restate what he had been told by the troopers who had held each wagon at Mora's city gates until the wagon master had been questioned. "Sire, the lightning storm appears to have scorched a large swathe of land at the entry to the Alol," he said. "We knew that six culverins were stationed at the Amina front line and it seems that four of them have been destroyed, but two remain and these are located one at each side of the entry to the valley."

Alberon turned to Morserat. "I thought your brother said all the cannons were destroyed?"

The Duke nodded. "That's what Orran's report said. Maybe two of the culverins were not irreparably damaged."

Alberon waved his hand dismissively. "Whatever the situation, two cannons or none, Bertalan will not be able to hold the border if we move quickly and attack the Amina lines with a large force of cavalry."

Holger responded first. "Sire, the waggoners have also told us that a large contingent of Amina cavalry rode into the Alol yesterday. They were riding under the grey wolf banner, which almost certainly means that Bertalan is reviewing the situation at the border. He is probably anticipating some reaction from us. He is a cautious man and he will have prepared his defensive positions just in case. As we know from experience, the entry to the Alol is difficult to attack."

Alberon laughed. "If my brother-in-law is at the Alol, so much the better. In a single move we can deal with that traitor to the Empire and gain a foothold for a full invasion of Amina."

Morserat hated his nephew's impetuousness, his recklessness and his arrogance; however, he also knew the risks of defying the Emperor. Nonetheless he had to try to inject some sense. "My Lord, a full-scale invasion of Amina will require us to assemble a large army which will take weeks. By the time our forces have mustered we will be approaching the rainy season and it would be unwise to march through mud again as we did two years ago. In addition, as per the treaties, most of the Doran cavalry remain near Iskala. We have a small number of riders, led by my brother, patrolling the Kermin Plain, but as Bertalan has shown no intention of marching his forces into Kermin we have less than one hundred Doran cavalry on this side of the Doran Mountains."

Alberon held up his hand. "My lord Duke, I hear what you are saying and I accept that to a degree your council is wise, but if it were not for the Amina cannons guarding the border I would have mobilised our forces in the early summer. Had my cannons not been destroyed in the fires at Sparsholt, we would have marched on Amina next spring. The destruction of the

Amina weapons changes the dynamics and we must demonstrate our courage and our intent. With your one hundred Doran horsemen and the Kermin light cavalry we should be able to field five or six hundred cavalry within a couple of days."

Despite risking the Emperor's wrath, Morserat decided to have one last try. "Alberon, we can probably put five hundred cavalry in the field quickly but whilst a cavalry force might secure the border they will not be able to hold it and Bertalan will simply pull back and wait for reinforcements from Tamin. For all we know he may already have more cannons being transported north. In addition we will have broken the 1508 treaties before we are ready to win a single battle, never mind marching on to invade Amina."

The blue eyes held the Duke in a cold stare and Morserat waited for the tirade that normally followed. He was surprised; Alberon spoke quietly. "I ignored your advice in 1507 my Lord Duke and it was a mistake. Let me consider what action I want to take and we will talk again tomorrow. For now, go and ready your Doran troopers and the Kermin cavalry. I will give you my orders in the morning."

Having started his return journey in the hills, Audun had kept to the higher ground for most of the morning. On the road below him the wagons were moving, and clearly the border had been reopened. Getting a lift on one of the carts was tempting, but he decided that he needed to be further from the Tamin Plain before joining the road. He knew that there was little likelihood that he would be recognised unless, by chance, he encountered the same waggoner with whom he had travelled south the day before.

It was close to midday when Audun's sore feet made the decision for him. He had travelled far enough on foot, and it was time to seek a more comfortable mode of transport.

The wagon master was a big man, ruddy cheeked and well muscled. He introduced himself as Jon and, indicating to the cart behind him, told Audun that he was carrying casks of Amina wine for the vintner's market in Mora. Jon clearly liked company, or at least he liked to talk. "It's unusual to pick up a traveller in the middle of the Alol, have you come from Tamin?" he asked.

Audun had anticipated the question. "No, my brother has a sheep farm in the east of the Alol and I have been visiting him," he replied. "I am now on my way back to Mora."

Jon clapped his hands together, excited at the opportunity to share news and gossip. "So you didn't pass by the Tamin Plain on your way across the Alol?"

Audun shook his head. Barely pausing to take a breath, the waggoner described the destruction he had seen on his way north. "And I don't suppose you have heard about the destruction at the border either?" he went on. "I should have had this load on the road a couple of days ago but the border was closed due to some sort of lightning storm there. Colleagues that have passed me on their way south tell me that the storm has destroyed the cannons that protect the border. It seems a strange coincidence that these two storms happened only a day or so apart and in such close proximity."

"Nature has a power of its own," was all Audun managed to say before the wagon master continued in a more conspiratorial tone. "Do you know what the people are saying?"

Audun again shook his head.

"Well the rumours are that the lightning and the fires are unnatural. I have heard that there was a similar so-called natural disaster on the Doran Plain a couple of weeks ago, although no one seems to know exactly what it was. Some of my friends were in Mora around the time that news spread of the incident in Doran and the rumours were that the destruction there was caused by a wizard."

Audun laughed. "Wizards, sorcerers and dragons only live in fairy tales."

Jon's look became more serious. "So you have heard some of the rumours? A dragon seems very unlikely to me, but a wizard? People are saying that the wizard had been asleep for centuries in a deep cave in the Doran Mountains and he was disturbed by the gold miners digging. One miner has claimed that as he cut into a segment of rock there was a sudden explosion in front of him and out from the dust stepped an old man wreathed in fire."

It amazed Audun how quickly the rumour about a wizard had developed. People's imaginations had already embellished the story to make it more plausible. It was also slightly concerning that the rumours, in a strange way, were getting closer to the truth.

However Jon was not finished. "I believe this wizard is intent on destroying Kermin and Amina or at least setting our two countries back on the path to war."

Audun looked quizzically at the other man. "What do you mean?"

"Well, if it is true that the defences at the border have been destroyed then it will not be long before the Emperor in Mora decides to mobilise his army to invade again as he tried to do two years ago. We may be lucky though, we are near the end of the summer and autumn is not really a time for campaigning."

It was not a situation Audun had really considered. "I don't understand," he said.

Jon looked across at Audun as though his companion was stupid. "You must know that in 1507 the forces of Kermin were intent on invading Amina to incorporate our country into the so-called Empire. The rain and our cannons stopped the invasion and since then the cannons at the border have been a deterrent. Without the cannons, the border and the Alol are exposed. The wizard must now be in the employ of the Emperor."

Audun was taken aback. "Why would this wizard, if he exists, do this? Why would he want to start a war?"

It was Jon's turn to laugh. "So despite your scepticism you do think it is possible that these 'natural disasters' could be the work of a wizard? As to what his motive might be, I have no idea, but I do know that the Emperor in Mora lusts for more power and wealth. He has coveted Amina for years, to the extent that he has managed to persuade our King to name the Kermin princes as heirs to the Amina throne. If the Emperor has formed an alliance with this wizard then that would explain why our cannons were destroyed."

Audun paused for a moment before asking his next question. "If we assume for a moment that there is some truth to the rumours, although I doubt it, then why destroy the fields in the Tamin Plain?"

It seemed the waggoner had already considered this. "It's obvious. Much of Amina's wealth is generated from our exports of wine, wheat and linen goods. The Tamin Plain grows most of the flax and the southern slopes of the Alol have most of the vineyards. Destroy these and you cripple our economy. For all I know these might be the last wine barrels I carry this year. The wineries will have to close down and the linen mills will be silent. No work for people will mean no wages, no wages means no food and unless the Amina treasury intervenes it could be a hard winter ahead for Amina's poorest citizens. It also means that there will be no taxes to fill the treasury, so the King will not be able to buy new cannons from Ackar, leaving the Alol border less well defended. That's why the Emperor must have paid the wizard to destroy the crops in the fields."

In the distance Audun could see that the valley was beginning to get wider. Jon confirmed what Audun was thinking. "The border's getting closer. We don't have far to go and we can see for ourselves what's happened there."

Audun had no need to see for himself; he already knew. Abruptly he patted the other man's shoulder. "Thanks for the lift Jon. I need to leave you here." Without another word he leapt down from the wagon. The wagon master's laughter and shout followed him. "Take care you don't accidentally bump into a wizard or a dragon."

Audun needed time to think, time to clear his mind and reflect on his actions and time to reconsider his plans. He retraced the path he had followed the morning before taking the hill path to the west until he reached the drover road and the Mina River. His destination was the small copse he had rested in two nights earlier.

As he walked, he considered what he had learnt from the waggoner. He had destroyed the Kermin and the Amina cannons in the belief that he could use his power to ensure peace. Instead, unwittingly, he had possibly brought war closer. The fields of fire on the Tamin Plain had been meant as punishment for the man responsible for ordering his grandfather's murder, but now he realised that the ordinary people of Amina would suffer.

Lost as he was in his own thoughts, Audun did not initially notice the man who stepped from the hillside onto the path fifty yards in front of him. When he did see him, he knew even in the fading light that this was no passing shepherd. As the man passed from shadow into the last rays of sunlight, the motif on the tunic was clear to see: a grey wolf. It had to be the man he had just been thinking about. This was Bertalan, the Amina King, walking alone.

With the stars flickering in the dark far above the leafy canopy of the copse, Audun rested with his back against a tree. He closed his eyes and let the burbling sound of the nearby river wash over him. For a moment he imagined he was back on board the *Swan*, following the stars to some new port. The image passed in a second and he reminded himself that he had left the sea to complete his mission of revenge. Again he asked himself why he had not taken the opportunity that had just been presented to him. The Amina King had been alone, unarmed and oblivious to his presence in the shadows a short distance behind. Audun already knew the answer; he had taken a moment to consider the consequences. That was the lesson he had been taught by the wagon master. The destruction of the forges on the Doran Plain was justified, but the obliteration of the Amina cannon on the other side of the hill was a mistake. He had created an opportunity for his father to renew his bid to extend his empire. The levelling of the fields on the Tamin Plain would hurt the Amina treasury but also the local people, another mistake. Had he acted earlier that evening and eliminated the Amina King, it would have been one more mistake. From what Audun understood of affairs of state, on the death of the king, Alberon's son, Aaron, would inherit the Amina throne. There could be no doubt that the son would swear fealty to the father, so Audun would have gifted Alberon the prize he coveted.

Audun opened his eyes and looked up to the sky. Orion, the Great Bear, the North Star, all fixed and reliable. How many miles had he travelled on the *Swan* trusting these heavenly bodies? Now he found himself trusting a red orb, an ancient alchemist and his own ability to control them both. He was beginning to learn that power was a fickle friend. Once released, it itself cared little for the consequences of its actions.

CHAPTER 12
A Wizard's Name

❖ ❖ ❖ ❖

Jon, with his wagonload of casks of Amina wine, was one of the first to arrive in Mora having witnessed the destruction on the Tamin Plain. Soon everyone in the vintners' market had heard about the fields of fire. The city was already awash with speculation as to what had happened at the Kermin Alol border a few days earlier. Many people had also heard about some sort of disaster on the Doran Plain near a place called Sparsholt. As the stories spread, so they grew and were embellished and personalised.

One woman said she had heard a story from a waggoner who had personally seen the wizard standing on southern slopes of the Alol bathed in fire as he destroyed the fields. She told others that her source had said the wizard was seven feet tall with eyes that bled with fire. Someone else knew a miner in the Doran Mountains who had witnessed the wizard break out from his grave in a great explosion of rock. For most of those who heard the stories, they confirmed one thing: it was no natural lightning storm that had struck the Amina cannons or destroyed the buildings on the Doran Plain.

As the tales spread, so did the fear. Mora's citizens remembered only too well the deprivations of the winter of 1507-08 when Amina's blockades had brought starvation and death to the city. If the wizard was intent on destruction and conquest, what would the coming winter bring? Others had a different fear, although it was tinged with hope; the believers said that it was written in The Book that this was the end of the world, as God had foretold.

Another explanation came from an unexpected source, a scribe who worked in the library and was one of Ianis' assistants. He had been given the task of answering the Empress Sylva's questions regarding the Aramin myth, 'Lex Talionis'. When the scribe heard the stories regarding the wizard and the destruction at the Alol and on the Tamin Plain, he came to a surprising conclusion. This must have been why the Empress had wanted to learn about this ancient text.

The scribe had read the ballad and knew that a child had escaped the destruction of Aram. The story told that the child would return and take his revenge. The scribe was convinced he had an answer and a name. The child was returning after a thousand years, looking for his revenge. The wizard's name was Adun. It would be a few days before another name would emerge. It had been etched in the scorched fields of flax; the wizard's name must be Arin.

Sylva had read Angus Ferguson's history *White Light Red Fire* a number of times, but she had found no clear answers in the book. Instinctively she agreed with Ianis's assessment that the story was a mix of fact and fiction. She had asked Ianis to do more research, and he had reported that other sources had allowed him to confirm that most of the details of the battles of the early 14th century recorded in *White Light Red Fire* were historical fact. However, whilst the sorcerer, Oien, had clearly been a real person, there was no corroborating evidence for his demise. Ianis concluded, and the Empress agreed, that the end of the story, the white light and the red stone, had to be fiction, written to bring the story to a satisfactory conclusion.

It had been several days since the Queen Mother had set Valdin and Ramon their task: 'find Audun and bring him to me in secret'. Neither man knew that the other had been given the same mission, but both men had kept the Queen informed. They had not had any success.

Ramon had concentrated his enquiries at Mora's port, where he knew many of the other captains. These acquaintances were curious to know why he had become a landlubber. Why was he not at sea, either on the *Swan* or *Lex Talionis*? Since his release from the confines of the castle Ramon had asked himself the same question, and had considered simply boarding a carrack and leaving Mora behind. However each time he considered approaching one of the ships to ask for passage, one thing held him back: curiosity. He now knew a lot of the back story of his stepson, but he did not understand how Audun could conjure fire at will, if indeed he could. He needed to stay. He needed to understand.

Ramon's reports confirmed to the Queen that the *Swan* continued to sail along the southern coast of Andore, trading as it had always done between Thos, Anelo and Tufle. One fact that did reinforce Ingrid's belief was that the captain of the *Swan* had not been seen in any of the ports for a couple of months.

Whilst Ramon's enquiries had been focused at the port, Valdin had been hoping to discover information in Mora's inns and its markets. He had not got closer to finding Audun, but he did have information which he knew he needed to report to the Queen.

Ingrid was in her private rooms when one of her maids announced the arrival of Valdin. She stood to greet the huntsman, who bowed as he entered the room.

Ingrid pointed to a seat. "Please sit Valdin. Have you found where Audun is?"

The huntsman shook his head. "No my lady, but I have other news I think you need to hear."

Ingrid returned to her seat. "Please continue, Valdin." So it was that the Queen learnt about the destruction of the Amina cannons and the charred remains of the fields on the Tamin Plain.

"Thank you Valdin, you were correct to bring this information to me. Now please return to your search for Audun."

The huntsman paused for a moment before continuing. "My lady, there are two other things you need to know."

Ingrid noted the man's reticence, unusual for the huntsman. "Well, are you going to tell me?"

"My lady, one of the rumours in the inns gives the wizard a name. He is Adun, a disinherited Aramin child from an ancient myth, supposedly arisen after hundreds of years from his grave in the Doran Mountains. It struck me as a strange coincidence that the child's name was so like that of the captain of the *Swan*."

It took Ingrid a moment to construct her response. "People come up with the strangest ideas when they are faced with the unexplainable. I can't imagine the captain of the *Swan* is more than twenty-five years old, and from what you have told me of him he certainly doesn't strike me as an all-powerful wizard. But it is a strange coincidence, for sure. Now what was the second thing you needed to tell me?"

"I was in the Black Bear Inn yesterday evening. It's close to the barracks, and the Captain of the Guard was sitting by himself in a corner of the inn. He had already consumed too much ale and was oblivious to all those around him, and he was having a rambling conversation with himself. You pay Vidur and me to be your ears and eyes in the city, and drunken conversations in the inns often result in important snippets of information. I sat at the next table and the Captain's mumblings made little sense to me, but they might to you."

"Well? What was Holger saying?"

"As I said, it made no real sense, but what I could hear from the mumblings was something to do with the Emperor, a son, and a sorcerer. The captain seemed to be trying to make sense of some puzzle he didn't understand. It was drunken ramblings, but I thought I should tell you."

The Queen hid her concern. "Valdin, I have just remembered that I have a task I need you to do for me. Come back this evening and I will give you your instructions."

The huntsman rose, bowed and replied, "Of course my lady."

Sylva had a visitor with her when Ingrid entered her rooms unannounced. Sylva rose to greet her mother-in-law. "Ingrid, this is an unexpected surprise."

The Empress turned to her visitor. "Thank you for coming, Captain Ramon. It is clear that the Queen needs to talk with me. I will call for you again later."

Ramon stood up to leave, but Ingrid interrupted. "It is best that the captain stays. He knows everything we know, and possibly more, so he might as well hear my news. He may have some useful insights."

So Ingrid shared her information with the other two. Although it had happened a few days earlier, neither the Queen nor the Empress had heard about the destruction of the Amina cannons.

Sylva was first to react. "Does Alberon know that the defences at the border have been destroyed? If he does, he is likely to make some stupid attempt to take advantage."

Ingrid shrugged. "I have only just been told about the lightning storm at the Alol, but Morserat has Doran cavalry patrolling the Kermin Plain, so he is likely to know something has happened at the border and may well have informed Alberon."

Ramon coughed and turned to Ingrid. "My lady, I apologise for not telling you at the time, I was rather distracted. When Holger was escorting me to meet with you after I was released from the dungeons we saw lightning in the distance and Holger thought the ammunition had exploded. At the time I thought it was odd, as the lightning bolts appeared to come from the hillside rather than from the sky."

It was the first time Sylva had heard about her husband's tirade and Ramon's imprisonment. She shook her head. "He can be such an impetuous fool."

Ingrid continued with her news. "One of the stories circulating in the city is that the wizard has a name, Adun."

Sylva had recently heard that name from Ianis, and Ramon reminded both ladies that he had told them about the Aramin myth when they had asked about the name of his carrack, *Lex Talionis*. He explained, "This is a myth, possibly thousands of years old. When the ancient tablets were found in the eastern Kermin Alol it took years to decipher the hieroglyphs. How could a thousand-year-old child return for his revenge?"

It was Sylva's turn to interrupt. "This may be so Ramon, but you and I have just been discussing Angus Ferguson's history of the early 14th century and this account suggests that at least two characters, Oien and Ala Moire, had lived for millennia."

Ramon nodded. "That is true, my lady, but we both agree this history is part fact and part fiction. The two names Adun and Audun are surely mere coincidence."

So it was that Ingrid learnt about the historical records of the sorcerer Oien in *White Light Red Fire*.

"If I were to accept that Audun had somehow

acquired, or inherited, this supernatural power, which I don't believe by the way, then why would he destroy the Amina cannons and crops?" said Ramon. "If he is seeking revenge on his father, then surely he has no grudge with Amina or the Amina King. It makes no sense. There must be some other explanation."

It was Ingrid who proposed action. She turned to Sylva, "We need to share some of our knowledge with your brother and learn more from him about what has happened in Amina."

Morserat and Holger were reporting back to Alberon. Morserat took the lead. "Sire, we can probably gather a force of eight hundred cavalry in a few days. We would need to wait on some Doran units to travel here from Iskala to add to those currently patrolling on the plain and add to the Kermin cavalry already here in Mora. However my advice remains the same. We may be able to take the border at the Alol, but a cavalry force will not be able to hold the ground for long."

Alberon was about to respond, but he was unexpectedly interrupted by Ingrid, who had walked into the council room unannounced. Morserat and Holger immediately stood up and bowed.

Alberon stared at his mother. "Mother we are in a meeting and I left instructions that we were not to be disturbed. Are the guards at the door sleeping?"

Ingrid pointed at the two other men. "You two

can leave now." For a moment the hazel eyes stared at Holger. It was a shame, but she had to protect her son and her grandsons.

Once they were alone, Ingrid's stare turned to her son. "I presume your meeting with Morserat and Holger was to plan how you could take advantage of the destruction of the Amina defences at the Alol?"

It always amazed Alberon that his mother was so well informed. He was even more surprised when she continued, "Maybe however you don't know about the destruction of fields on the Tamin Plain, or that the city is full of rumours that a wizard called Adun is at large and seeking his revenge."

"So even the people now know that my bastard son was born of a witch!" responded Alberon. "They will be pleased when I find him and have him burnt at the stake."

Ingrid shook her head. "No, you seem to have conveniently forgotten that Adun was the child from the Aramin myth of a thousand years ago. You also seem to forget that you are Audun's father and the fact that your son is the sorcerer, the wizard, might make the people think and act differently." Ingrid hoped her decision to act would stop that particular rumour getting out. "Now I do hope you were not planning to try to take advantage of the destruction of the Amina cannons," she continued.

Alberon looked away. "Of course not, mother."

Ingrid snapped her reply. "You mean of course I was, mother, and I am telling you again that you will not. You will order Morserat to stand down any troops he has being readied, and if you do not, then I will."

Alberon stood and raised his voice. "Mother, you continue to countermand my orders, and I will not stand for it."

Ingrid smiled. "Then I suggest you sit down again. You don't seem to understand. If it is Audun who has somehow obtained this power, his revenge is targeted at Bertalan as well as at us. We need to reach out to Sylva's brother and understand what is happening in Amina, for the safety and security of both our countries."

The person who was the topic of the conversations in Mora was still waiting at the Kermin Alol border. Bertalan had overseen the construction of additional defences at the mouth of the valley and was waiting for Silson to arrive with additional reinforcements. He knew that if his brother-in-law were to mount any sort of attack on the Amina positions, it would have to be with cavalry. It would take several weeks for Alberon to raise a foot army, and by then Bertalan would have been able to call up his divisions of halberdiers. Bartos was already patrolling the plain to the north with enough cavalry to at least hamper any initial advance from Kermin units. Bartos had also sent a few men further north travelling with the merchants' wagons. They would be the early warning if any Kermin forces were gathering near Mora.

It was early afternoon when the large troop of Amina cavalry reached the northern end of the Alol. The Duke of Amina led the company. Silson dismounted and saluted his king. Bertalan's instructions were brief. "Get your men to set up their tents on either side of the main road. Bartos will be back here later and he can take command then. With the cavalry we already have patrolling the plain, and your men, we should be able to withstand any approach from Mora. Now I need you to tell me the full details of what has happened on the Tamin Plain."

Having passed on his orders to his captains, Silson made his way over to what had been Daunt's headquarters tent, which was now occupied by the King. Bertalan indicated for the Duke to take a seat.

"So Silson, your messenger outlined what has happened on the Tamin Plain but perhaps you can fill me in on all the details," said Bertalan.

Silson described in detail the charred ruins of the flax fields and the destruction of the vineyards. Then he told the King about the strange message in one of the flax fields.

At this point Bertalan stopped him. "Have you found out what Lex Talionis means and who Arin is?"

Silson nodded. "Yes and no. Our scribes tell me that Lex Talionis roughly means 'an eye for an eye', or more simply 'revenge'. However, Arin is a common name in Amina, and I can think of no connection between the words and the name."

"It is strange that the wording is 'For Arin', suggesting that whoever Arin is, he is not the perpetrator," said Bertalan. He rose from his seat, walked over to the side of the tent and passed Silson a piece of metal. "The same message was left here amongst the wreckage of the culverins."

Silson stared at the piece of metal for a long moment, trying to gather his thoughts. "My lord, there were two other oddities with the storm at the Plain. I was walking Tamin's city walls when I saw the first lightning strikes. It was odd that they appeared to come from above the Plain, from the hills in the Alol, and not from the sky. Stranger still, the villagers in the nearby settlement heard no thunder. I have never heard of lightning without thunder, let alone of it being able to write messages.'

Bertalan shook his head. "I don't know what's happening, or why, but these events are not the work of natural forces. The lookouts here on the eastern hill also said that the lightning strikes appeared to come from the opposite side of the valley, from the western hills and not from the sky. I need to contact my sister and find out from her what links there are to the events here and what happened on the Doran Plain a few weeks ago."

Audun had spent most of the morning in the copse close to the Mina River. He needed more time to think and to plan. Having spent some of the previous night contemplating the stars in the night sky, he had felt a strong pull to leave all this behind and return to his simple life on the *Swan*. He knew he had no real desire for power; indeed power increasingly frightened him. Then his thoughts would turn to his mother, Ragna, dying of a broken heart, and his grandfather, Arin, dying in a Tamin dungeon. The desire to avenge his family once again overcame the pull of the sea.

It was late morning before he made his decision. It was mid-August and harvest time. The farms in the eastern Kermin Plain, close to the Aramin Forest, would be looking for casual workers. A few weeks toiling in the fields might help him clarify his thoughts.

By now it was a familiar route, south on the drover road close to the river, then east on the track to the crest of the hill that overlooked the main road. As he descended to the main road, Audun had to step back as a large cohort of Amina cavalry passed him, galloping north. He was pleased; hopefully these reinforcements would hold back any attempt by his father to attack the border.

Audun was not to know, but in Mora his father had

made his decision. He could defy his mother, but would Morserat obey his commands? Maybe the Duke was right and an attempt to take the border with a cavalry force was not a sensible option.

Morserat entered the council room, and Alberon invited him to sit. "Morserat, I have decided to heed your advice. Despite the fact that the Amina forces have been weakened, a cavalry attack would be reckless, particularly if they still have some functional cannons. Now I want you to plan a full-scale invasion for next spring. You will have my cannons ready by then, won't you?"

Morserat was relieved; a lot could change in nine months. He replied, "Yes my lord, I think that is a wise decision."

Once the cavalry troops had passed, Audun joined some waggoners who had stopped their journey to share news and a midday meal. The lone traveller was welcomed, and as he shared some of the cheese and bread he listened to the gossip. It hadn't taken long for the stories to travel and Audun listened intently as he learnt about the wizard called Adun and the debate that the name was wrong, the wizard was called Arin and he was intent on destroying Mora and Tamin. Those that followed The Way added that it had been foretold in The Book and this was the end of the world.

Audun was surprised and concerned. The gossip and the rumours were too close to the truth, and whilst he did not intend to destroy the cities, he remembered his nightmares and his wrath as he had pointed the staff and released the red fire. Was the red orb still set on a path of destruction? Could he control the red fire?

He listened and said nothing until one of the waggoners turned to him. "Well Mr Traveller, what have you learnt on your wanderings?"

Caught unaware, Audun hesitated before responding with a question. "I had heard about some sort of destruction in Doran, but that it was caused by a dragon?"

The waggoner laughed. "Old news and nonsense, no one believes in dragons."

Audun joined the laughter. "I have been working on a remote farm in the west of the Alol and only old news gets there. Please though, tell me where did these wizard's names come from and who really believes in wizards?"

So Audun learnt about the 'first-hand witness accounts' and that the name Adun had travelled south from Mora, whilst clearly the wizard was called Arin, as he had left his name burnt into the Tamin Plain.

Audun thanked the waggoners for sharing their meal with him and moved off towards the eastern hills. Once more the laughter and shouts followed him. "Watch out for dragons!" Audun turned and waved a farewell as he started to follow the sheep track that led up into the hills.

As he walked, Audun considered his situation. He was the wizard, the sorcerer, and fortunately he did not meet the descriptions of the 'eye witnesses'. However, the names were more of a concern: Arin, his grandfather, and Adun, the mythical Aramin child, with a name so close to his own. Adun was the name he had used when he had introduced himself to Arvid, and the name he was known by in the Golden Fleece in Mora. It confirmed his decision to disappear for a while in some remote farm in the east. Maybe it was a quirk of fate, but he was now walking in the direction of the forest that had supposedly been home to the Aramin child in the long distant past.

It was early evening when Valdin returned to the Queen's rooms for his instructions. Ingrid indicated for the huntsman to take a seat. "Valdin, what I am going to ask you to do for me will seem strange, it is very risky for you and you must never tell anyone about it, not even your brother. I will fully understand if you refuse this mission and there will be no repercussions. First though, is there any news that you need to share with me?"

Valdin took a sip of the wine he had been offered and nodded. "There is one new piece of gossip, my lady. Apparently the wizard has another name, or maybe there is more than one wizard. The wagon masters who have travelled here from Tamin say that the name was burnt into the charred ground on the Tamin Plain."

Ingrid gave the huntsman a curious look. "And what is this new name?"

"The name that was reportedly inscribed in one of the burnt flax fields is Arin."

Ingrid paused for a second; the name was not unfamiliar, although it was more common in Amina than in Kermin. She would need to think, but now she needed to give her instructions.

"As I have said, Valdin, I would fully understand if you refuse this contract, but I will pay you handsomely."

Valdin rose from his seat. "I am at your command, my lady." With that the huntsman rose and with a bow left the room.

As Ingrid turned to go back to her private rooms her portrait on the wall caught her eye, painted twenty-six years ago. She sighed; she had looked so young back then. A moment later the sigh turned into a gasp. The portrait had been painted by an artist from Tamin who was Ragna's father and Audun's grandfather. His name was Arin.

Feeling slightly faint, Ingrid sat back down and looked at the portrait for some long moments, remembering. Twenty-six years ago, Arin had been commissioned to do her portrait, and his fourteen-year-old daughter had mixed the paints. Even at fourteen she was a pretty young thing, and Ingrid was pleased when the girl agreed to stay behind once the painting was completed and join her household ladies. Twenty-three years ago, Alberon had been infatuated with the girl, and Ingrid had never noticed it, never anticipated the love affair or the child. Now it seemed certain that Alberon's bastard son, her grandson, was the wizard, the sorcerer, but how was it possible? How could he have acquired such unnatural powers?

As she stood looking at the painting, other more recent disclosures came to mind: the letter Sylva had sent to her brother asking him to find the illegitimate child and deal with it, and Ramon's description of Ragna and the boy's hurried flight from Tamin. Now it made sense; Audun was seeking his revenge on both royal families. He held both guilty for whatever had happened to his family. She shook her head. It still seemed unbelievable, but the evidence all seemed to lead to the same conclusion.

Fortunately Arin was a relatively common name and hopefully no one in Mora would remember a painter of that name from twenty-six years ago. For now she would keep this part of the puzzle to herself.

Holger was staggering back from the Black Bear towards the barracks. In his drunken state he did not see, or hear, the shadow slip out of the doorway and move behind him. With the alcohol dulling his senses,

Holger felt shock but no pain as the dagger was swept expertly across his throat.

CHAPTER 13

Hillfoot

❖ ❖ ❖ ❖

Amleth, Holger's second in command, was surprised when his captain did not arrive for their normal morning briefing. Holger was a stickler for order, discipline and most of all time keeping. He was never late. By mid-morning Amleth was getting increasingly concerned, as Holger did not appear to be anywhere in the castle or in his rooms. Amleth was coming to the only conclusion that he could think of: Holger must have been sent on some secret mission for the Emperor.

Six guardsmen were waiting for Amleth at the castle gate, ready to begin their morning tour of the city, when a boy came running up to them. One of the guards recognised him; he was the son of the landlord of the

Black Bear. So it was that twenty minutes later Amleth discovered why his captain had missed their morning meeting. Holger's body was lying at the end of the alleyway that led from the main street to the rear of the Inn.

Amleth was plunged into shock, and later regretted his rough interrogation of Samuel, the landlord, a man he knew well. Yes, Holger had been drinking in the inn late into the evening. Yes, he was drunk when he got up to leave. No, the landlord had not seen anyone leave with the captain, indeed from memory he thought that Holger had been the only person left in the inn that late in the evening. Being a professional, Amleth had already checked, and found that Holger did not appear to have been robbed. It appeared to be a motiveless, meaningless murder of his commander and friend.

Samuel knew the majority of his customers and during the rest of the morning arrests were made across the city. Amleth personally interrogated each one, but only confirmed what Samuel had already told him. Holger had spent the evening drinking alone in a corner of the inn and none of the regulars could remember him talking, other than to order his next ale. They had all left the inn with the captain still drinking.

In the castle the news was met with a variety of reactions. Alberon vowed he would tear the city apart until he found the murderer, and when he did the punishment would be extreme. Sylva retired to her rooms in floods of tears. Posters appeared around the city offering a generous reward for any information that led to the arrest of the culprit. Amleth ordered guardsmen to interrogate everyone living within half a mile of the Black Bear. It was all to no avail. The murderer seemed to have stepped out of the night and vanished back into it again.

In her rooms, Ingrid also shed tears. She had known Holger for years. She liked the man and admired his honesty, his loyalty and solidity. However, his death had been necessary. With growing concern in the city about the intentions of the sorcerer, or wizard, she could not allow any hint of a rumour linking the Emperor to the perpetrator of the destruction in Doran or Amina. Ingrid knew the guilty party, but in reality she considered Alberon himself to be the murderer. Without his reckless tirade in front of Holger, her action would not have been required.

The Queen had also fretted over the issue of another Captain, Ramon. By now he knew almost the entire story but Ingrid had decided that Audun's stepfather could be trusted to keep his knowledge secret. He would not put his stepson at even greater risk and besides she had another mission for Captain Ramon.

It would be several weeks before Ramon would find out about Holger's murder. By coincidence, on the same morning when Amleth had been wondering about Holger's absence, Ramon was already on a carrack that was transporting a cargo from Mora to Tufle. He had been given his instructions by the Queen and carried a letter of introduction from the Empress to her brother, King Bertalan.

Following the reports from the Kermin Alol and the Tamin Plain, Ingrid and Sylva had agreed that they needed to share information with the Amina King. The question was, what information? Sylva was reluctant to disclose the nature of the works that had been destroyed on the Doran Plain, concerned that it would be a betrayal of her husband. Ingrid was less worried. Whilst she expected that Alberon would already be rebuilding the ironworks at Sparsholt, she would do whatever was in her power to stop her son going back to war. Indeed, she thought that if Bertalan knew of Alberon's plans then Amina would be prepared, and that might be enough to make Alberon consider more carefully before embarking on another stupid military campaign.

So Ramon had his instructions, but for now he was just pleased to be free from the confines of Mora Castle. The carrack was cutting effortlessly through the light swell of the Eastern Sea, and it would be a couple of days before it would reach Tufle, giving time to consider, time to think.

The last few weeks had been a whirlwind for Ramon, accused of raising a wizard, chained in Mora's dungeon, sentenced to death by fire and then in the end receiving some explanations. Audun, the Emperor's illegitimate son seeking his revenge? That was plausible, but the idea that he could somehow conjure up supernatural powers seemed quite unbelievable.

At the same time as Ramon was sailing south, Audun continued his journey east through the Kermin Alol. Having learnt about the rumours that were circulating and the various names that were being given to the wizard, he knew he needed to lie low for a time. If he had unknowingly left evidence behind him at Sparsholt as he had done on the Tamin Plain, then it was highly probable that his father would by now suspect his hand in the destruction of the ironworks. If the Empress had communicated with her brother, his identity might also be known in Tamin.

As the August sun rose higher, warming the day, Audun sat on a small knoll close to a burbling brook. In the distance smoke rose from a cluster of cottages on the Kermin Plain. Further to the east the fringes of the Aramin forest were just visible. In the fields the farm workers were gathering the harvest. The village would be his destination for the evening, but for now he would sit for a while and think.

His first thought was of his stepfather. Was Ramon safe and well? During his time in Mora, Audun had not been able to obtain any information about what had happened to Ramon. Clearly the Emperor had wanted to deal with his bastard son in Mora and had imprisoned his stepfather to try to entice him there. The fact that Ramon had become entangled in his web of revenge was an unfortunate consequence of the word games he had played with his father. It was too late for regret though. Audun knew he could wield unimaginable power, but he also knew that was not the answer. What was the answer? Was there one?

Audun reflected back on the three months he had spent in Mora and his battle of wills with the orb, with Oien. Did he now truly control the power? This led to another question that he had not found an answer to. Who had delivered the staff, and why? He remembered his shock as the red fire had filled the small cottage when it had been left at the cottage door.

The cottage, rented for six months from Arvid. Why had he introduced himself as Adun, the name all of the clientele in the Golden Fleece knew him by, the name that now seemed to be given to the wizard? Surely with a bit of searching, his father would find out where he was living. But then if he had used his own name, it would be the same. Adun or Audun, the wizard, the sorcerer, the destroyer, would that be his legacy? Would that be the summation of his search for vengeance? He shuddered; it was at the same time too much and too little.

His thoughts returned to his own words, 'unimaginable power'. It was a conundrum. Audun knew that he could stand on the Kermin Plain and let his anger flow through the staff and he could raze Mora to the ground. He could deliver the same punishment to the Amina King if Tamin was destroyed by the red fire. He would avenge his mother, his grandfather and his family, but at what cost? In Mora it was most likely that Ramon would be consumed along with the city, as would one hundred thousand innocent citizens.

Unimaginable power which he could not, or at least, would not, use. Red fire that was fuelled by his wild anger, blue lightning that was conjured by his cold fury. Neither was the answer. However it was no more possible to imagine that he could walk up to Mora Castle's gates and demand justice from the Emperor, the Empress and the Dowager Queen.

Audun lay back in the grass, listening to the sound of the tumbling stream. It had been two years since he had stolen the orb from the cave below Aldene Castle. He had waited patiently for the power of the orb to be revealed. He had learnt patience. He could wait until his forward path became clearer. For now it would be the remote village and the fields.

Whilst Audun was listening to the babbling stream, Ramon was enjoying the sound of the waves and the entertainment provided by the dolphins. He had found a corner near the prow of the carrack where he could sit undisturbed and think. Think about his stepson, and things unbelievable.

It had been almost ten years since Ragna and her son had boarded the *Swan* for the journey from Tufle to Boretar. Ramon's thoughts drifted back to the mother whom he had grown to love as a sister rather than a housekeeper. She had become a good friend in the three years that she had cared for his house in Boretar. The insinuation that she was a witch was simply preposterous, but equally the evidence that her son had unnatural powers was compelling. Ramon turned his thoughts to his stepson. What had he missed in the ten years that had passed by as Audun had grown up?

Ramon was proud of his stepson. Audun had grown up to be a skilled helmsman, an excellent ship's captain and a wily businessman. A year ago Ramon had made him an equal partner in his business and Audun's negotiating skills had been instrumental in making the profits grow, allowing Ramon to purchase the new carrack, *Lex Talionis*. Remembering the name also reminded Ramon of Audun's insistence that this was what the carrack should be called. Now he at least partly understood why.

What else? Ramon searched through his memories of the past ten years. Two things then struck him. Firstly, it was unusual that the thirteen-year-old Audun could read and write. It almost certainly meant that Ragna could too, but she had never mentioned it. Ramon guessed that Ragna had probably learnt the skills whilst she was Ingrid's maid and had taught her son.

Secondly, Ramon had been surprised by the boy's interest in history, particularly the history of the early 14th century. He remembered Audun's excitement when he had been able to visit David Burnett's library in Aldene. Burnett, he recalled, had given Audun a present of the newly printed *White Light Red Fire*, the same book he had been discussing with the Empress Sylva only a couple of days ago. That was a strange coincidence.

Ramon then also remembered Audun's first voyage captaining the *Swan,* a return journey to Aldene after Ramon had broken his leg. That must have been two years ago, when Amina and Kermin were at war. Ramon let his thoughts drift through all he had learnt in the past few days. He now knew many of the secrets of Audun's history, but could there be more recent secrets, and did those secrets have their origins in Aldene?

It was late afternoon when Audun descended from the Alol hills and walked into the village of Hillfoot. It was typical of the many hamlets and small villages that dotted the Kermin Plain. The wattle and daub cottages with their thatched roofs sat on either side of a hard-packed earthen path that led through the village. The place was situated, as its name implied, just at a point where the eastern Alol Hills sloped down to join the Kermin Plain. The village seemed to be slumbering in the August sunshine. The only activity was pigs snuffling about in the vegetable middens at the sides of the cottages and hens searching for scraps in the front gardens. Aptly named "The End of The Road", the inn stood on the eastern side of the village.

Although Hillfoot was remote, and not on any busy road, the village had harvest rights to acres of wheat, barley and oats and the inn provided accommodation for the itinerant workers who arrived each year at harvest time. A short distance further to the east, where a brook tumbled down from the Alol, was a watermill. The End of the Road was also where the waggoners from Mora would spent the night before loading their wagons with the mill's produce and transporting the ground grain to Mora's markets. Close by the mill were the grain stores.

Audun took in his surroundings. It was a peaceful, idyllic location and he realised that although Hillfoot was remote, thanks to the crops and the watermill it was a relatively prosperous village. As he reached the front door of the inn he could hear the shouts of the workers as they cut, scythed and bundled the harvest. He hoped that in the morning he would be able to join them.

A shout came from the rear of the inn. "Hello there, can I help you?"

The owner of the voice appeared from the side alleyway. The man was tall and slim with his grey hair tied back in a pony tail. Audun assessed him to be in his early fifties, but he looked fit, and the tanned skin suggested that he must live an outdoor life.

Audun walked over and offered his hand. "Yes, I hope you can. I was looking to gain some employment working in the fields. My name is Ragnar."

Audun had decided that although Hillfoot was remote it was quite likely that the waggoners had told stories of the wizard and his names, so he had decided to revert to the name his mother had used years ago to disguise her identity when they had travelled on the *Swan*.

The other man took the offered hand. "Welcome to Hillfoot, Ragnar. My name is Anders. We have enough hands working the fields, but as the grain is harvested I could do with help in the mill and the grain stores. Would that be suitable for you?"

Audun smiled. "That would be fine. I was travelling from Tamin to Mora to look for work, but on the journey I decided that I had had enough of city living and autumn in the country would be a welcome change."

Anders nodded. "That's understandable, I hate the cities. Give me a little time to sort out some tasks here in the inn, then I will get you settled at the mill. You can enjoy the sunshine with a tankard of my best ale as a welcome gift."

Over a second tankard of ale, Audun found out that Master Anders was the village headman and that he owned both the inn and the mill. This was a surprise to

Audun, as someone with such wealth would normally have a grand house in Mora and hire others to manage their land. Anders explained that his brother was called Aracir and was Chancellor of Kermin. Anders had lived in the city but he hated it, so he had decided to move to the country and the lands that had been bequeathed to him and his brother by their father. Audun knew the name of the Chancellor, but for another reason. The letter from his mother was tucked at the bottom of his sack next to the casket holding the orb.

It was early evening, and Audun had settled into his small room on the upper floor of the mill. Having tucked his sack and the staff under the bed, he decided it was time for some supper. He thought it sensible not to take the staff with him, as it had been the object of many questions from the waggoners as he had travelled from Mora. Each time he had been asked, he had explained that it was a relic that had been in his family's possession for centuries, but it was also distinctive and something that could identify him. For the umpteenth time he wondered who had delivered the staff to the cottage in Mora.

On leaving the mill, Audun noticed a camp fire a short distance to the east. The men gathered round it appeared to be armed and ready for action. It seemed strange that a remote village would need to deploy armed guards at night.

The End of the Road was doing a roaring trade. The farmhands had returned from their day's work in the fields and were enjoying their evening refreshments. As Audun paused at the inn's front door, he was surprised to see weapons carefully laid against the side wall. A random mix of swords, spears and bows, they seemed to have been put aside, but they were also ready for action. Maybe Hillfoot was not such a peaceful place after all. Audun thought he would need to get an explanation from Master Anders.

As he entered the inn the heat was the first thing that hit Audun, followed by the noise. Master Anders had clearly spotted the newcomer's arrival and hurried across to greet him. "Well Master Ragnar, you can see that Hillfoot is not so quiet of an evening once the workers return from the fields. I assumed you would come over for your meal and I have kept a small table for you over here. Are you all settled in to your room?"

Audun nodded. "Yes, the room is fine thank you, but I am wondering about the weapons at the door and the guards outside the mill?"

Anders frowned. "Yes, that may well seem odd to you, but I am busy at the moment. The crowd will disperse for their beds in an hour or so and I can come and talk with you. In the meantime I will send the maid over to get you your drink and your meal."

Audun sat back, enjoying the noise of the chatter and the laughter. He hoped that he could return to a normal life for a few weeks here in Hillfoot whilst he pondered on his plans.

The sound of a lute being tuned cut through the noise and a few moments later the bard began to sing. Audun was focused on his food and largely ignored the first three well-known ballads. His attention changed when the minstrel hit a loud chord and announced, "I hope you all like my new song. It's called 'The Wizard'." The crowd cheered as the minstrel plucked his strings and cleared his voice. So his song began.

The wizard broke out from his mountain grave
As his red fire filled the cave
The miners ran to escape their doom
All in its path red fire would consume

The fire would destroy Sparsholt
Before cannons at the Alol melt
On Tamin Plain the flax would burn
And reveal a name… Arin

The time of the wizard is here
Destruction, death and fear
Some say the world will end
Others say a child is seeking revenge

I am a minstrel and not a seer
All I know is...
The time of the wizard is here
Destruction, death and fear

The applause filled the room as the minstrel repeated his last lines several times before taking a bow. The words "destruction, death and fear" seemed to echo around the room long after the last chord had faded.

Audun was lost in thought, and it took him a moment to realise that Master Anders had taken the seat opposite him. "Well Ragnar, you were asking about the weapons at the door and the guards to the east," he said. "The minstrel's song is not the reason, in case you were wondering. I can't imagine Hillfoot would be of any interest to a wizard. We worry about a threat much closer to us here. The Aramin Forest is a mile or so to our east and despite the many attempts of the rulers in Mora to bring the tribes under the control of the Kermin crown, none have succeeded. The Aramin are ferocious warriors and renowned for their prowess with bow and arrow. Most of the time they leave us in peace, but at harvest time with the grain stores filling up we attract their attention. Last September we lost almost a third of our grain in their raids, and this year I am determined to stop it. Hence all the farm workers carry some sort of weapon, and the men camped to the east are soldiers from the Kermin army paid for by my brother. This year we will be ready for the raiders."

Audun looked across at the other man. "From what I hear the Aramin are a dangerous foe. Would it not be better to just give them a portion of the harvest rather than risk lives in a fight?"

Anders spat out his reply. "They are scum, and this year I will teach them a lesson if they dare to attempt to raid the stores."

As Anders left to deal with some customers arguing loudly on the other side of the room, Audun reflected on his words: "I can't imagine Hillfoot would be of any interest to a wizard." Audun smiled. How true that was, unless the wizard was trying to escape from a destiny of destruction, death and fear.

CHAPTER 14

An Unexpected Arrival

❖ ❖ ❖ ❖

Ramon arrived in Tufle to find the port decorated in holiday style. Flags flew from all the ships docked at the port and flower displays were laid out in front of the warehouses and shops. Ramon was a regular traveller to Tufle and Tamin and he knew that no public holidays were held in late August. Intrigued, he enquired of one of the dockhands who were helping to settle the carrack in its mooring berth. The man laughed as he replied, "It's a miracle. The King has just announced a week's holiday. Queen Aisha has been blessed with the birth of a baby boy."

Ramon understood the politics in the southern lands. King Bertalan and Queen Aisha had been married for over fifteen years and had remained childless. This in turn meant that eleven-year-old Aaron and nine-year-old Egil, the Empress Sylva's sons, had been named in the peace treaties of 1508 as the heirs to the Amina throne. This dynastic solution suited the Emperor. If Alberon could not bring Amina into the Empire by use of force, he would acquire it by right of inheritance when one of his sons acceded to the Amina throne and swore allegiance to the Empire. Ramon knew Alberon would not view the news of the birth of the Amina Prince as a reason to celebrate.

After some further enquiries, he learnt that the King and Queen had kept the pregnancy a secret until the baby was safely delivered. All of Amina was celebrating with the royal family. None of the people of Amina wanted to be ruled by the Emperor in Mora.

As Ramon travelled along the river Amin on a small cargo boat that was transporting goods from Tufle to Tamin, he wondered if the birth of the Amina prince would change his mission to King Bertalan. Indeed, with the celebrations going on in the city would he even be allowed to see the King?

He carried three letters with him. One was an introduction from Sylva; the other two were sealed. One was a personal message from the Empress to her brother and the other was from Queen Ingrid. It was the Queen who had insisted that Ramon should take on this role as royal messenger. Ingrid trusted the captain because he knew most of the story. She could have engaged one of the huntsmen to deliver her letter, but there was a risk that they would learn some of her secrets. Ramon had his instructions.

Tamin's streets were thronged with revellers as Ramon made his way up towards the castle. The guards at the castle gate were dismissive. "The King and Queen are celebrating the birth of their son and they're not interested in any messages from Mora," said one.

Ramon was persistent. "My introduction letter is from the King's sister, the Empress, and the messages I carry are urgent. Find me someone who can deal with this, and find them now." The captain was used to being obeyed.

It was a short while later that Silson, Duke of Amina, arrived at the castle gate. He scanned the introductory letter and turned to Ramon. "You'd better come with me. The King will allow you a short audience, as the request comes from his sister."

Ramon was escorted through the castle to the Royal Family's private apartments. It was clear that the King and Queen were not going to be doing any official business on this momentous day. Bertalan was sitting at a window looking out over Tamin as Ramon was ushered into the room.

The king pointed to a seat at a table close by. "Please make yourself comfortable, Captain... Ramon, I believe?"

Ramon bowed. "Thank you sire, and congratulations on the birth of your son. I apologise for disturbing you on such an auspicious day but my messages are urgent."

Bertalan rose and took the seat opposite Ramon. "Well, you'd better let me see what my sister has to tell me."

Ramon passed across the first letter and replied, "I also have a letter from Queen Ingrid."

A long silence followed as the King read the letters and then read them again. Eventually he looked across the table and studied the other man's face for a moment. "So, Captain Ramon, you are privy to the inner conversations between my sister and her mother-in-law? How very strange. My sister's letter is a reminder of another letter she sent nine years ago. Her request then was to search the Artist Quarter and find and arrest a woman called Ragna and her son. I was asked to hold them until Sylva sent troops to escort them back to Mora, where they faced some sort of charge of treason against the Empire. As far as I remember the family were never found. I presume you are going to explain to me the connection between this and the message burnt into the flax field on the Tamin Plain."

Ramon was about to reply when Bertalan held up his hand. "I assume you know what is written in these letters?"

Ramon shook his head. "No sire, I do not know the details, but I have my instructions, and the things I must tell you are not written down."

Bertalan looked back down at the letters. "So if I am to believe what the Queen says, her son was in breach of the treaties and was rearming, building cannons at his own ironworks in this place called Sparsholt. Quite clever, I suppose, by the strict letter of the treaties, Alberon was not prohibited from building his own weapons, only from importing them from Ackar. My sister says you can tell me what 'Lex Talionis' means in the context of the message on the Tamin Plain."

This was where Ramon's instructions became somewhat trickier. He had to steer a course between truth and rumour. First he told Bertalan about the Aramin child, Adun, and the myth that was the source of one of the names that some rumours gave to the wizard. The words of the ancient ballad also explained to some degree the associated words, 'Lex Talionis'. Ramon explained that these same words had been left as a message within the ruins of the ironworks at Sparsholt.

Bertalan leant forward and gave the other man a long stare. "Are you really asking me to believe that some long-dead Aramin child has come back to life and has decided to destroy my cannons at the Alol and leave the fields on the Tamin Plain a ruin of ash?"

Ramon held the stare for a moment. "No sire, not quite. Your sister and the Queen have instructed me to tell you that they believe a disinherited son has somehow acquired unnatural powers and is seeking revenge on those he holds responsible for his family's deaths."

Far to the east, that disinherited son was working hard. Audun was used to the physical tasks that went with captaining the *Swan*, but this work only involved the loading and unloading of goods at the ports and was interspersed with more relaxing times at sea.

With the large wagons full of grain being transported to the mill each day, Audun had little time for relaxation. The grain had to be unloaded from the wagons, hoisted to the upper floor of the mill and then, once processed, it had to be bagged and moved to the nearby grain store.

The physical effort was balm to Audun as he managed to leave behind his anger and his desire for revenge, lost in the simple pleasure of hard labour. Within a few days Master Anders had also become as much a friend as an employer and the pair would spend a long lunch at the End of the Road, sharing stories. Anders told of his experiences at the court in Mora, and as a result Audun learnt more about his father and the Emperor's family. In return Audun described the lands that were familiar to him, the busy port at Thos, the city of Boretar, Aldene, Bala and the towering Inger Mountains. All the while Audun was only known by his chosen name of Ragnar.

Audun had been at Hillfoot for several days when one lunch time Master Anders, for some reason, wanted to learn more about the northern land of Bala. Audun described the old town of Aldene, the cobbled streets and some of the town's history. He paused as he remembered David Burnett, the cave, the casket, the red stone and his desire for vengeance. The casket, the stone and the staff remained hidden under the bed in his attic room in the mill. Audun wondered, was he simply hiding from his destiny for a while, or was he going forget it, and leave it all behind here in Hillfoot?

Ramon was again seated opposite King Bertalan the day after their first meeting. "Captain, I have read the messages you delivered several times and I am still not sure what reply to send back with you," said the King. "You can confirm for my sister and the Queen that their suspicions are correct. The destruction on the Tamin Plain and at the Alol did not have a natural cause. Witnesses say that the lightning, as it appeared, did not come from the sky but from the higher slopes in both places. And there are no reports of thunder accompanying the lightning. At the Alol there was also a message left etched into the remains of one of the pieces of iron."

Bertalan passed the fragment to Ramon, who had seen a similar piece that had been left in the remains of the destruction of the cannons near Sparsholt.

"Now captain, maybe you would be good enough to

explain the link between my sister's letter of nine years ago and recent events."

This was another moment where Ramon needed to balance truth and fiction. "Sire, the woman Ragna was found guilty of being a witch and her son was therefore declared a sorcerer. Both were sentenced to death in their absence and this sentence still remains and would be exacted if either were to enter Kermin. Your sister believes that the wizard could be the son seeking revenge."

Bertalan shook his head. "Why would this son seek vengeance on Amina rather than Kermin? And who was Arin?"

Ramon paused. "We don't know sire, but maybe you did find the family, and Arin was part of it."

"Well, if we are being threatened by a single man who can wield such destructive power then it is not clear to me what we can do to prevent him, other than to hope he makes a mistake and we can bring him to justice. One other thing puzzles me though. If this person can destroy acres of farmland and turn cannons into useless lumps of iron, why has he not turned his power on either of our cities?"

Ramon shook his head. "I don't know, my lord. I find all of this rather difficult to believe. It is as though I am reading some fictional story but also acting it out in real life."

Bertalan stood up from the table and walked over to

the window seat where he had been sitting the previous day. Slowly he turned, and his voice sharpened. "Captain Ramon, I have another message that you will deliver to my brother-in-law. If he does rearm and plans to try to invade Amina again, then he will be met with an iron fist. Now I will fight, not just to protect my country but to ensure that the birthright of my newborn son is preserved. Tell Alberon that if he threatens at the Alol I will march my armies and my cannons across the Kermin Plain and leave Mora in ruins. Tell him."

"I will pass your message to your sister, my lord, as I have no access to the Emperor." Ramon replied.

Bertalan laughed. "Don't worry captain, you will return to Mora with two other messengers who will have access to the Emperor." He signalled to the guard at the door.

Ramon did not recognise either of the new arrivals. The young man was tall and seemed to be nervous in the presence of the King. The boy was much less shy and ran across to him. "Uncle, how nice to see you! Have you called me so that I can meet my newborn cousin?"

Bertalan ruffled the lad's head and laughed again. "You will meet your cousin later today Aaron, and then you will be going home to Mora to be reunited with your own family."

Bertalan made the introductions, although after the first moment they were not necessary. Ramon knew that the young nobleman was Edin, Duke of Aramin and the boy was Aaron, Prince of Kermin, eldest son of Sylva and Alberon. The treaties of 1508 had confirmed Aaron as first in line to the Amina throne in the event that Bertalan and Aisha remained childless. The boy was being tutored for nine months each year in Tamin. The Duke had been instructed to remain in Tamin as company for him. With the birth of the Amina Prince, there was no need for Aaron to remain in Tamin.

"The carrack called the *Erth* is moored at Tufle and the Captain has instructions to take the three of you back to Mora," said Bertalan. "At the request of my sister, the *Erth* is carrying additional supplies to help to ensure that the people of Mora do not starve again this winter. I do hope that they recognise my generosity. As for your wizard, captain, we don't know who he is or where he is, so it seems to me that the next move is up to him."

As fate would have it, the wizard's next move would be forced upon him.

CHAPTER 15

The Cult of the Staff

❖ ❖ ❖ ❖

The messenger from Tamin arrived at Mora Castle at the same time as the *Erth* was casting off from its moorings in Tufle. The letter he carried was addressed to Sylva and was to be delivered to her in person.

The Empress was in her private rooms discussing recent events with Queen Ingrid. Sylva was irritated when her lady in waiting interrupted the conversation. "What do you want?" she snapped.

The noblewoman curtseyed. "My lady, a messenger has just arrived from Tamin with an urgent message from your brother. His instructions are to deliver it to you in person."

Sylva shook her head. "Tell him to wait. I will see him shortly."

It was Ingrid who intervened. "You had better read the message, Sylva. By now Ramon should have met with Bertalan and this may be your brother's response."

The messenger was ushered into the room and Sylva took the letter with an air of irritation; she had important things she had to discuss with her mother-in-law. Sylva flattened out the scroll and the first lines made her catch her breath with a gasp. She turned to Ingrid. "I cannot believe this!"

The Queen immediately took more interest. "What does Bertalan say? Is it a response to Captain Ramon's visit?"

Sylva shook her head and read the letter out loud. It was short and to the point. *"My Dear Sister, I am sure you will be delighted to hear that Aisha and I have been blessed. Today Aisha gave birth to our son. He is a healthy boy and we have decided to name him in memory of our father. Prince Berka will now become heir to the Amina throne and there is no need for your son to remain in Tamin. Aaron will travel home in the next few days on the Erth together with the additional supplies you requested. I do hope you can visit us soon to meet your nephew in person."* It was signed by Bertalan.

Sylva was lost for words, so Ingrid was the first to speak. "Well, I suppose that clarifies the succession rights to the Amina throne. It is probably as well that Alberon is in Iskala. This announcement will undoubtedly accelerate his desire to mount an invasion again as soon as he has his weapons. However, we need to caution him and remind him that there are many hazards on the road between being born a prince and becoming a king. Presumably Aaron will remain second in line to the throne?"

Sylva sighed. "Well at least Aaron will be coming home rather than being forced to stay in Tamin. We are on the cusp of autumn and Alberon will not be able to raise an army before winter, so hopefully we have some months to try, this time, to successfully influence his future actions."

Ingrid shrugged. "Let's hope we have more success than we did a couple of years ago. As you know, Alberon is not good at taking any council that opposes his impetuous decisions. Sylva, you asked me here to tell me about something new that you had learnt with regard to Audun. I will leave you to distil this current news and I will come back later."

With that the Queen departed, leaving Sylva lost in her own thoughts and concerns. She knew Ingrid was correct. Alberon would see this birth of an Amina Prince as a block to his planned expansion of the Empire. Holding him back from making rash decisions would be a challenge.

Fortunately the Emperor was not in Mora to receive the

news from Tamin. A day earlier he had departed for Iskala with a large troop of Kermin and Doran cavalry. The news from Doran, delivered by Soren, was of some concern. King Aster of Soll had passed away and the throne had passed to his grandson, William Norward. Alberon had suddenly realised that he had forgotten the dynastic connections. William Norward was the son of Lord Norward, who had been married to the daughter of King Aster. He was the pompous commander in chief whom Alberon had declared to be a traitor, and who had been beheaded at his command on New Year's Day in 1508. Now William, Norward's son, was King of Soll.

King William had acted quickly following his coronation. He had been instructed by the Duke of Doran to travel to Iskala to swear fealty to the Emperor and the Empire. Morserat's messenger returned to Iskala with William's response. The new King had declared Soll independent from the Empire and refused to pay the tithe that was due. To emphasise his intent, wrapped up with the reply letter, was the forefinger of Morserat's messenger. This was the news that Soren had reported to the Emperor a few days earlier, and Alberon had immediately ordered the cavalry troop to assemble and ride with him to Iskala. He vowed he would treat the son the same as he had the father. William was declared a traitor to the Empire and was outlawed, with a price on his head.

It was late afternoon when Ingrid returned to continue her talk with the Empress. Initially the pair reflected on the news from Amina and discussed how they would try to control Alberon's reactions. It was Ingrid who changed the subject. "Sylva you asked me here this morning to discuss another topic and we were interrupted by the message from your brother."

Sylva nodded. "Yes, I have been given some strange information from the Keeper of the Books and I have asked him to join us so that he can tell you his story in person."

A few minutes later Ianis was escorted into the room. The librarian bowed deeply to the Empress and then to the Queen, his nervousness obvious. Ianis was comfortable in the presence of his books, but standing in front of the two royal ladies had him shaking.

Sylva had met the man several times and understood his reaction. "Ianis, for goodness sake sit down before you fall down. Have a sip of the wine to calm yourself and then tell my mother-in-law what you have learnt from your scribe."

Ianis did as instructed and after a couple of sips of the wine he began his story. He addressed the Queen directly, as he had already briefed the Empress.

"Your Highness, I found out a couple of days ago that one of my scribes is a member of a strange cult. What I learnt from this man may be relevant to the rumours of the sorcerer, or the wizard, as some call him.

The group is called 'the cult of the staff', and their origin dates back at least two hundred years. I have looked through our archives and there is no written mention of such a cult, so I can only relay what my scribe has told me." He paused. Sylva grew impatient.

"Ianis, please get on with your report. We do not have all day to wait on you finding your words."

Ianis blushed. "Apologies, my lady, I want to make sure I don't miss out any details. This scribe was born and brought up in Bala, the country in the north of the island of Aldene. Bala is unique in that it does not have a monarchy but a clan structure where the clan chiefs are the authority. The head of all the clans is the chief of Clan Cameron. The Empress might remember this from reading *White Light Red Fire*. My scribe is a member of Clan Blair, whose lands lie to the east of the capital, Aldene. The clan name means "open plain" and their motto is 'Virtute Tutus', 'By Virtue Safe'."

"Please get to the staff," snapped Sylva.

Ianis bowed slightly. "Yes, my lady. My scribe tells the story like this. Two centuries ago an ancient relic was found in the Blair lands. It was a staff with strange runes carved into the shaft that no one could decipher. Supposedly the chief of the clan at that time had a strange dream where an old man dressed in amber and black told the chief where the staff was to be found and said it had to be protected by the clan and had to travel wherever future dreams dictated. Over time the staff took on an almost religious significance and the cult of the staff became the protectors of the relic. Apparently the relic was hidden in a shrine built into a cave in the Blair lands. The location was only known to a few members of the clan.

"A number of years ago selected members of the cult were sent south to Boretar, Tamin and here to Mora. This resulted from another dream that the current chief of Clan Blair had. In that dream the clan chief had been told that it was time for the staff to begin its journey."

Ingrid held up her hand. "Ianis, this is all fascinating, but what has it to do with the events of the past months in Doran and in Amina?"

Ianis once more apologised. "I am sorry, my lady. I get lost too easily in history and forget to get to the point. According to my scribe, the staff left the cave in Bala a few years ago, in the hands of someone called the Guardian. The Guardian travelled to Boretar and remained there for two years in the house of one of the cult members. Earlier this year the Guardian arrived at my scribe's house. The man describes the event with reverence. He was able to see and touch the relic. The Guardian apparently only stayed for a couple of days before leaving. My scribe says he was told that the staff had now to complete its journey, a journey that it had been waiting for hundreds of years to begin."

Ingrid looked over to Sylva. "I'm sorry, I do not

understand the relevance of this history to recent events."

Sylva thanked Ianis and asked him to leave before she replied. "Ianis enjoys telling the long story. Apparently the Blair history also gives the staff another name, 'the staff of power'. Improbable as it may seem, is it possible that it was brought to Mora for Audun. It may simply be a coincidence, but Ianis' scribe's information suggests that the staff arrived in Mora only a few weeks before the destruction of the ironworks at Sparsholt. Captain Ramon has explained to us that his stepson was fascinated by the history of early fourteenth century Bala. Maybe Audun knew about the staff. Maybe he is a member of the cult. Perhaps, if he has it, the staff is the source of his power."

Had they but known it, the relic under discussion was for the moment resting peacefully under the bed in the attic room in the Mill at Hillfoot.

CHAPTER 16

Juice of the Yew

❖ ❖ ❖ ❖

Located far to the north, Soll was locked in snow and ice for four or five months each year. The smallholdings scattered across the southern region, close to the Doran border, provided a subsistence living for some of the population. Further north, the tundra and the reindeer ignored the border with Esimore and large herds travelled south in the winter, to return north again once the snows had cleared. Soll's capital, Marmilt, was no more than a large village. The King's castle was a large wooden longhouse perched on the motte whilst the wooden walls of the palisade surrounded the bailey and the wooden houses of the village.

In 1496 King Aster of Soll had agreed to swear fealty

to the Emperor in return for a significant dowry payment of Kermin gold. Alberon was already king of Doran and Kermin, and the extension of his rule to include Soll allowed him to crown himself Emperor of the North. Having accepted the oaths of King Aster, Alberon paid no attention to the northern land. The King of Soll had to renew his oaths every few years and this was done in a simple ceremony in Iskala. The Emperor had never visited Marmilt. Soll was useful in name only; it held no value for the Empire or the Emperor. As a result Alberon was ignorant of the people and their customs.

From a distance Soll may have seemed backward and primitive to the Emperor, but it did have its own rare skills and profession. The southern smallholdings were, in general, tended by the women and old folk of the families. The men were hunters. The northern territories were home to an array of wild animals, as well as the reindeer. Bison, elk, and the now rare auroch still roamed the northern tundra. The eastern woodlands of yew and pine were home to brown bears and grey wolves. Soll's hunters were experts with the crossbow. The weapon was constructed from the local materials of yew wood and reindeer horn. Reindeer sinew formed the bow string. Soll's hunters were also mercenaries and had marched with the Emperor's army to the fateful battle at the Kermin Alol in 1507.

Alberon arrived in Iskala as the late August sun was

creating a red, orange, purple and blue painting in the western sky above the Doran Mountains. But the Emperor was not interested in the sky; he wanted to know what was happening on the ground, and why it had been allowed to take place.

Morserat was in the council room in Iskala Castle when Alberon charged in. "What is this nonsense that Soren has reported to me? The new King of Soll has declared independence from the Empire and you sit here enjoying your supper. By now you should have a troop of Doran cavalry out to arrest the outlaw!"

The Duke of Doran stood and bowed to his nephew. "Welcome back to Iskala, my lord. I do have men out on the Doran Plain searching for the new King of Soll."

Alberon raised his voice. "The new King of Soll? You mean the traitor, the outlaw and the son of a traitor. I want his head the same way as I took the head of his father. I will lead a troop of cavalry myself and go and burn down his pathetic capital. What is it called?"

Morserat knew that the Emperor's anger was often extreme and irrational. "It is called Marmilt, and I have only visited it once. It is really only a small village. My men will find this King William and bring him here. Tomorrow we will ride to Sparsholt and you can review the progress being made on your ironworks. There is no need for you to ride to Soll when my men can do the job for you."

For the next hour Morserat briefed Alberon on the

current situation. It had been a month earlier that King Aster had passed away, and with only his daughter as his direct heir, the crown had skipped a generation and had passed to the daughter's son, William Norward. Morserat had been part of Alberon's father's council alongside William's father. The two had never been friends, but Lord Norward had always given wise council to Elrik and afterwards to Alberon. Morserat was certain that Norward had never been a traitor. His weakness had been his over pompous nature. His death at the end of the axe had been a travesty, the charges trumped up by the Emperor to hide his own failures in the disasters that had resulted from the 1507 war with Amina. But now was not the time to revisit the past.

Morserat explained to Alberon that on his coronation two weeks ago the new king had declared Soll a sovereign country and declared that his people would free themselves from the oppression of the Emperor and his Empire. In the last few days, settlements in the north of Doran had been raided by Soll hunters. Morserat added that the raiders stole sheep and cattle, but unless the villagers resisted, none of Doran's people had been injured in the raids. The crossbowmen, it seemed, had held their strings under the orders of their new king.

Alberon's temper was beginning to fray. "So you have bandits stealing your people's livestock? Indeed my people's livestock! And you sit here and tell me that you have troops searching for this traitor. Why have you not readied a large cavalry force and gone into Soll and burnt this Marmilt, or whatever it's called, to the ground?"

Morserat realised that his reply would sting the Emperor, but he went ahead anyway. "It seems to me that kings often make rash decisions for which their people pay the price. William Norward will not have returned to Marmilt, and he will not stay to fight a battle with highly trained light cavalry. On such an approach his hunters will simply vanish into the wilderness in the north, well out of our reach. It is King William you want to punish, not the people of Soll. My men will find him and you can have your execution of the guilty party."

Alberon noted the insinuation and was about to respond angrily, but Morserat quickly continued. "There are two other things you should know, my lord. Firstly the Soll king sent two messages back when I demanded that he come here to take his oaths. The first was that the Soll hunters were not robbing Doran but were simply taking back what they had paid for in ten years of paying the annual tithe to the Empire. Soren has told you already that the second message contained my messenger's forefinger, but it also contained this." Alberon opened the package. Inside was a crossbow bolt. The tip of the wood was wickedly barbed with a piece of sharpened reindeer horn.

Alberon turned the bolt in his hand. "What do you think this is supposed to mean?"

Morserat shrugged. "The wrap around the bolt was addressed specifically 'For the Emperor'. I presume it is some sort of threat."

Alberon laughed. "So the puny king of Soll would threaten his Emperor? His bravado will echo thinly when I have his head separated from his body. I will leave your men to capture the traitor and bring him to my justice. Tomorrow I hope to see significant progress at the ironworks."

As is often the case, servants are the invisible watchers and listeners. The man had remained in the shadows at the back of the council room, only occasionally stepping forward to refill the wine glasses. Neither the Duke nor the Emperor knew that the servant's home village was the place they had been discussing, Marmilt. Now the listener had a task to fulfil for his new king.

At the same time as Alberon was discussing events in Soll with Morserat, Valdin was reporting to the Queen. Ingrid had some new instructions for the huntsman. She went straight to the point.

"Valdin, I have another task for you. Earlier this year a traveller from the country of Bala visited Mora. He travelled here from Boretar a few months ago and is supposed to have brought some ancient relic with him, a staff. This person is apparently its guardian. Some sort of ancient power is said to reside in the staff. I need you to find the guardian, and more importantly the staff. I don't know if the man, or the relic, are still here in Mora or they have moved on. I suggest you start your search by talking with one of the scribes who work with Ianis in the library. The scribe is a member of an organisation supposedly called 'the cult of the staff' and he is probably the best starting point for your search. When you find the staff, you will bring it to me in secret. Now have you made any progress in your search for the Captain of the *Swan*?"

"I know from my enquiries at the docks that the *Swan* continues to trade around Andore and at times across the Middle Sea to Tufle," replied Valdin. "Apparently Audun has not been seen with his ship for several months. By coincidence, earlier today I was in a tavern called the Golden Fleece, which is on the edge of the merchants' quarter. I listened in to the bar conversation, which seemed to be largely an argument about the name of the wizard. One snippet of conversation caught my attention. Apparently someone called Adun had moved into the area a few months ago but hadn't visited the inn for a couple of weeks. I asked the serving maid if she knew this Adun. She did, and she told me that the man had rented a cottage not far from the tavern. When I asked her to describe him all she could say was, "he has the most beautiful blue eyes". Tomorrow I will pay a visit to the owner of the cottage, someone called Arvid."

Ingrid leant forward. "So you think that this Adun person could be Audun?"

Valdin nodded. "It seems possible, my lady."

Ingrid smiled. "Excellent. Please go and find Audun and the staff and bring both of them to me. Now you may leave."

An early September fog clung to the Doran Plain as Alberon and Morserat, together with a small troop of Doran cavalry, left Iskala to make their way to Sparsholt and the ironworks. The village seemed eerily quiet as the riders approached. The forges, situated further to the north, were still hidden by the fog.

The troop did not need to stop at the village, but the deep silence puzzled Alberon and he reined in as the outline of the houses became visible through the fog. He turned to Morserat. "Something isn't right here. Surely there should be some noise coming from the village and some people about."

"The fog is probably deadening any sounds, and with this weather the people must have stayed indoors. Master Henry and his smiths are probably keeping warm at their forges and no doubt they'll be there waiting for us. We should move on."

Just as the Duke turned to nudge his mount forward, sounds did come from the village: the ominous twanging of crossbow strings. The first bolt hit Alberon high on his left shoulder, near his neck. The second bolt hit the Emperor's horse in the rump, causing the beast to rear up and throw the Emperor to the ground. In the moments of confusion that followed, two more bolts took two of the cavalrymen from their mounts.

Morserat shouted to his men. "Soll hunters are in the village! Get them!" As the troopers raced across the open ground to the buildings, Morserat dismounted to attend to his Emperor. The tip of the bolt was embedded deep in Alberon's shoulder. The shaft lay on the ground nearby, having snapped off when Alberon fell from his horse.

Over the years Morserat had seen many wounded men, and whilst the wound to the Emperor looked serious, Morserat judged that it should not be fatal if the bleeding could be quickly stopped. Using his knife to cut strips from his cloak, the Duke tightly bound the Emperor's shoulder. The head of the bolt, which Morserat knew would be a sharpened piece of reindeer horn, would need to be removed, but that was a job for a skilled surgeon.

As the cavalrymen returned in ones and twos, Morserat issued his orders. One trooper was despatched to Iskala to bring the Duke's surgeon to Sparsholt with all speed. Others found a cart in the village and the Emperor was carefully transported to the nearest house, which turned out to be that of Wayland Henry. As the Emperor drifted in and out of consciousness, all Morserat could do was wait.

Gradually as the troopers' reports came in, what had happened became clearer. During the night twenty

Soll hunters, all armed with crossbows, had entered Sparsholt and rounded up everyone from their houses. The villagers had been shepherded to an empty barn half a mile from the settlement and locked in. The threat had been explicit: if any tried to escape or made any noise they would die at the end of a crossbow bolt.

There was now no sign of the attackers, who had simply vanished into the fog. Wayland Henry was one of the first to return to the village and on entering his house the big man burst into tears at the sight of his Emperor lying wounded on the large bed. Henry loudly insisted there was nothing that the villagers could have done to stop the attack. Morserat calmed the smith down; he knew that the inhabitants of Sparsholt were simple working people, not warriors. There was little they could have done in the face of twenty drawn crossbows.

While Morserat sat waiting for the arrival of his surgeon, he found himself unconsciously fiddling with the shaft of the quarrel. With a start he suddenly noticed something he had missed earlier. Carefully burnt into the wood were three words: 'FOR OUR FATHER'. So this had been no random attack. William Norward, newly crowned King of Soll, had been here in person to avenge his father.

Morserat had ordered his cavalrymen to search the Plain for the perpetrators of the attack, and more troops had been called from Iskala to comb the countryside.

The Duke knew it was probably a futile gesture. By the nature of their trade Soll's hunters were experts at blending into the background of the countryside when stalking their prey. The fog lying on the Plain would be a bonus to them, but even on a clear day Doran's troopers could pass within a few yards of a Soll hunter without spotting him.

In fact William and his younger brother John were already north of the ironworks and making their way back to Marmilt. John Norward, three years younger than his brother, had been against the venture, fearing that taking the step of attacking the Emperor would bring a large army to Marmilt's wooden palisade and the capital of Soll would be raised to the ground.

A week earlier, William had been adamant. "The Emperor takes all the wealth of my country in his tithes and more importantly he had our father executed on a whim to cover up his own failings," he had said. "The border raids in the north of Doran and my declarations as King of Soll were all designed to draw the Emperor from his comforts in Mora and to come here to deal with me in person. Now we know he is coming to Iskala, we will be waiting for him near his precious ironworks, which he is sure to visit."

The two brothers were now making a rapid escape back to their homeland. The rest of the Soll raiding party had left Sparsholt in the early morning. Two hunters could probably avoid detection by the Doran cavalry units, but twenty could not.

William and John slipped into a small copse as they heard the sound of riders approaching. In a hushed whisper John voiced his question. "Do you think we killed him?"

William paused for a moment before replying. "I don't know. The fog was both a blessing and a curse. It has covered our escape, but it made the shot more difficult to take. The bolt found its mark, but whether fatal or not, time, and the juice of the yew, will determine."

Waiting until the sound of horses had passed John continued, "Whatever the outcome, you know that Soll cannot resist a major assault from Doran and Kermin forces. You are declared outlaw and you will be hunted until they find you. Then your head will roll at the end of the axe just like our father's."

William smiled. "If that is to be my fate, then so be it, at least I will have struck a blow for freedom for Soll and revenge for the death of our father. For now that is enough. And my timing is not random. In a few days' time the snow will fall and Soll will be beyond the reach of any army."

It was mid-afternoon before the Duke's surgeon arrived at Sparsholt. Master Bradstone had treated many wounded soldiers in his time, but this was different;

this was no soldier, this was the Emperor. However, his professional training quickly overcame his concerns. He persuaded himself that this was just another patient whose wounds he hoped he could heal.

With Alberon drifting in and out of consciousness, the surgeon went to work. Carefully he probed the wound with his fingers, searching for the tip of the quarrel. After a few moments he turned to Morserat. "It's a pity the shaft snapped, it makes extracting the tip much riskier."

Morserat nodded. "It happened when he was thrown from his horse."

Bradstone turned to Wayland Henry, who was sitting on the floor at the side of the room. "I presume you are the master of the house?" Henry nodded. "Then I need you to find me honey and wine. Please get me both quickly."

Glad to be of use, Henry jumped to his feet. "Yes sir, at once."

Five minutes later Henry was back, carrying a flagon of wine and a large jar of honey. Bradstone took a long swig of the wine and then went to his bag. The instrument he took out had two threaded tongs attached to a threaded centre rod. Bradstone turned to Morserat. "If I can locate the end of the shaft, this should get it out. First though, the honey. In a moment I will need the two of you to hold the Emperor still whilst I try to extract the tip."

Carefully Bradstone poured the honey into the wound. Then, leaving the golden liquid to soak in for a minute, he started to prime his instrument. He nodded to the two other men, who took their positions restraining the Emperor, and then he started to probe the wound.

After what felt like an age, but was in fact less than a minute, he started to wind in the threaded central rod. Suddenly, with an ugly gurgling noise, the tip of the bolt came out. Casting his instrument to the side, Bradstone took another long swig of the wine and then poured the rest of the flagon over the wound. The unconscious Emperor lay prone on the bed. Bradstone checked and found a steady pulse. He let out a sigh of relief.

Turning to Morserat and wiping the sweat from his brow, Bradstone nodded to the Duke. "Well, that's the difficult bit done. Hopefully we are in time and the wound will heal. Now let's look at what did the damage."

As he pulled the sharpened bit of antler horn away from his instrument, the surgeon's face took on a serious, concerned look. Morserat noticed immediately. "What's the matter? What's wrong?"

Bradstone passed the Duke the piece of horn. "You said the bolt was fired from a Soll hunter's crossbow. In my younger days I visited many lands trying to gain knowledge from locals about herbs and medicines. Back then I visited Marmilt in Soll. The hunters' crossbow bolts are capable of bringing down most of the animals they hunt, but not the auroch. To kill an auroch the hunters would fire three bolts into the animal, each of them coated with what they call 'the juice of the yew'."

Morserat did not understand. "What is the juice of the yew?"

Bradstone grew more serious. "It's a poison. The sharpened reindeer horn that will form the tip of the bolt is left in the putrefying body of an animal for a week and then left to dry. Once dried, the tip is further soaked in a juice made from ground yew berries and leaves. The auroch doesn't die from the bolts – it dies a short while later from the poison. Look at the tip you hold in your hand. It's black, and the blood it's coated in is already turning green. Like the auroch, the Emperor won't die from the wound, but unless I can get him back to Iskala and try to find an antidote to the poison, the juice of the yew will kill him."

CHAPTER 17

Trouble at the Mill

❖ ❖ ❖ ❖

Sylva was waiting at the dockside in Mora as the *Erth* came into view downriver. The cavalryman whom Amleth had sent to the mouth of the Morel to watch for the carrack's arrival had reported an hour earlier, and Sylva wanted to be at the dock to welcome her son home. Once the mooring ropes had been secured, Edin and Aaron were the first to disembark. Ignoring royal etiquette, Sylva ran over to greet her son with a warm embrace. As was fitting for the return of a Prince, a troop of Kermin cavalry waited patiently, holding the Empress's horse and a black stallion for the Prince.

Typical of an eleven-year-old, Aaron was

embarrassed. "Don't fuss so mother, people are watching."

Sylva smiled. "I don't care Aaron, I'm just delighted to have you home. How is your new baby cousin?"

Aaron was more excited about the stallion. "Is the horse for me? I've been doing a lot of cavalry training with Uncle Bertalan's horsemen. Yes, little Berka seems to be fine for a baby."

The Duke of Aramin stood in the background whilst the mother and son were reunited, and it was clear Sylva hadn't given any thought to Erin. "My Lord Duke, I am sorry, I didn't think. We should have brought an extra mount."

Erin smiled. "It is not a problem, my lady. I have two legs and it will be nice to walk round Mora's streets again after such a long time away in Tamin."

Suddenly Sylva realised that there were two travellers she had forgotten about. Embarrassed now, she shook her head. "Captain Ramon, in my excitement to come and greet Aaron I have not made a good job of arranging the welcoming party."

Ramon bowed. "My lady, like the Duke, my legs are fine and I will be happy to share the walk with him and maybe a jug of ale on the way."

Sylva laughed. "Not too many jugs, captain. I need you to be sober when you report to me this afternoon to give me my brother's messages."

Ramon nodded. "Of course, my lady, I will visit you later as you request."

With an excited Prince mounted on the back of the stallion, the cavalrymen wheeled their horses round and at a steady trot rode back up the hill towards the castle.

The two men, who had become friends during the sea journey from Tamin, set out on foot. Some would consider it a coincidence, others fate, that the inn the pair selected for their jug of ale was the Golden Fleece. Erin and Ramon had only taken their first sips from their tankards when they were interrupted. Ramon stood to shake the other man's hand, noticing again the serpent tattoo. "Valdin! It has been a while."

The huntsman smiled. "Welcome back to Mora, captain. I hear you are now a messenger for the Queen."

Ramon nodded. "And for the Empress, and I need to report to her shortly."

Valdin shrugged. "We all have our duties to perform, but right now I need to speak with you in private for a moment."

Ramon apologised to the Duke and followed the huntsman out to the courtyard at the rear of the inn. He now knew the origin of the viper tattoo. He had discovered the answer in a book he had found in the Emperor's library during his house arrest in the castle. The blade that the serpent was wrapped around was a skilatu, the weapon of choice of the assassins who had lived in the Doran Mountains a hundred years earlier.

As Ramon had learnt more about Audun's history, like his stepson he had pondered if Valdin had been sent to Boretar by the Emperor to kill Audun. It was one piece of the jigsaw that had not found its place.

Valdin went straight to the point. "Captain, I believe I may have found where Audun has been hiding. There's a regular client of this inn called Adun. He arrived in Mora a few months ago and he's renting a cottage from the man I am talking with at the table across the room from where you were sitting with the Duke of Aramin. Adun's description is so close to that of Audun that I have to believe they are one and the same person. As he has not been seen for a few weeks, together with rumours of the possible name of the wizard, or sorcerer, the locals are speculating that he is the wizard. There's no proof of course, but there is an odd coincidence. This Adun was sometimes seen carrying an old wooden staff that was marked with strange motifs."

Ramon was equally direct. "Valdin, I have never seen Audun carry a staff, and he certainly has no need of a support. I have a different question for you. Were you sent to Boretar to murder Audun at the orders of the Emperor?"

Ramon could tell that the question was a surprise as Valdin replied. "No, those were not my orders, and if they had been your stepson would be dead, but why this question?"

Ramon pointed to the tattoo. "I know this is the

brand of the assassins, and once I knew that, it was an obvious question."

Valdin smiled. "Yes, it's the brand of my ancestors, but that was not my task in Boretar. If it had been I wouldn't have failed. However I have a new task from the Queen, to find an ancient staff that was carried to Mora a few months ago, and it seems to me that this relic, which originates from Bala, could now be in Audun's possession."

Ramon was bemused. "What's so important about some ancient staff?"

Valdin smiled. "I only get told what I am required to do, not what the reasons are. The Queen said that in history the staff was called the 'staff of power'."

Ramon was well versed in ancient text and histories. He responded, "I have never heard of a 'staff of power', and if there was such a thing then I'm sure it would have some historical references."

Valdin shrugged. "Whatever you say, captain, I only know what my task is. If you want more information, perhaps you should ask the Queen. Now the man I am sitting with is called Arvid and he is renting the cottage to Adun. I am about to go with him to search the cottage. You are welcome to join us if you are interested."

Ramon shook his head. "I am interested, but I am tasked with reporting to the Empress this afternoon and I may already be late. Would you be able to meet me back here this evening and tell me what you found out?"

Valdin rose and shook the other man's hand. "Later this evening I will be here waiting for you. And by the way, I will let you buy the ale."

Ramon nodded. "Agreed, until later then."

After a hard day's work at the mill and in the grain store Audun had decided that he needed to find some space to think about his forward plans. Passing time in Hillfoot was pleasant enough, but he knew this country retreat could not last forever. Winter was on the horizon, and he needed to decide where the changing of the season would take him.

He chose to follow the mill stream, whose source was higher up in the eastern Alol hills. His choice of route had two purposes: firstly it gave him space and fresh air, and secondly, Anders had noted that the mill stream flow had reduced over the past few days and perhaps Audun could find out if the stream had been blocked in some way.

After a thirty-minute climb, Audun paused to look back down to the valley below. The scene took his breath away. With the setting September sun, Hillfoot was bathed in a glorious red glow. Audun gasped and checked that the orb was still located in his bag and the staff remained inert in his hand. The vista below him was too similar to his earlier nightmares of the red fire destroying cities and armies.

Relieved that nature's colour was responsible for the light falling below, he was about to turn to continue his ascent when he heard shouts. From the edge of the forest, fire arrows were targeting the mill. The Aramin were attacking Hillfoot, or at least the mill and the grain stores. Audun felt his anger rise, red and raw; these were his friends who were being attacked.

In a moment the orb and the staff had become one and the red fire was licking down hungrily over the hieroglyphs. Audun focused his anger and the red fire leapt from the tip of the staff, making the edge of the forest burst into flames. Ignoring his promise to himself to avoid using his power to take lives, he continued to blast holes in the eastern edge of the forest, the place where the arrows were coming from.

Subduing his anger for a moment, Audun surveyed the effects of his destruction. Then he noticed a large group of tribesmen making for the grain stores. The attack on the mill was a distraction; the stores were the target. Again the red fire leapt from the tip of the staff and the attacking force was incinerated. It was all over in moments.

Audun slumped down on the grass, appalled at what he had done. So much for his promise not to take lives. He had not acted with cold fury but in a red rage, and the orb and staff had responded accordingly, with furious red fire, not cool blue lightning. Below him, the fires in the forest and around the mill were gradually guttering out.

Shaking himself free from the impact of his actions, Audun continued to climb. On the flat land near the summit of the hill, he reached the source of the mill stream and found the reason for the reduction of flow at the mill; a crude dam had been built to block the waterway. The cold fury that built inside was more anger at his own lack of control than with the dam itself. Nonetheless the orb responded with a blue-white glow as lightning bolts blew the dam to smithereens.

As Audun separated the orb from the staff a familiar voice echoed in his head: *Your anger is good Audun. Your power lies in your anger.*

The September sun which was setting Hillfoot aglow was reflecting off Mora Castle's golden turrets as Ramon walked along the castle walls to the Queen's rooms. The maid ushered him into the same turret room as his previous meetings, and there waiting were the Queen and the Empress. "Welcome back to Mora Captain Ramon," said Ingrid. "What news do you bring from Tamin?"

Ramon took a sip of the offered wine before replying. "King Bertalan sends his best wishes to you both. I arrived in Tamin just after the new Prince was born and the city was in holiday mood. Nonetheless the King was gracious enough to grant me an audience. He told me that he could confirm that the incidents at the Kermin Alol and in the Tamin Plain were not caused by natural events. Apparently in both cases the lightning struck without there being any accompanying thunder and the bolts seemed to come from the hillside, not the sky. In both cases the wizard left his message 'for Arin', although the name means nothing to the King."

Sylva leant forward. "Did my brother remember my letter asking him to seek out Ragna and her son?"

Ramon nodded. "Yes my lady, he did, but as far as he could remember the family were never found."

Ingrid of course now knew the connection to the name Arin, but for now she would keep that part of the story to herself, so she changed the subject. "What was Bertalan's reaction to the news that the Emperor was developing weapons at the ironworks at Sparsholt?"

Ramon remembered clearly Bertalan's reaction. "The King actually laughed. He recognised that although the action of the Emperor broke the spirit of the treaties, they did not break the letter of the agreement. However he added a further message that I was to deliver to the Emperor. He said to tell the Emperor that if Kermin were to invade Amina again, then he would march his forces and his cannons across the Kermin Plain and destroy Mora. He said he now not only had to protect his country but he also had to defend the rights of his newborn son."

Sylva nodded. "That is understandable." She turned to Ingrid. "We know what Alberon's reaction will be to the birth of the Amina Prince. Bertalan's threat is likely to make him even more determined to take immediate action."

Ingrid's voice took on a sharp edge. "Well, we need to ensure that my son does not act with impetuous stupidity. Fortunately we are at the edge of winter and there will be no time for Alberon to raise an army before the snows come. That will give us the time we need."

The Queen was interrupted by a polite knock at the door. "Come," she said.

A maid entered. "My lady, there is a messenger from Iskala waiting here to see you and the Empress."

Ingrid responded. "Well show him in, for goodness sake."

It was a weary, dust-covered Soren that entered the room and bowed to the Queen.

Sylva was quick with her rebuke. "Soren, you might at least have taken a moment to clean up before entering the Queen's rooms."

Soren bowed again, clearly very agitated. "I am sorry my lady, there was no time. My message is too urgent."

Sylva snapped. "There is always time for polite etiquette when presenting one's self, young man."

Soren shook his head as though trying to focus on his message.

Ingrid was growing impatient. "Well get on with

it Soren, before you are left standing there in a pile of dust."

When it came the message was blurted out staccato. "The Emperor has been badly wounded by a crossbow bolt."

Both women leapt to their feet and shouted out, "What!"

Ingrid regained control first. "Never mind the dirt, Soren, you must sit down and tell us it all."

Soren did as commanded and gave his report in full. Ingrid was annoyed; she prided herself that despite her relative isolation she was kept well informed of important events, both in Kermin and further afield.

She shook her head. "Soren, I apologise I am clearly slightly out of touch. Let me be sure I understand correctly. King Aster died a few weeks ago and his grandson inherited the throne of Soll."

Soren nodded. "That is correct, my lady.

Ingrid continued. "And the grandson is William Norward, the son of Lord Norward, who was an advisor to my husband and my son and who was executed on the forecourt outside this window a couple of years ago."

"Yes my lady."

"And Morserat thinks William Norward was responsible for the attack on the Emperor."

"Yes, that is what my uncle thinks."

Ingrid seemed to shrink slightly in her seat before

asking her next question. "How serious is the Emperor's wound?"

Soren paused as though composing himself to give the answer. "The surgeon managed to remove the arrow tip, but he is concerned that it may have been poisoned. Soll hunters at times use poisoned quarrels to kill their prey. I'm told that the wound itself may not be fatal, but the poison can be. The surgeon is searching for an antidote."

Sylva let out a gasp in anguish. "He might die?"

Soren answered as honestly as he could. "At the moment we don't know, my lady. I am told he drifts in and out of consciousness. Clearly the surgeon and the physicians are very concerned."

Ingrid was, as ever, practical. "Soren, go and get cleaned up and get some rest, then I need you to arrange transport for us to Iskala. We will leave tomorrow, as early as possible. The Empress will want her own mount, whilst I will require a carriage. You should probably instruct one of your Doran cavalrymen to ride ahead to Iskala to inform Morserat of our plan."

Soren bowed again. "All will be ready by tomorrow, my lady." With those words, he left the room.

Ingrid turned to Ramon. "I think this has rather disrupted our discussion, captain. No doubt the news will quickly travel to Mora on the grapevine, but for now please don't disclose what you know to anyone else."

Ramon rose to leave. "I have one last question, Your Highness. Am I free now to leave Mora? The *Swan* was docked at Tufle when I arrived there and I would like to return to the sea. Before you ask, Audun was not with the ship, but I have asked Vasilli, who is the current captain, to bring the *Swan* to Mora and when she leaves I would, with your permission, like to be on board."

Ingrid nodded. "From what we have learnt from Soren, the Emperor is in no condition to disagree, so you have my permission to return to your normal life. If it is possible though, I would like you to meet with me tomorrow before we leave for Iskala. I have some questions that you might be able to answer about an ancient relic from Bala."

A purple dusk was settling over Hillfoot as Audun looked down on the village. As dark closed in, candlelight shone from some of the cottages and from the inn. He had become used to the weariness that had drained him when he had exerted the power of the orb and staff at the Alol and at the Tamin Plain. Strangely, this time the release of the red fire seemed to have been less taxing. Audun considered this as he looked down at the peaceful lights flickering below. The red fire driven by his wild anger was less controllable, but also less draining. The cold fire, the blue lightning, was more in his control, but it took much more effort.

Audun sat for many a long moment considering. Red

fire released in an angry temper, blue lightning released in a cold fury; was either really controllable? What now? Could he simply walk back down to Hillfoot and pretend that he had not seen the destruction that he had unleashed on the attackers at the Mill? Had fate chosen for him, and was it time to end his country retreat? The questions were many. The answers were few.

The violet, red, orange and blue hues of sunset painted the sky over the Kermin Plain as Ramon returned to the Golden Fleece. Valdin was sitting in a quiet corner, and true to his word he had instructed the barmaid to charge Ramon for his jug of ale. Ramon paid for his and Valdin's jugs and joined the huntsman.

Ramon started with a question. "Did you confirm that Audun had lived at the cottage?"

Valdin looked directly at the other man. "The cottage was largely empty. Indeed it seemed largely unlived in, which was strange as Arvid confirmed that this Adun person had first rented the cottage in June. I did find this though, and wondered if it could be Audun's." Valdin handed Ramon the well-thumbed copy of *White Light Red Fire*.

Ramon caught his breath. He remembered well the copy of the book gifted to Audun by David Burnett during a visit to Aldene a few years earlier. It was the first printed copy of Angus Ferguson's history of the Bala wars of the early 14th century.

Ramon nodded. "Audun certainly owned a copy of this book, and it was a gift he treasured. This could be his."

Valdin frowned. "In some ways that's a pity."

Ramon looked puzzled. "I don't understand? I thought you were tasked with finding Audun. If this is definitely his, then presumably you have completed your task."

Valdin paused for a moment. "I found something else in the cottage. In a corner of the main room, largely out of sight, was an old box stuffed with clothes. Hidden at the bottom of the box were some remnants of clothing that had been shredded with a knife. They were badly stained with blood. The owner of the cottage, this Arvid, has been arrested on suspicion of murdering Holger, the Captain of the Guard. Obviously he denies any knowledge of the shredded clothing."

Ramon had been at sea when Holger was murdered, so he knew nothing of the background. "Valdin, I'm afraid I am missing some of this story. You'd better explain."

Valdin described how Captain Holger had been found dead behind the Black Bear.

Ramon asked the obvious question. "Why would anyone do that? And why would this Arvid do it?"

Valdin, of course, was keen to find an alternative suspect. "Well, it seems this Arvid is a known thief and burglar, although he has never been caught. Perhaps

Holger knew this and planned to trap him and to arrest him. The punishment for a burglar who is caught in Mora is quite severe. If Arvid was found guilty of robbery, the best he could expect is to lose his right hand. Maybe that's why he targeted Holger. Of course, if he's found guilty of the captain's murder then the punishment will be much more severe."

Ramon shook his head. "I don't understand how this connects to Audun."

Valdin took a long swig of his ale before replying. "Captain, I would have thought that was fairly obvious. Arvid denies any knowledge of the bloodstained clothing and of course blames his tenant, Adun. If it is indeed Audun who was renting the cottage then he is very likely to be arrested on his return to Mora and charged with Holger's murder. It would then be one man's word against another's."

Ramon slowly took in this information. "But Audun would have no motive or grudge against Holger. That accusation makes no sense."

"I have met your stepson and personally I doubt he could be a murderer. I also doubt he is a sorcerer, but suppose Holger had believed the rumours that the sorcerer was called Adun and that someone with that name lived in the cottage and regularly visited the Golden Fleece? If Audun had found out that Holger was making such enquiries, then he would possibly have had a reason to keep the Captain quiet."

Ramon suddenly realised that the huntsmen was too close to the truth about Holger's knowledge, and might also be close to explaining the reason for the Captain of the Guard's murder. "Interesting speculation, Valdin, but I don't know how you make the leap of logic from the sorcerer, if he exists at all, being named Adun to Audun being the sorcerer."

Valdin smiled. "My brother and I are the eyes and ears of the Queen. We gather information, and sometimes we come to our own conclusions. I probably know more than you think I do. There is, however, one other explanation. The cottage originally belonged to Arvid's sister-in-law and her husband. The pair perished in the pestilence of nine years ago. They left behind an orphan son, whose name is Raimund. Arvid and his family took the orphan into their own home and the boy lived with them for a few years before running away. Arvid claims that if the bloodstained clothes were not from his tenant, then they must have been left by his nephew, who he has not seen for several years. There is no proof of course that this Raimund exists, and indeed no reason I can think of as to why a fourteen-year-old boy would have a grudge against the Captain of the Guard. That leaves Audun, or Adun, as Arvid's only alibi."

1509 had been an uneventful year for Raimund and the other members of the Den of Thieves. The old warehouse with its badly cracked front façade and weed-filled roof garden remained standing and so far had avoided the fate of the neighbouring buildings, which had been demolished in early 1508 to provide wood for fuel for Mora's residents. Raimund and Aleana continued to take an occasional purse in the markets, but with harsh laws in place to punish pickpockets if they were caught, Rafe insisted that the pair only ever took one or two purses, and only when they were certain that they would not get caught. The secret passageway that ran between the Den and the Emperor's warehouse remained undetected and an occasional underground trip could bolster the Den's funds. Aracir had never returned to the warehouse to audit the contents, so the small, expensive items that were removed were never missed.

Raimund and Aleana remained the very best of friends, and as they had grown to maturity, nature had taken its course and the two friends had become lovers. They were inseparable.

Raimund seldom passed the old cottage that had been his childhood home, but on one occasion recently he had seen a young man leave it; a young man with blond hair tied back in a pony tail and startlingly blue eyes, carrying a staff covered in strange motifs. His uncle and aunt must have at last found someone to buy or rent the cottage. In the four years since he had run away, he had managed to avoid Arvid and his aunt,

Astrid, although he had seen them at the markets. With the passing of time he had grown, and he hoped that even if he bumped into his relatives, they would not recognise him.

It was only in the occasional nightmare that Raimund relived the botched raid on the jeweller's shop of four years ago. He would wake drenched in sweat, seeing again the jeweller falling across him with Arvid's knife protruding from his chest and the man's blood pumping out over his clothing. Aleana would hold him tight and comfort him until he quietened down and drifted back to sleep.

He shared everything with Aleana, apart from the story of the murder. In the morning she would ask what had troubled his dreams, but he could not tell her. He was not a murderer. As for the bloodstained clothing which he had shredded that night and hidden in the bottom of his father's old trunk, he had long since put it out of his mind.

CHAPTER 18

The Guardian

❖ ❖ ❖ ❖

Audun was sitting in a quiet corner in the End of the Road listening to the chatter of the farm workers. Inevitably all the conversations revolved around the events of earlier that evening. As often happens with momentous events, the observers all had different views, depending on their point of observation and their personal view of the world. The consensus that gradually developed was largely based on the reality of their world view. The conflagrations at the edge of the forest must have been a result of the fires that the Aramin had lit to prime their fire arrows. These must have somehow got out of control. It was also the common opinion that the fire that consumed the tribesmen who were attacking the grain store must have been caused by stray arrows from their comrades in the forest.

The few who invoked the possibility of a wizard were generally talked down. "Why would an all-powerful wizard come to protect Hillfoot? Why would he even be in this part of the Alol? Apart from in stories and folklore, did wizards actually exist anyway?"

One person who had a different perspective was Anders. He was the only one who knew that Audun had set off to walk in the hills earlier that afternoon. He took the seat opposite Audun, whom he knew as Ragnar. "Well Master Ragnar, I see the mill stream is flowing freely again. Thank you. What was the problem?"

Audun hesitated for a moment before replying. It was a relief that the farm workers seemed to have discounted the possibility of the wizard, but the headman might have a different view. "There was a blockage at the source of the stream," he said. "Fallen rocks I presume, which I removed and the full flow returned."

Anders laughed. "Fallen rocks I doubt. More probably placed there by the Aramin so that they could cross the mill stream and get into the grain store. That's more likely."

Audun shrugged. "There was no one else on the hill other than myself, so I assumed that the dam was just a coincidence. The upper slopes above the source of the stream are strewn with large boulders."

Anders held the other man's eyes for a long moment. "Did you see the fires that happened here in the village, and the Aramin attack?"

Audun knew he needed to be careful. "As I climbed the slope I heard the shouts, but the sunset was shining low over Hillfoot, so it was difficult to pick up what was happening on the ground below." Audun had decided that this was his safe ground. "As best I could tell, it looked like fires had been lit on the edge of the forest and suddenly went out of control," he continued. "From my position I didn't see what happened to the attack on the grain store."

Before Anders could ask another question, Audun asked, "Did anyone get hurt in the attack? Was any damage done?"

Anders shook his head. "No, we were lucky. No one was hurt and we were ready for the fire arrows that struck the mill. However there was something strange about this attack. In previous years the Aramin have used similar tactics – reduce the flow of the mill stream to make it easy to cross, start the raid as though the mill is the target and then send a raiding party to steal the grain from the store. When the stream's flow dropped it was a warning, so we were ready. In the past though, the fires in the forest were small and controlled to light the arrows, and the fire arrows themselves could not have wiped out the raiding party. The bar talk may discount some sort of sorcery. Personally I am not so ready to dismiss the idea."

Anders gazed more closely at the other man. Audun held the gaze for a moment. "As I have said, there was no one else but me on the hillside."

Anders nodded. "And that's what makes me wonder. In the meantime I have another puzzle you might be able to solve for me. You see the big man with the ginger hair sitting on the opposite side of the room?"

Audun looked over to the other side of the bar. "Yes, but I don't know him, if that's what you are asking."

Anders eyes narrowed. "Are you sure, Master Ragnar? Master ginger hair is not from these parts, indeed his accent suggests he comes from one of the countries on Andore. He is seeking someone called Audun."

Audun tried to hide his shock. "I don't know anyone of that name, Master Anders."

Anders pointed to Audun's side. "Strange that, because the big man said that it was likely that Audun would be in possession of an ancient staff with strange runes carved into the wood. What he described was just like the one lying beside you."

Audun suddenly realised that he had been careless. Normally the staff and the orb would be hidden under the bed in his room, but on coming down from the hillside he had carried both into the inn. The staff's strangeness had often prompted inquisitive questions, so he relied on his standard response.

"The staff has been in my family for generations, so I don't know why it would be of interest to the man over there or indeed how it links to this Audun person," he said. "Anyway Master Anders, I am tired from my walk in the hills so I think I will retire to my room."

Anders smiled. "Rest well, Ragnar, or is it Audun or maybe Adun? If it is the latter I owe you thanks for your intervention in the Aramin attack."

"I think we should stick with Ragnar," said Audun quietly. "Goodnight."

As he left the inn, Audun could feel the big man's eyes follow him. He needed time to consider this new situation and decide how best to react.

Soren and his troop of cavalry were waiting calmly in Mora Castle's forecourt. The Empress's palfrey was pawing the ground less patiently. Ingrid and Sylva were in the former's apartments, meeting with Ramon.

Ingrid opened the conversation. "Captain, thank you for coming to meet with us. When do you plan to leave Mora?"

Ramon shrugged. "I don't know exactly, but I would hope the *Swan* arrives in the next week or so and I'll sail with her."

Ingrid nodded. "You go with my thanks and blessing, captain. But first I have a question for you about something that we have found out that may be relevant to Audun. Do you know anything about a Bala organisation called 'The Cult of the Staff'?"

Ramon shook his head. "No, I have never heard of such an organisation."

"Do you suppose Audun could have learnt about the staff? Apparently it is also called the 'Staff of Power'. It's an ancient relic that supposedly was found by the Blair clan in Bala and has been protected by them over the centuries."

Again Ramon shook his head. "I know something of the Bala history and Audun is well read on the ancient histories of Bala, but I can recall no mention of such a relic. It's possible that Audun gained some new knowledge the last time he visited Bala, which was a few years ago when he took command of the *Swan* after I was injured in an accident. He has never talked to me about this staff or mentioned it. Why do you think this might have relevance?"

Sylva now took the lead and explained what she and the Queen had learned from Ianis and his scribe. Ramon was intrigued and surprised.

"So you think Audun has acquired this staff and it's this power that has enabled him to deliver the sorcery?"

Sylva nodded. "It may be a coincidence, but it seems possible, considering the time that Audun arrived here in Mora was supposedly similar to the arrival of the Guardian and the staff. But maybe it's just folklore.

Like everything concerning your stepson, it's hard to distinguish between what is reality and what is myth."

Ramon turned to the Queen. "You know of course that your man Valdin thinks he might have found where Audun has been living in Mora, and that the person he has identified is called Adun and has been seen carrying an ancient staff covered with runes?"

Sylva frowned; she knew nothing about Valdin and his tasks. She turned to her mother-in-law. "Ingrid, we promised each other that we would share any information we gathered. Are you keeping secrets from me again?"

Ingrid looked across at her daughter-in-law. "No, I am not keeping secrets my dear. Disconnected bits of information that may have no substance, yes. If Valdin had discovered any real proof, you would be the first to know. Anyway, we have kept Soren and his troopers waiting too long. We need to leave for Iskala. On the journey I'll share with you the few snippets I have found out. Thank you Captain Ramon, you may leave us now."

Ramon stood and bowed. "I hope when you get to Iskala you find the Emperor is recovering from his wound."

Audun had decided that for the moment he would stick with his normal routine. However, with Anders being suspicious of his true identity, it was also clear that his time in Hillfoot had to be coming to an end. His dilemma was deciding what to do next: return to Mora, move to Tamin or some other choice? He was lost in his ponderings as he crossed between the Mill and the Grain Store, and failed to hear the stranger approach from the village behind him.

"Audun, I need to talk with you."

Startled out of his ruminations, Audun spun round, his right hand dropping to the dagger at his waist. He came face to face with the big man with the ginger hair who had been sitting in the opposite corner of the inn the previous night. Taking a deep breath to calm his racing heart, Audun responded. "I'm sorry sir, I think you have mistaken me for someone else. My name is Ragnar. I don't know anyone called Audun."

The other man let out a growl of frustration, and for a moment Audun imagined he was in a conversation with a bear. The image was reinforced by the size of the man and the thick ginger hair of his beard.

"Audun, I know who you are and I know the history of the staff," said the man. He pointed to the charred ground where the Aramin attackers had been incinerated. "I also know how you did that. The master has told me I need to talk with you."

Audun suddenly recognised the accent. "You're from Bala and from your accent, from the east of Aldene. However I repeat, I don't know anyone called Audun."

The bear growled again, the words slightly muffled

by the beard. "Audun, let's walk over to the side of the grain store and sit in the sun. If you don't want to walk over I will be forced to carry you. You will talk with me."

Audun's hand was still poised over his dagger. The bear thrust out his paw and the huge right hand held Audun's arm in a vice-like grip. "Forget it, boy. If necessary I will break your arm before you can draw it." The vice tightened threateningly.

With little option, Audun followed the man over to the wall surrounding the grain store and sat down. "Who are you, and what do you want with me?"

The man laughed. "Oh, so you have suddenly remembered your real name."

Audun shrugged. "I simply repeat my question. Who are you and what do you want with me?"

The bear tugged at his ginger beard. "My name is Alexander Blair of Balthayock and I am the Guardian of the Staff."

A dozen different questions came to Audun's mind, but he decided to continue to play ignorance. "Well, Master Alexander Blair of Balthayock, so now I have your name, but what is it that you want with me, and what is this staff you are referring to?"

The man from Bala turned towards Audun, his amber eyes glinting in the sunlight. "I am sent by our master to correct your waywardness. The staff you know about, the Staff of Power, enabled you to deliver the destruction here." Again Master Blair pointed at the charred ground only a short distance away. "It is the same staff that was resting at your side in the inn last night."

Audun was intrigued, but determined to stick to his story. "The old staff has been in my family for generations. It is an heirloom and I don't know about it possessing any magical power."

The amber eyes narrowed and the growl got deeper. "Let's stop playing games, Audun. Our master sent me on a long journey over many years to deliver the staff to you in Mora. My instructions are to tell you to stop playing with your power in these ridiculous actions you are taking in your attempt to gain your vengeance. All you have succeeded in doing is to make the powers in these lands aware of your presence. You have a throne to claim, and the power that goes with that throne will gift you real power, the power the master needs."

Master Alexander Blair of Balthayock's voice took on the tone of an adult speaking to a naughty child as he explained to Audun the history of the staff.

Audun was surprised. In the time it had been in his possession, the staff had not demonstrated any inherent power and Audun had assumed that it was only useful as a conduit for the power in the orb. Alexander Blair had made no mention of the orb, although he had mentioned the master several times.

CHAPTER 19

Iskala

❖ ❖ ❖ ❖

When Ingrid and Sylva arrived in Iskala, they were taken straight to the royal apartments. Alberon appeared shrunken in the great bed. The canopy was pulled open and the Emperor was surrounded by agitated physicians, all clamouring to be heard. Master Bradstone was clearly in charge, and he hastened his colleagues out of the room as the two women entered.

While Sylva ran across the room to her husband's bedside, Ingrid addressed the physician. "Well?"

Master Bradstone seemed to be searching for the right words. "My colleagues and I were discussing the Emperor's condition as you arrived, my lady. There is no known antidote to the juice of the yew. Nothing we have tried has any effect. The poison is killing the Emperor and we seem powerless to stop it."

Alberon groaned and turned over in the bed without regaining consciousness. The movement caused the bandage on his shoulder to slip, revealing his wound. Sylva gasped at the blackened flesh and gagged at the smell of putrefaction emanating from the wound.

"Surely you can do something to reduce the decay in his flesh?" she stammered.

Bradstone moved swiftly over to his patient and reset the bandage. "I'm sorry my lady, it is the way with the poison. He will either succeed in fighting off the seeping decay or he will succumb to the juice."

Audun turned to Alexander Blair. "Who is this master you keep on referring to?"

Blair looked surprised. "You do not know? Yet you have been under his instruction these past two years."

Audun feigned ignorance. "I have?"

Blair continued. "The old man only visits me in dreams. Dressed always in black with amber fire as his companion, he is older than the mountains. He is the fire of othium and he comes with an ancient name, Oien. He demands you take your throne and raise his armies. You will rebuild for him the glory of the second age."

Audun knew something of the history of the second age. "I will not be responsible for the destruction of cities and the deaths of innocent people."

Blair waved his hand towards the charred ground near the grain store. "Just as you were not responsible for the deaths of the tribesmen there."

"The tribesmen were hit with their own fire arrows. I was walking in the Alol when the tribesmen attacked," Audun said.

Blair smiled. "Of course you were Audun. But now it is time to fulfil your destiny. We need to return to Mora."

Audun shrugged. "I will return to Mora, but in my own time. Now I have work to do in the granary." With that Audun got up and left, leaving Blair sitting alone in the September sunshine.

That evening in the End of the Road there was no sign of Master Blair. Anders was deep in conversation with a well-dressed stranger, but when he spotted Audun he waved him over to the table and introduced the stranger. "Ragnar, I would like to introduce my brother, Aracir," he said. After pleasantries were exchanged, Anders explained that his brother was visiting Hillfoot for the annual harvest festival which was due the next week.

"My brother also brings momentous news," Anders continued. "It seems that the Emperor has been severely wounded by a bolt from a Soll hunter's crossbow. He is in Iskala, critically wounded. It is rumoured that the Soll hunter was none other than William Norward, the new king of Soll and the son of Lord Norward who was executed by the Emperor in 1508."

Audun did not know how to take this news. It seemed his revenge had been taken by another grieving son. He stammered out the only words he could think of. "Is the Emperor dying?"

Aracir responded. "He is critically wounded. The Soll bolt was poisoned and the physicians know of no antidote, so we must all wait and pray."

Audun did not know what else to say, so shaking the other man's hand he bid Aracir a good night and left the Inn. Outside he was confronted by Alexander Blair. The big man had also heard the news. "We must go now to Mora," he said. "Now is the time to claim your crown."

Audun pushed past the Bala man. He needed time and space to think out the consequences of Aracir's news. Stopping for a moment, he turned to Blair and said "While the Emperor still lives there is no throne to claim." Then he walked back to the Mill.

Ingrid had returned to Mora the previous day. There was nothing she could do in Iskala, and with the Emperor lingering between life and death, someone had to deal with the day-to-day running of the Empire. Sylva had remained in Iskala to tend to her husband, although in reality there was little she could do. Alberon had not regained consciousness, and the black decay on his shoulder seemed to be spreading. It was ten days since the attack and the Emperor's condition was deteriorating. Nothing the physicians did seemed to make any difference.

Finally, with Sylva by his side, the Emperor succumbed to the juice. He was just six months shy of his fortieth birthday.

Soren, as ever, was the messenger and he took the news to Ingrid in Mora. As in 1495 when her husband had been killed by an exploding cannon, the city was ordered to spend a month in mourning. All the citizens of Mora had to wear something black on their clothing.

Riders were despatched to take the news to Bertalan in Tamin and to the outlying regions of Kermin. A rider arrived in Hillfoot as the sun was setting over the western Alol. Aracir was to return with haste to Mora. Audun noted the sudden activity around the Inn as Aracir prepared to depart.

And so Audun learned that his father had died. Now it was time to return to Mora, although he still did not know what he was going to do.

The boy found Ramon in his rooms in Mora Castle. It was the news Ramon had been waiting for. The *Swan* had just moored at Mora's dockside and Vasilli had sent the boy to fetch the captain. Thirty minutes later, the *Swan* was heading south on the Morel towards the open sea.

Audun was approaching Mora on the main road

from the Alol. He immediately recognised the *Swan* as it left the harbour and saw his stepfather on the deck. Ramon was free.

Audun returned to his small cottage in the tradesmen's quarter, but he had no sooner stowed his bag containing the casket and the red orb than the door was thrown open. It was Valdin.

"Audun, or maybe it is Adun, I have been looking for you for some time. None of your friends at the Golden Fleece knew where you had disappeared to. Maybe it was wizard's business? Anyway, you are to come with me."

Audun considered resisting, but he knew that Valdin would not be denied. "Where are we to go, and for what purpose?"

Valdin smiled. "I know a lady who is very keen to meet you. Please come with me."

Audun followed Valdin out of the tradesmen's quarter and up the main street. Audun thought initially that their destination was Mora Castle. As a result he was surprised when Valdin turned into a side street some way before the castle gate. It was a wide street, and by the size of the houses it was home to many of the city's wealthy citizens. Audun was further intrigued when Valdin turned into the third door. The two men standing outside the house nodded a welcome as Audun followed Valdin through the doorway. The pair were clearly on guard duty, but wore no uniforms to identify themselves.

Audun followed Valdin up to the third floor, where the Huntsman pushed open a door and indicated for Audun to take a seat. The room was richly furnished, with fine paintings decorating the walls. Audun recognised the portrait hanging on the wall opposite him; it was of the man he had first met only a couple of days earlier. He was clearly in the house of Aracir, Chancellor of Kermin, and the man for whom he had a letter from his mother. The letter was still stowed in his bag back at the cottage, next to the orb.

Footfalls in the hallway, outside the door, alerted Audun to the fact that they had company. The steps were light, a woman's step, Audun suddenly thought. A moment later the woman entered the room. Her light brown hair was tinged with grey, and the rich black velvet gown she wore spoke to her status. The hazel eyes swept the room. In that instant Audun knew with certainty the identity of his visitor.

"Good morning, grandmother. Have you come to offer me my crown?"

Alphabetical List of Characters

❖ ❖ ❖ ❖

- Aaron – first son of Alberon and Sylva
- Aisha – wife of Bertalan
- Alastair Munro – Known as The Eldest of Bala
- Alberon – King of Kermin and Doran and Emperor of the North
- Aleana – A member of the Den of Thieves
- Alexander Blair of Balthayock – Guardian of the Staff
- Amelia – Audun's grandmother
- Amleth – Holger's second in command of the Guard in Mora
- Anders – Headman in Hillfoot and Aracir's brother
- Angus Ferguson – 14th century warrior poet

- Aracir – Chancellor of Kermin
- Arin – Audun's grandfather
- Arvid – Raimund's uncle – a petty thief
- Aster – King of Soll
- Astrid – Raimund's aunt
- Audun – Alberon's illegitimate son and Captain of the *Swan*
- Bartos – Commander of the King's Guard in Tamin and cousin of Bertalan
- Berin – Duke of Alol – Half-brother to Bertalan and Sylva – killed in the 1507 battle in the Kermin Alol
- Berka – Bertalan and Aisha's son and Prince of Amina
- Bertalan – King of Amina and Alberon's brother-in-law
- Bradstone – The Duke of Doran's personal surgeon
- David Burnett – an old historian living in Aldene
- Danill – Vasilli's brother and helmsman on The *Swan*
- James Daunt – Captain of the Amina gunners
- Elrik – second son of Alberon and Sylva named after his grandfather
- Edin – Duke of Aranin and Alberon's cousin

- Garan – The fourteenth century Ackar Prince who became Dewar the Third and earned the title – The Peacemaker.
- Holger – Captain of the City Guard in Mora and Captain of the King's Guard
- Ianis – The Keeper of the Books in Mora
- Ingrid – Dowager Queen, Alberon's mother
- Jon – A wagon master
- Morserat – Duke of Doran
- John Norward – Younger brother of William Norward
- William Norward – son of Lord Norward, executed for treason in 1508. Grandson of King Aster of Soll and heir apparent to the crown
- Oien – An alchemist from the Second Age
- Orran – Morserat's brother and Soren's father, a Captain of the Doran light cavalry
- Osian – A Kermin master gunner
- Rafe – Master of the Den of Thieves
- Ragna – Alberon's teenage lover and Audun's mother
- Raimund – A thief
- Ramon – Master of *Lex Talionis* and Audun's stepfather
- Samuel – Landlord of the Black Bear

- Silson – Duke of Amina and Commander in Chief of the Amina armies
- Soren – Nephew of Morserat, son of Orran
- Sylva – Wife of Alberon and Bertalan's sister. The Empress.
- Valdin – Vidur's brother and fellow huntsman
- Vasilli – First mate on the *Swan* and on *Lex Talionis*
- Vidur – a huntsman (also known as Ferdinand)
- Wayland Henry – A Kermin Master smith

Geography of the Lands

❖ ❖ ❖ ❖

The large island of Andore is home to several independent countries. In the north, Bala has its border with Ackar at the old wall. South of Ackar is Lett, whilst further south are Toria, Ciren and Arance. Ember is an independent Dukedom in the east of Arance. To the north-east the island is bounded by the Eastern Sea, which separates the island from the eastern lands of Esimore, Soll, Doran and Kermin. To the south is the Middle Sea across which is Andore's southern neighbour, Amina. Lying between Middle Sea and the Western Sea are the islands of Elat and Lat. The Greater Sea runs the length of the island to the west. By the early 16th Century there had been little conflict between the nations. The legacy of the King called the Peacemaker had lasted for nearly two hundred years.

Kermin and Doran

Kermin and Doran have long lived in harmony with ancient treaties committing each to the protection of the other. Marriages between the two royal families further cemented the bonds between the countries. Doran is the most northerly of these lands and is separated from Kermin by the Doran Mountains. Doran is a relatively poor country with small farms scattered across the Doran Plain. The capital, Iskala, sits on a rocky outcrop on the northern slopes of the Doran Mountains. Winter snow blocks the high mountain passes and for four months each year Doran is cut off from its southern neighbour.

Kermin, by contrast, is a rich country. The Kermin Plain is home to fertile farmlands and extensive pastures. The gold in the Doran Mountains is mined on the Kermin side of the border and this provides much of the Emperor's wealth. Kermin's capital, Mora, is an impressive city sitting on the banks of the river Morel, which flows south-west from the Doran Mountains into the Eastern Sea. The Morel is wide as it flows past the city and the port bustles with activity as goods are imported from, and exported to, most of the known world. To the east of Kermin is the large Aramin forest, home to the Aramin tribes. The border between Kermin and Amina is the Kermin Alol, which is rugged hill country, populated mostly by herds of sheep and cattle.

The hills rise steeply from the valleys, cutting the Alol into several distinct sectors with the trade roads hugging the valley floors.

Amina

South of the Kermin Alol is Amina with its vineyards, wheat fields and acres of flax. Tamin is the capital city, and the Amin River flows close to the city walls. Further north the river Mina flows south and west from the Kermin Alol into the Middle Sea. Amina's port is Tufle, and further south near the coast is the small town of Slat. The port at Tufle is connected to Tamin by the river Amin and a constant stream of small boats transport goods to and from the city. Wheat, wine and linen are amongst Amina's main exports. Carracks and caravels constantly crisscross the Middle Sea making Tufle the busiest port in any of the lands and a key source of Amina's wealth. Tufle also has the largest ship building yards in the south and most of the vessels sailing the Middle Sea and the Eastern Sea were built in Tufle. The Vale of Tember stretches out to the south of Tamin and is the country's breadbasket.

Ackar and Lett

Ackar is the richest country on the island of Andore, with large farms and a busy river port at the capital,

Boretar. The Tar River flows through Boretar's port to the Greater Sea. To the north-east, closer to the border with Bala, is the second city of Erbea. The Erb flows past Erbea after it has been joined from the north by the Bari. Ackar is the most populous of the countries and is rich with the trade that flows in and out of Boretar. In the mid-13th century Ackar nobles gradually extended their power into their southern neighbour. By 1280 the countries agreed to a union and so Ackar and Lett became the most powerful country on the island.

Lett is slightly smaller than its northern neighbour and less wealthy. The capital city is named after the country, Lett lies inland. Olet is the country's port on the Greater Sea and the extensive shipyards at Olet build most of the vessels that ply their trade up and down that sea. The shipyards get their raw materials from the Forest of Lett, which extends down beyond the Lett border into Ciren and on south into Toria. South of Boretar and close to the border with Lett are the Ackar ironworks. The ironworks produce metal components and equipment used in agriculture, shipbuilding and armaments. These products are widely exported from the port at Olet.

Bala

Bala's border starts north of Ackar at the old wall. Bala is segmented by two great mountain ranges. North of the capital, Aldene, are the Inger Mountains and in the far north the Coe Mountains. The only route through the Inger Mountains is the Pass of Ing. Winter snow means that the pass is blocked for several months each year. To the north-west of The Inger Mountains is the province of Banora. Bala's capital is smaller than the great southern cities of Boretar, Tamin and Mora. Aldene has two distinct districts; The Old Town, with its grey stone houses, cobbled streets and the castle perched on its rocky crag, is encircled by the old town walls and has remained unchanged for centuries. Outside the town walls is the New Town with its warehouses and the homes of Bala's merchants. The New Town had been built in the late 14th century following the development of Bala's only port at Elde. A broad road connects the port to the town. Bala is a reasonably prosperous country due to its exports of woollen products and deer pelts.

Toria, Ciren and Arance

Ciren and Arance share a border with their northern neighbour, Lett. Toria borders Ciren to the west and Arance borders it to the east. Arance has rich farmlands and in the east the province of Ember, whose capital is Anua, is home to the Ember Horse Lords. Ember is renowned for its thoroughbred horses, and Ember stallions grace the stables of the royal families in every country.

Ciren is rich in natural resources with the Forest of Lett providing the wood for the shipwrights in Olet. Ciren mines supply the iron ore for the Ackar ironworks and its quarries the stones for Boretar's buildings. Ciren's capital is the small town of Cire.

Toria is a small country perched on the south-west edge of the island of Andore. Toria is blessed with a benevolent climate and its vineyards, fields of rye and potato farms produce the raw materials for its main exports. Toria's wineries and distilleries provide the finest wines and spirits and are exported widely. Toria's busy port at Thos looks out across the Western Sea and in the distance the island of Elat can be seen on the horizon. The other great port on the southern coast of Andore is Anelo in the south of Arance. Here the Ember horses are loaded onto carracks for their journey to the horse markets in Boretar.

Elat and Lat

Lying between the southern shores of Toria and the northern shores of Amina are the twin islands of Elat and Lat. The islands are of little value other than as possible staging posts for crossing the Middle Sea. The water lying between the islands forms a shallow channel connecting the Middle Sea to the Western Sea, the Straits of Elat. However this water is too shallow for any large boat to navigate and holds no value. The islands do however hold a curiosity, as the shallows evaporate in the summer months so the waters turn purple as the salt becomes concentrated in the narrows.

Esimore and Soll

Esimore and Soll are situated in the far north and are separated from Andore by the Eastern Sea. Esimore is the most northern country and it is largely tundra, with great herds of reindeer roaming free and tended by the few nomadic herdsmen who call the land home.

The northern tundra runs across the border between Esimore and Soll and the reindeer are not constrained by any frontier. As a result Soll's main source of income comes from the reindeer hides that are exported south to Doran and Kermin. To the south Soll borders Doran, and like its neighbour it is a poor land dotted with small peasants' crofts. Winters here are long and cold and most of the population are subsistence farmers. In 1496 under threat of invasion from the south and bribed by Kermin gold the King of Soll swore fealty to the Kermin King and Soll became the third member of the Empire.

THE EMPEROR, THE SON and THE THIEF

Printed in Great Britain
by Amazon